Alleged
Wheatland
Local Amish woman allegedly attacked, but refuses to testify
—*The Wheatland Post*

Brent's gut tightened as he read the article. Sarah's story would now be fodder for public scrutiny and gossip. He scanned the article quickly. The paper quoted "unnamed sources" at the police department, and referred to Sarah only as "the Amish widow."

Rage rolled right through him, mingling with his feelings for Sarah. He'd thought he had plenty of time to convince her to testify before the media got involved.

But he'd waited too long, and he knew why.

He'd waited too long because he liked Sarah and respected her feelings.

He'd waited too long because he enjoyed spending time with Sarah, and if he'd pushed too hard, she'd have refused to see him.

He'd waited too long because…he wanted to kiss her.

He'd been a fool. He'd known what needed to be done and he'd lost focus.

Brent McCade was not the kind of man to be a fool twice.

Dear Reader,

When I was a teenager I saw my first Amish quilt. It was startling to the eye, shocking almost. The bold pattern, the endless lines of quilting, the clashing colors against black bore no resemblance to the pastel calico quilts I was familiar with. The quilt was utterly different, simple yet complex...and oddly compelling. The memory of it stayed with me.

Years later, my husband, young son and I sometimes drove through a tiny Amish settlement in Southeastern Michigan. There we looked at rows of black buggies parked at a house for church services, clotheslines full of dark, plain wash, calves tied up in the front yards, children playing outside a one-room schoolhouse. Amish life was utterly different, simple yet complex...and oddly compelling.

My fascination with the Amish led to the inevitable writer's question, "what if," and ultimately, to Sarah and Brent's story. After all, to a romance writer, there is no love story more satisfying to write...or more compelling...than one of forbidden love.

This is a book I've had somewhere in my heart for years, and I hope you enjoy it.

Linda Markowiak

RELUCTANT WITNESS
Linda Markowiak

Harlequin Books

TORONTO • NEW YORK • LONDON
AMSTERDAM • PARIS • SYDNEY • HAMBURG
STOCKHOLM • ATHENS • TOKYO • MILAN
MADRID • WARSAW • BUDAPEST • AUCKLAND

ISBN 0-373-70785-1

RELUCTANT WITNESS

For Zilla and Paula,
editors who are willing to take risks
for the sake of the story.

And for Jim and Stevie, in memory of all those drives down
country back roads. City or country…it makes no
difference. I love you both, wherever we are.

CHAPTER ONE

SARAH YODER yearned to draw faces.

Drawing faces was forbidden.

Yet Sarah knew that if she ever started to draw a face, she'd work boldly. She'd eschew the pen and ink she used to create the scenes of Amish farm life that filled portfolios upstairs. Instead, she'd take up a thick-leaded pencil, even a piece of charcoal. She could almost feel the weight of the tool in her hand. And then she'd draw—big, slanted lines of cheek and jaw, eyes—expressive eyes, using a few strokes to capture the distinct character of the individual.

But Sarah was Amish, and the reproduction of Amish faces was forbidden. There were many reasons for the ban, some religious, some just facts of life, here in central Ohio and in Amish settlements everywhere. To create a face was to give too much emphasis to the individual. The Amish were to be loyal to their group of believers, and above all, separate from the outside world.

Sarah thought she'd overcome the urge to draw faces years ago. But over the last two months, this one desire had eaten at her. She was still so angry. Scared, sometimes, too. Because two months ago Sarah Yoder, Amish woman and widow, had learned how cruel the outside world—non-Amish faces—could be, had learned in the most terrifying way pos-

sible why the Amish kept themselves separate and
apart. But she'd also learned how hard it was to obey
the Amish injunction to turn the other cheek, and
something inside her wanted to…burst out. To do
something defiant and angry and perhaps healing.
Then maybe she could be as inwardly serene as she
tried to be on the outside; then maybe she could feel
truly Amish once again.

*It's over, all of it. Even if it doesn't seem over.
Even if in your heart it'll never be over.* Picking one
of the livelier hymns, Sarah hummed, a determined,
decisive sound. Work helped her forget. So, with a
diligence that had become automatic, she smoothed a
piece of pinkish fabric on the table. Carefully, so as
to waste as little fabric as possible, she aligned the
pattern for the face of the rag doll she was cutting
out. The doll would have no features, just a blank,
round piece of cloth where a face should be, because
Amish dolls never had faces.

The tourists were as fascinated with these dolls as
Amish girls were. Despite her mood, Sarah felt her
lips soften. Though many of the beliefs of her faith
might be hard to accept, the Amish love of children
and family was not one of them. In fact, her father
and brother, her cousins and their children, meant
more to her than anything else.

So perhaps this doll she was making, the one that
would have a blue dress to go with its black apron
and bonnet, should go to one of the Amish children.

"Sarah."

She jumped.

"Sorry. I didn't mean to scare you." Her fifteen-
year-old brother, Levi Stolzfus, stood in the open
doorway of her shop.

Sarah turned toward him. When her husband, Jacob, had died five years ago, Sarah had returned to her father's house to help with the housework. Later, her father and Levi had helped her build her shop onto the back of the farmhouse. Now her eyes met his, and his gaze skittered away. "Levi, I'm fine. It's all right."

His Adam's apple, too prominent in his skinny neck, bobbed as he swallowed. "I just came to tell you, a car is turning in at the gate."

She raised her eyebrows at the soberness of his tone. Someone coming was nothing new. For more than three years, there had been a sign at the road, inviting tourists in to buy fabric, dolls or completed quilts, or to attend one of the classes on quilt making she taught.

"There are two men in the car," Levi added. "English men."

"English" was the Amish term for any outsider, regardless of their actual origin.

Her heart gave a thump. But she made sure her tone was calm and quiet. "There're probably coming to buy quilts for their wives. Just tourists."

"I'll stay here with you until they leave," Levi offered.

Sarah hesitated. She wanted so much to be able to tell him to go back out to the fields, where her father and a couple of hired hands were bringing in the first cutting of hay. That there was no reason to hang around the shop. But her father was too far away to hear her if she called. Except for Levi, she was alone. "Thank you," she said.

Levi smiled. The Amish didn't thank each other

often. What was the need to thank another for helping out? Thinking of others first was the Amish way.

She heard the crunch of gravel, the slam of car doors, the sound of footsteps on the porch. A shadow fell across her worktable. Holding the pattern between her fingers, Sarah didn't look up for a moment. When she did, the sun coming in through the open doorway threw two bodies into shadowy relief.

The first man was Norman Bauer. "Levi, hello. And Sarah, how are you?" The voice of the elderly prosecuting attorney was kind. Norman was a distant cousin from a branch of the family that had left the Amish faith a few generations ago. She'd known Norman for only two months. He was a gentle man. And because of his ties to the Amish community, he understood...everything.

Norman had visited her shop several times in the last weeks to purchase a couple of quilts. In his own way, Norman was trying to help her.

"I'm doing well, as I hope you are," she answered.

Norman stepped aside, and the man who had been behind him came into the shop. He was tall, and so dark in hair and dress, so broad in the shoulder that for a second, with the sun behind him, she thought he was Amish. His suit jacket was draped over his arm, and his black suspenders made vigorous slashes down his chest.

A tiny shiver of fear went through her because he was a stranger and a man. Then his gaze captured hers. She looked up into gray eyes that were as clear as the rocky pond shallows, clear and very, very direct. Honest eyes, she thought suddenly, topping features that were regular and spare, a mouth that was firm. The English women would call him handsome.

Even the Amish women, who weren't supposed to focus on the outer features of a human being, would not be able to help noticing his extraordinary looks.

Her hand curled around that imaginary piece of charcoal.

"Sarah, this is Brent McCade," Norman said. "He's the new assistant prosecuting attorney, just moved here from Toledo."

"Mrs. Yoder." Brent McCade held out his hand.

Sarah shook it. His palm was warm, dry, but for some reason, hers felt a little damp. "Please call me Sarah, in the Amish way," she said, quickly withdrawing her hand from his and lowering her eyes.

"Sarah," he corrected himself. "Well, then please call me Brent."

His tone made her look up. And something in those gray eyes made it hard for her to look away. When she realized she was staring, she dropped her own gaze. All of a sudden, she felt an odd sensation in her stomach, as though she'd been overheated and taken a drink of cold water from the well. It was the same way she'd felt when she was a young girl, and Jacob had invited her to a sing. It had been years since she'd felt that way. Those years had been filled with chores and outward acceptance, but also disappointment and loss.

It shocked her thoroughly that she should have this feeling about an English man.

"You're not what I expected," Brent said abruptly. Then he added a quick, "Sorry."

Sarah felt a flash of annoyance at his comment, and silently rebuked herself for the reaction.

Norman cleared his throat and said, "I'll show Brent around the shop."

"Please go ahead. Perhaps your wife would like a quilt," she said to Brent. The dolls she sold helped with expenses, but the quilts she made herself and commissioned from other Amish women, were how she made her living.

"Brent doesn't have a wife. Never had time for one, did you?" Smiling, Norman thumped Brent on the shoulder. Brent's mouth thinned and he looked away.

Never had time for a wife, Sarah repeated to herself as she watched him move around the store. Norman's comment shouldn't have sent a flash of relief through her. She should feel sorry for Brent McCade instead, that he didn't know how to value the love and support of a wife, that he apparently didn't know that family was the most important thing in the world.

Now that Levi had seen it was Norman who had come calling, he told Sarah he was going back to the hay field. Smiling her thanks again, she held out his straw hat and promised to take a jug of water soon to the field.

Then she went back to the doll on the cutting table, marking the patterns for the arms and legs. The work required no concentration, and she found herself thinking about Brent McCade. Over the last couple of years, men had tried to court her. She was only twenty-nine, and she could still have a family of her own. The men were nice, good Amish citizens, their faces familiar to her since childhood. None of them had ever affected her the way Brent McCade had with one look. *Silly,* she chided herself. *He's just a handsome English man.*

He was circling the shop, restless, almost prowling. His eyes squinted against the dimness as he flipped over a price tag to read it. The Amish used no electricity in their homes or businesses. In her peripheral vision, she could see him stop and stand before a display of yellow cottons, a frown on his face. Brent dominated the space, as though the shop was simply too small to accommodate him.

She told herself not to be irked by his comment about her not being what he'd expected. After all, she was used to misconceptions about her Amishness. The tourists weren't always tactful.

But she found herself dwelling on the comment anyway. Brent was from Toledo, a big city, where many women were professionals—doctors and presidents of corporations. They had their hair styled and did outlandish things to their fingernails with paint.

He must find her plain, which of course she was. *That much* he'd certainly have expected, if he knew anything about Amish dress. He probably also thought she was shy, the way she'd quickly disengaged her hand from his, the way she'd cast her eyes down. Yet to her own people, her boldness, curiosity and rather hot temperament were sources of comment and correction, character traits she'd spent a lifetime trying to curb.

Brent McCade had probably had no contact with the Amish before moving to Wheatland. Norman would have told him the basics. He would have explained that the Amish kept themselves separate from the outside world. They dressed modestly in unpatterned clothing, the women in dresses, aprons and white prayer caps. They had no electricity, television or telephones. For transportation, they used a horse and buggy. Norman respected the faith. But not everyone in Wheatland did, and maybe Brent had al-

ready heard things. He was a lawyer; he must know
a lot of people. Two months ago, she couldn't have
said exactly what a lawyer did.

Now she knew. He helped enforce the English law.

The Amish believed in getting along with their
neighbors, but they didn't resort to the English law if
there was trouble. Actually, they didn't understand
much of the English law. For example, last month
Amos Troyer had been arrested for shooting an owl.
The owls were a protected species, but all Amos had
known was that the owls were attacking his hens. In
the fall, David Bontrager had been arrested because
he hadn't worn an orange vest while hunting. Wearing the colorful vest went against the Amish faith. In
both cases, the men had refused to defend themselves.
They'd simply paid their fines and gone about their
business.

And only two months ago, Sarah Yoder had
shocked them all—the police, the former assistant attorney and even Norman, when she'd carried the tenets of her faith to what Norman had sadly said was
the extreme.

Now, over in the corner, Brent McCade had his
hands on a quilt. *The* quilt. A Sunshine and Shadow
pattern, her favorite because of the bold rush of color,
the vibrancy of thousands of tiny squares. It was her
best work, with swirls of tiny hand stitches, sewn in
the days when Jacob's accidental death had been a
constant ache in her heart. It had hung in the corner
of her shop for years, away from the windows so the
sunlight wouldn't fade the fabric. She took orders for
it, but it wasn't a popular quilt. Outsiders favored pastels, so the quilts would match their bedrooms.

Yet of all the quilts, Brent had stopped at this one.

He had his broad, male hand on the quilt she'd been making her husband, the quilt that, if Jacob had lived, she would have placed on the bed they'd shared. "That quilt is not for sale," she said sharply.

Brent dropped his hand immediately and turned toward her. "Look, Mrs....Sarah. I've been standing here thinking of how to make small talk with you, and I realize...things are not what I pictured. When I decided to come here, Norman suggested that I be gentle. That maybe we could talk a bit before you heard my suggestion."

Brent gave a small shrug, and Sarah understood. They didn't know each other, and she was Amish, he English. There was no common ground to form the basis for small talk, and Brent didn't strike her as the type who dwelled on the weather. "So this is awkward," he added.

He took a couple of steps toward her, then stopped, his fingers drumming a restless beat on the edge of the cutting table. "What I have to say will make you uncomfortable, but I'm the kind of man who says what's on my mind."

Norman was standing farther away, off to her right by a stack of quilt tops waiting to be put in the quilting frame. He smiled at her in encouragement, and Sarah began to have an inkling of what was on Brent's mind. She took a deep breath and put her chin up. "Then perhaps you'd better just say what you came to say."

He faced her fully, the table between them. "I want to take another look at your case. The case of the man who...attacked you."

Stay calm, she ordered herself. "You mean, the man who *raped* me." No matter what, she'd call the

crime what it was, that English word that sounded so
hard and cruel.

A fleeting shadow crossed his face, but he kept his
gaze on hers. "If you prefer. First off, I want to say
how very sorry I am for what happened to you."

She searched his face. He had honest eyes, but
nothing about him suggested any real understanding.
The clothes he wore were beautifully cut, his material
wealth apparent. By the English measure of success,
he must be very successful. The gulf between her
world and his was obvious. She'd been taught to
search for good in everyone, but she didn't know
Brent. Anyway, were English men really sorry for
Amish women, under any circumstances?

Abruptly, her mind flashed back to that night two
months ago. Another English man. *You deserve it,
Amish girl. You have holier-than-thou ways and hide
that golden hair*—Randy West's hands had fisted,
tugging at her hair—*but you want it bad, don't you?
All you Amish girls must really want it bad...*

But it wasn't that night. It was today in her shop,
where things were familiar and safe. Brent McCade
must never think she lacked courage. "Thank you for
your sympathy," she said, falling back on the English
politeness. "But it doesn't change anything. I told
Norman I wouldn't testify in court, and my decision
was—and is—final."

"I warned you," Norman said to Brent. To Sarah
he said, "I still don't agree with your decision,
but—"

"Look," Brent interrupted. "I understand your re-
luctance. Often, rape victims don't want to testify.
Many women feel this way, it's not because you're
Amish. A rape victim doesn't want to see her attacker

again, she doesn't want to face him in court and answer questions. She doesn't want to look at all those strangers in the courtroom. I understand."

He didn't understand. How could he? He was a man, and a man from a different world. "I'm an Amish woman." She closed her eyes for a second. Did she really have to explain this again? It had been so hard the first time. "I'll take your word for it that an English woman would find those things difficult. But at least she would be facing her own kind. And she would surely speak more comfortably, about...sexual matters." Though Sarah was a widow, a farmer who had seen animals mate, she felt her cheeks flame. This felt like a violation of a kind, having to face a strange man—*this* man, who'd made her insides flutter for a moment—and speak of sexual matters.

As far as she was concerned, the discussion was at an end. She bent over her table. Taking up her cutting wheel, she cut the fabric in a satisfying, long sweep.

"Sarah." Unexpectedly, his hand came out, across the table toward hers.

Abruptly, she stopped cutting. She had to, because otherwise the foolhardy man would've lost a finger. She clutched her wheel and waited.

His hand closed over her own fist, over her knuckles and the handle of the wheel. "Look at me," he said softly, persuasively.

His voice was strong, compelling her to look up.

"I'm sickened by what happened to you. I'm *not* part of the problem. What I want to do is fix it."

Her temper snapped and she tugged her hand away. "You can't fix this! It happened. How will putting that man in jail change anything?"

His fist rapped the table, hard. "Because he'll be locked up. Hasn't it occurred to you that he might do it again? That you might not be safe?"

Of course it had occurred to her. "I'm careful now. I don't walk alone at night. My brother always—"

"Another woman, then! Maybe even another Amish woman. Do you want another woman to go through what you have? Think, Sarah."

She'd thought. She didn't need Brent McCade to remind her of the threat to other women. *All you Amish girls want it bad...* Amish, English, it made no difference. She wouldn't wish that hideous fear and sick feeling of loss and shame on any other woman.

In the beginning, she'd been so angry at the violation of her body that she had cooperated with the authorities fully. She'd started to tell the police everything. She'd cried, but a female police officer had held her hand, and at that moment, Sarah hadn't cared that the woman was English, just that she was a woman.

It was only later, when her father had come for her, that things had changed. At home, her friend Rebecca had helped her bathe, and the Amish community had met to decide what to do about her rape, that things had changed. Daniel Yoder was the bishop, and he was also Jacob's father. He was a man she'd loved and trusted for years. He was the head of their faith, who kept the faithful from the individualism that, if allowed, would eventually lead to the death of the community.

Daniel wouldn't let her participate in the lineup the police had arranged. He wouldn't let her testify. To be passive, to accept, was the Amish way. The Amish community that ringed the hills west of Wheatland might be two thousand strong, but Sarah's church district was much smaller. She knew everyone in her community, and they knew her. They supported her as best they could, tried to ease her hurt. On long evenings they'd brought their sewing and sat with her. The whole community had prayed that God would bring healing to her shattered heart. They'd also prayed for Randy West, that God would forgive him his terrible crime.

But they would not support the English law. They would remain separate and apart, even in this.

Someday, Sarah hoped, she could share in the prayer for forgiveness. Now her own prayers were more blunt. *Dear God, don't let him hurt another woman!* But she could not go against the bishop. The consequences of defying a direct order of the bishop would be staggering. Her own people might shun her.

Shunning was the worst thing that could happen to an Amish person. Community cohesiveness was vital to their survival, and every Amish person understood that if they broke with the community, with the teaching of the bishop, they'd be shunned. When a person was shunned, they were completely cut off from Amish life. No one could speak with the person or do business with them. No one could sit down and eat with them. And the shunning went on until the person repented.

"I'll pray for those women," she said now. But it was hard to believe that Randy West would change. She'd looked into his eyes and felt the crazy kind of fever in him.

Brent made a sound of disgust.

She should ask him to leave. But for some reason,

she wanted him to understand. "We're passive, even when it's hard." *Even when it's nearly impossible.* "Our men don't fight in wars, even when our own freedom is at stake. When we were persecuted, we went willingly to prison. Vengeance belongs to God."

"I don't believe that," Brent said, his voice ringing with conviction. "What's more, I don't think you believe that. I read the police report, and I know everything that happened that night. I don't think you believe in being passive, because you blackened both his eyes, Sarah. You fought. Hard."

She flushed. She hadn't been able to admit to her own people how she'd fought Randy West. If she told them, she'd be compelled to admit she was glad she'd fought. The memory of her struggle was helping her heal.

"That doesn't change anything," she said. Testifying was forbidden, and that was that. Daniel was interpreting the faith, and who was she to say he wasn't right? The good of the community had to come first. To risk losing all that she knew, all that she'd been raised to be, just to testify in an English court and have the satisfaction of *maybe* seeing Randy West go to jail...

So Brent McCade came into her shop and thought that with one conversation he was going to change the beliefs of a lifetime? Even for an English man, he must be arrogant.

"Brent, I think you should give Sarah some time to think things over," Norman cut in, quiet but firm. "You've pushed hard enough for one day."

That fist came down again. "Norm, for God's sake, she's wrong, and if you'd give me some time—"

"Enough for now," Norman said. "Goodbye, Sarah."

Brent's mouth thinned until it was no more than a white line, and for a moment, Sarah thought he might just stay there, rooted in her shop until, by some force of will, he'd get her to change her mind. But with one long look at her, he turned to go.

That look seemed to search for something deep inside her that she knew wasn't there. She understood he was doing his job with an intensity that was deeply felt.

"I'll be back, Sarah."

Perhaps her understanding of his motives—and her Amishness—stopped her from telling him never to darken her door again.

CHAPTER TWO

"I TOLD YOU," Norm said with a certain satisfaction, stroking his gray mustache thoughtfully. Implied, but not added, was the word *son*.

Brent tried not to react to the paternalism. He owed Norm, and these days he could count his supporters on one finger. He bit into his rare cheeseburger and looked around the Essen Haus restaurant. There were just a few tourists here, those who'd managed to run the gauntlet of restaurants over on Main Street that featured "genuine" Amish food.

Some of the town's businessmen were having lunch. Norm had pointed them out, the dry cleaner and the insurance salespeople. At one table, a big man was laughing. In the corner were three Amish men, their faces as calm and grave as their clothing. The businessmen ignored them; the tourists at the next table stared. Brent shook his head. He'd had a couple of weeks to get used to the town, with its weird mix of Amish, tourists and locals, but he still couldn't get over that he'd actually ended up in a place like this.

Norm followed Brent's gaze. "You'll have to learn that things are different in Wheatland. You've read books about the Amish, but this is the real thing."

"Okay, so the Amish lead a different kind of life." That was the understatement of the century. He put down his burger. "How does that change the fact that a crime was committed and it's our duty to prosecute it?''

"I've always believed it's the victim's choice whether to press a case," Norm said quietly. "Anyway, we both know that without Sarah's testimony, you don't have enough evidence."

Brent pushed aside his plate. He'd never imagined he'd have to persuade another prosecutor that they ought to put a rapist away. He leaned over the table, intent. "The woman was *raped*. I know prosecution is hard on a woman, like I told Mrs.—Sarah. But it's been a long time since I couldn't persuade one to take on the guy who did it. The process is hard, but going through it heals them, Norm, as much as anything can."

"I agree. But Sarah's Amish."

"Sarah's also a woman." Brent paused at his own words. His first sight of Sarah Yoder had practically stopped him in his tracks. She was Amish, all right, from that white cap on her head to her stiff black shoes. But she was also most definitely a woman. Her skin was flawless, her hair golden, her features rounded and feminine.

Uncomfortable now, and not sure exactly why, Brent put his mind to the task of convincing his boss. "Look. You know the son of a bitch will do it again. As soon as he's sure she really won't do anything to help us catch him, he'll get bold. Maybe real bold."

Suddenly, the greasy beef he'd eaten felt like a hard ball in his stomach. Brent ignored the discomfort. "It's my job to put creeps like that in jail. All I need is a little cooperation. Is that too much to ask of that..." Somehow he couldn't come up with the right word for someone with a strikingly beautiful face, callused fingertips and clothes that made her look like one of the Pilgrims at the first Thanksgiving. "That woman," he finally said. "How can she calmly tell me she'll *pray* for those other women he might attack? I'll learn, will I? Well, I don't think so."

Norm gave him a level look, then smiled slowly. "We've always avoided confrontation in the prosecutor's office here, gotten along with everybody. Maybe I'm about to see some change. I have a feeling you're going to give me trouble."

"No matter what, I've got to do my job."

"In spite of what happened in Toledo?"

"*Because* of what happened in Toledo." He had wondered if Norm believed any of the accusations that had been leveled at Brent. Norm had hired him, but that didn't mean he truly believed in him. Wheatland was a growing county with a growing crime rate, but it still had a small, rural budget. Brent's fall from grace was an opportunity for Wheatland to get the kind of talent and expertise that didn't come the way of a small-town prosecutor's office very often.

Norm signaled for the check. "Funny, you've never asked me whether I believed all the crap they accused you of back in Toledo."

"It doesn't matter." Brent shrugged. He was curious, but it really didn't matter. Because now he was in this dinky town starting over. Alone again, because Jennifer, his fiancée, had left him amid all the controversy. It still hurt. So now that his whole life had fallen apart, what did it matter what Norm thought?

"It doesn't matter?" Norm repeated incredulously. "It doesn't matter whether or not I think you're innocent?"

Whatever tiny kernel of innocence Brent had possessed had died the day he'd discovered that Thacker Cavanaugh, his friend, mentor and boss, was going to let him take the fall for an alleged violation of attorney ethics. That accusation had made Brent an overnight pariah, resulted in an expensive lawsuit against the county and put an end to a promising career—for now. By the time the rumor mill had finished with him, it hadn't mattered that the state bar investigators had concluded that there wasn't enough evidence against him.

He still had his license to practice law and he had a plan. In a small town, his conviction percentage ought to be spectacular. He'd stay here a year or so, give Norm a fair payback for hiring him, quietly rebuild his reputation, then move on to a bigger community with bigger cases. Once he was back in the limelight, his career would take off again.

The waitress brought the check, and Norm stood up slowly. Norm was a good guy. They'd met a few years ago at a statewide bar conference. Norm had a quiet intelligence that Brent had sensed immediately. Over time, they'd become friendly, to the extent an older, rural prosecutor and an up-and-coming city crusader could be friends.

Now Brent was grateful for the connection. Without it, he might not even be able to make a living nowadays. "Look, Norm, I know it's payback time. So I intend to give you your money's worth here."

Norm smiled at him. "That was something I never doubted for a moment." He sobered immediately. "But I won't have you harassing Sarah."

Brent went still. He was grateful to Norm. But, God, he hated still having to answer to a boss. By this time in his career he should be the county prosecutor himself somewhere, directing other attorneys. "Are you forbidding me to pursue this case?" he asked tightly.

Norm laid a hand on his shoulder. "No. Go over there and talk to Sarah again if you want, but try to reach some understanding with her. If she complains, though, I'll take you off the case. I don't want trouble over this."

"I hardly think the Amish are going to organize a lynch mob," Brent said dryly. Deep down he knew he was going to prosecute Sarah Yoder's case. In ten years, he'd never put a case aside. He wasn't idealistic, he assured himself. It just angered him that a woman had been raped, and he couldn't do his job.

They paid the bill for lunch and went out onto the sidewalk. The street was crowded with tourists. Shops advertised Amish souvenirs. Blank-faced dolls in one window. Had Sarah Yoder made one of them? It would be impossible to tell. Except for the color of their dresses, they all looked the same—cotton dolls with pinafore-like aprons and prayer caps made out of some white, translucent fabric.

Suddenly, Brent had a flashing vision of Sarah— her small, work-rough hands manipulating the pattern, another vision of her fisting those hands and giving Randy West two black eyes. There was a contradiction here. An intriguing contradiction for any trial lawyer. Why would a woman who'd shown that much outrage—and courage—while she was being violated, later refuse to prosecute her attacker? When Brent figured out that puzzle, maybe he could persuade her to do the right thing. But it wasn't going to be easy. There had been a determined set to that mouth.

He and Norm walked past the next store window.

In it were plaster figures of an Amish boy and girl, bent at the waist and kissing. Next to them was a whirligig, an outlandishly folkish Amish man chopping wood, twirling his arms in the false wind of an electric fan. Sheesh.

They crossed to the corner, where a dark buggy came clattering along, with a stone-faced man holding the reins. The man faced straight ahead, ignoring the stares of the tourists.

As Brent and Norm waited for the light to change, the woman next to him poked her companion in the ribs. "I told you they have real Amish here. Get your camera, Floyd. Come on," she added more sharply. "He's getting away!"

Floyd aimed with his camera, snapped frantically, presumably catching the rear of the retreating buggy. Too bad the buggy was between Floyd and the horse, Brent thought wryly. If not, Floyd and his wife would have been able to take home a picture of a horse's ass, a gen-u-ine Amish horse's ass. Suddenly, the tourists seemed to be everywhere, clutching shopping bags, pointing and staring at the few Amish who dared walk the streets.

"What is the fascination with the Amish?" That was something the books didn't begin to explain. "Why do tourists come here to buy junk and stare at people who live like—" He stopped, sure Norm wouldn't like what he'd been about to say. *Like relics, people out of history, people out of sync.* "At people who don't drive cars?" he finished.

They headed toward the courthouse. A huge Victorian building, it dominated the town square. It was a monolith to the ambition of its founders, ambition Brent could readily understand. *Maybe a judgeship eventually.* He was only thirty-four. He had time to get back on track.

"It's the whole lifestyle. Slow down, Brent," Norm added, beginning to puff from the pace Brent had unconsciously set. "I think the tourists respond somehow to the idea that the Amish don't value material possessions the way we do." Norm stopped on the sidewalk, and Brent stopped, too. A couple of the town's public defenders waved as they headed into the building for the one o'clock arraignments. They didn't hurry. Brent himself had an almost lazy afternoon scheduled, nothing like his city practice had been.

"It's ironic," Norm said. "My mother was friends with an Amish woman. That woman had the same kind of problems as other people. But all the non-Amish see are the quaint idiosyncrasies. The clothes, the buggies." Norm started to walk again. "The tourists, the outside world, well, they romanticize the Amish. They don't think about the reality of that cold buggy seat in the winter. The Amish are evidence that all's right with the world, if it can still support that kind of...spirituality."

They stopped at the door of the courthouse. Norm put a hand on his shoulder. "I took a chance hiring you. You're an outsider. With the things said about you in Toledo, I'd be a fool not to watch you real close. But that's not my way. I'd rather give you a chance. But I want to make sure you understand something. So far, nobody knows about the rape of Sarah Yoder, outside of a few police officers and some of the Amish. Not even the *Wheatland Post* picked up the story. If this case goes to trial, you need to keep things low-key. I don't want a media circus."

A media circus? Over the rape of an Amish widow. Sure, the media would be riveted. Brent was stunned as the implications sank in.

All he needed was one really big case to jump-start his career...

But the media attention would be hard for Sarah to bear. He'd been through it himself. Reporters had crowded around, the lenses of their cameras right in his face when he'd come out of the courthouse in Toledo that day. *Do you have a comment, Mr. McCade, on the report that you wanted a conviction in the Samuelson case so bad that you hid evidence pointing to the defendant's innocence? That you planned to let an innocent man be executed to advance your career? Your buddy Thacker Cavanaugh says it was you, that you had the file, that you knew all along...*

No Amish woman could withstand that kind of scrutiny. Even he, the crusading lawyer-on-the-make, had almost cracked under the pressure.

But Sarah Yoder had been the victim of a despicable crime. She deserved justice. Damn it, justice was his job.

There were ways to shield witnesses. He could get the cooperation of the judge. Sarah wouldn't have to have cameras in the courtroom, at least. He felt a surge of protectiveness that wasn't wholly professional. He wouldn't let anybody manhandle Sarah. He thought fleetingly of other women he'd represented over the years—women who'd shown extraordinary courage in the face of a system that was sometimes harsh.

He wouldn't examine his motives too closely. He had a job to do. He had to think of it this way: she needed justice. He needed a breakout case. It was a win-win situation.

"I'm going to buy a quilt," Brent said abruptly. "Specially designed. It might take a while to pick out just the right quilt for my living-room wall."

Norm didn't miss the underlying message. "Get to know Sarah. She's a fine woman, and on your way to winning your case, she might just teach you something about life."

A couple of minutes later, Brent headed down the hall to his office. Norm was cryptic sometimes, he thought. What on earth could a woman like Sarah teach him about life? This thing with Sarah Yoder was about a case. A very, very good case that Brent McCade was going to prosecute...and win.

WHEN BRENT'S sleek red car turned in at the farm, Levi sped across the barnyard. Sarah came from the kitchen doorway and met her brother on the steps of the shop, wiping her hands on a dish towel.

"It's Brent," she said, her stomach giving a little pinch of awareness. "I recognize the car."

Levi grinned at her. "I recognize the car, too."

She smiled back. These last two months had been hard on all of them, but perhaps hardest on Levi. Maybe because they were a small family, by Amish standards anyway, she and Levi had always been close. Levi had been the one to find her, after...

"I *love* that car," Levi said. "A real Jaguar, and that baby is *red*." He rolled his eyes heavenward and make a smacking motion with his lips.

Sarah smiled again, though it felt strained. She forced a lilt into her voice. "Been up late at night reading again?"

Sarah reached up and gave the brim of Levi's straw hat a tug. Levi had a forbidden flashlight and an auto-racing magazine tucked between his mattress and box springs. Sarah had seen them when she'd changed the sheets.

She should chastise Levi for his unseemly interest in fast cars, but instead she'd quietly replaced both magazine and flashlight. Levi was "sowing his wild oats." That was the Amish term for a time of adolescence in which the strict rules of Amish behavior were relaxed. Everyone hoped teenagers, if permitted a certain amount of freedom, would get the rebelliousness out of their systems in preparation for a lifetime as good Amish citizens.

Besides, Sarah could hardly chide Levi unless she was prepared to chide herself for all those pen-and-ink drawings in her own room. Those drawings weren't strictly forbidden, but they were a tangible expression of individuality that was simply not right. Earlier in her life, she'd been torn about her Amishness. She'd even thought about not joining the Amish church as she came of age. But that had been before she'd fallen in love with Jacob. Most of all, she couldn't chide Levi because she too thought Brent's car was pretty, and in years past, she'd often ached to ride in a fast car, to see the whole world go whooshing by, flashing scenes of color and light.

She'd learned to bury such impulses, as Levi must. "The car is colorful, like a candy apple," she said. "But remember, a buggy will get you to the same places."

"But not so fast." Levi sighed. "Think of it, Sarah. You just touch your foot to a little pedal, and off it goes."

"Have you tried driving?" she asked sharply. Some of the wilder Amish boys did, she knew.

Levi shook his head. "No, so don't worry about what Father will say. But I sure would like to. To fly down the road, with all the girls looking..." He stopped and a blush tinged his ears.

"Katie Hershburger would be most impressed of all," Sarah teased, relieved that Levi still apparently exercised some control over his behavior. "I noticed you went out in the open buggy last Sunday night." At one of the auctions recently, Levi had purchased a used open buggy. A courting buggy. He was growing up.

The car stopped in the parking place in front of the shop. Brent got out, wearing a cotton shirt and a pair of jeans. Those jeans were much tighter than any trousers worn by Amish men. She'd pictured him in a suit, but this was Saturday, a day that many of the English didn't work.

"Hello, Sarah," Brent said quietly, walking toward her.

Wheatland was experiencing a June heat spell. And it was almost noon, so she was flushed from the heat of the oven. That's why she felt so uncomfortably warm, Sarah reasoned. "Brent. What brings you here?"

"I came to look at quilts."

He had tried to turn her life upside down a week ago. She faced him squarely. "Just to look at quilts?"

"You're a direct woman, Sarah." His eyes warmed, and she had the oddest impression that she'd pleased him somehow.

But of course there could be no warmth between them, no sharing. "Just for quilts?" she repeated.

"Today, just for quilts." His gaze turned to Levi. "Levi, isn't it?" He held out his hand. Levi hesitated at the unfamiliar gesture, then with a kind of defiant shrug to Sarah, he shook Brent's hand vigorously.

Oh, that was all she needed, Sarah thought in disgust. Brent cajoling Levi into one of the English ways. "Come in," she invited abruptly, heading up the steps and across the porch to the door of her shop. "You can look at the quilts, but you'll have to hurry. It's nearly time for our noon meal, and I'm baking."

He got to the door ahead of her. As she reached for the handle, he reached, too. His hand closed over hers, and again she had that sensation of power, of sheer masculine...bigness. A bigness that should have frightened her, but didn't.

It did rattle her, though. Quickly, she called to Levi to check on the bread in the oven.

"In a minute." Levi was circling that fancy car, running a reverent hand over the hood.

"Now, Levi! Unless you want a burned dinner." He looked up at her sharp tone, but did as she asked. Their mother had died giving birth to Levi. So he was used to Sarah's mothering.

Brent was still waiting for her to go ahead of him into the shop. "You'll need to decide quickly," she reminded him.

The dim shop was a few degrees cooler than the outside. From behind her, he said, "If I don't have time to decide today, I'll have to come back, won't I?"

Her temper flared. "For heaven's sake. What kind of quilt do you want?"

"I don't know." His gaze sought Jacob's quilt, draped in its corner. "I want to see them all."

Brent was obviously not going to hurry. If she brushed him off, she'd only give him an excuse to return. She was in the business of selling quilts, and she couldn't bar the door.

Of course he wasn't really here for a quilt. She might be a naive Amish woman, but she was no fool. He wanted to talk about the case again. Hadn't he almost admitted it, there on the driveway? Well, at least he hadn't lied.

Perhaps Levi and her father would eat without her. If so, she could stay in the shop and wait out Brent McCade. He wouldn't have any excuse to return.

"What do you call this pattern?" Brent asked, indicating Jacob's quilt.

"It's a Sunshine and Shadow," she said, surrendering to the inevitable. "It's one of the three traditional patterns, coming originally out of the first Amish settlement in America." Brent was looking at her with such intensity, he made her nervous. So she kept talking. "Real Amish quilts are made with plain fabrics. No calicos or other prints, like the quilts you're probably familiar with. Women used to make their quilts out of scraps they had left over from other sewing, and our clothes are all plain."

His gaze took in her plain green dress, but he said nothing.

"When I make a quilt for the tourists, I make it with pastels and printed cloth. Actually, then the pattern isn't Sunshine and Shadow any longer. It's called Trip Around the World because when the English adapted it to their own scraps, they renamed it." Heaven above, she thought, she really needed to get a grip on herself. What with this history lesson, Brent would be here all day.

"You'll want darker fabrics, being a man." Now, why had that comment made her blush? She hurried on. "You could pick out your own fabrics." But she knew immediately how absurd that notion was—that Brent McCade, lawyer, powerful man in the English world, would choose his own fabric.

She went over to the browns. "I have this leafy print. No flowers for a man's quilt. You can trust me to choose the colors and prints. You won't need to come back. When the quilt's finished, Levi can deliver it."

Brent strode over. He regarded the bolt of fabric intently. "I don't think I want prints. There's something about that quilt—" he indicated Jacob's quilt again "—that's more like what I want. Maybe in the browns, though, not so much turquoise. I want to pick everything out. Take my time."

"Sarah, dinner!" It was her father's voice, coming toward the shop.

"Excuse me," she said quickly. For some reason, she felt as if she'd been caught by her father doing something faintly disreputable, talking about Jacob's quilt with this English man.

"Sarah!" Her father's voice was more commanding than before.

"I'm sorry. I need to go. My *vater* gets hungry from working so hard in the fields." Unconsciously, she'd slipped into Pennsylvania Dutch, a German dialect, for the one word.

Brent gestured impatiently. "And your father dictates what hours you spend with your customers?"

She had not expected sarcasm, and it reminded her that whether or not Brent appreciated a quilt that few tourists did, he had no respect for her or her lifestyle.

"The father is the head of the Amish family." She could have said more, but there was no point. What did it matter if Brent understood she loved her father, and had been taught from childhood to respect his authority?

She'd been angry with her father after the rape because she thought he'd support what she wanted to do, as he'd done when she'd wanted to open a shop and let tourists onto the farm. But he'd sided with the bishop. He'd really had no choice, but...

God forgive her, she hadn't spoken to him for days.

Until that time six weeks ago, when he'd explained again that the community didn't want her to have to talk about something so private with strangers. Besides, God took care of vengeance. He'd been stern. So she'd thrown down her quilting hoop and gone upstairs, where she'd felt furious and lonely and misunderstood.

Later that night, she'd seen a light in the barn. She'd thought perhaps a cow was calving, and needed help with the birth. Instead, she'd discovered Adam Stolzfus, her grave and careful father, with his face buried in the hide of one of their mares, sobbing. She'd felt a rush of love for him so strong it weakened her knees. It was a reminder from God Himself that the whole community suffered with her.

The sound of her father's footsteps brought her back to the present. Brent hadn't budged. Her father came to the doorway. "Sarah, Levi said you knew it was dinnertime—" He stopped as he caught sight of Brent, and looked at him with guarded eyes. "I noticed the car. I figured you were an English woman buying a quilt." He paused, then, "I'm Adam Stolzfus."

Brent stepped forward and held out his hand. Her father didn't take it. "I'm Brent McCade. I'm a friend of Norman Bauer's. We work together."

Over these last months, her father had come to trust Norman in a way he trusted no other English man. His eyes warmed. "Then, you're our friend, too."

Sarah knew in that instant exactly what was coming next.

"Have you had dinner?" Adam asked cordially.

"No, I haven't eaten, and now that you mention it, I realize how hungry I am." Brent looked pleased with himself. Very arrogant and...*English* and pleased.

"Then you'll join us." It was a statement, though her father meant to be courteous. "Sarah is an excellent cook. She bakes on Saturdays."

Sarah gave one last try. "*Vater,* Brent is a lawyer, like Norman. Surely he has to get back to the office." Then she remembered it was Saturday. With one quick forbidden look at those tight jeans, she knew she was beaten.

So she wasn't surprised to hear Brent say, "I'm not doing a thing. And I'd love to stay for lunch...for dinner."

CHAPTER THREE

BEFORE GOING INSIDE, Brent washed his hands at the washstand set up on the porch. Adam Stolzfus led the way, and Brent had to resist the urge to let Sarah go before him. Obviously, that wasn't the Amish way, and Brent was determined to do nothing wrong. He'd spent the last week, every night until the wee hours, reading about the Amish and their culture.

Because of that, he was unprepared for the sight of Sarah's kitchen. It looked so...*normal,* when he'd been expecting...he didn't know exactly what. There was the usual run of countertops and cabinets. There was also a large collection of the kind of fancy bits of china his mother had accumulated, little teapots and cups, pickle dishes and God knew what.

He felt an odd, quick wash of sensation that he vaguely recognized as nostalgia. For what? Certainly not for his childhood. Not for a rented tract house with dingy paneling and peeling wallpaper, and a little china collection that was sticky with dust and the residue of tobacco smoke.

Quelling the memory, he took another look around, his careful, lawyer's eye seeing what he'd first missed. The stove was funny-looking—it must burn wood—and there was a hand pump at the kitchen sink. On the counter, smoke-dark cookie sheets and

pans held baked goods. There were several kinds of
cookies, and loaves of white and brown bread.

Adam and Levi sat down at the table. Sarah set an
extra place. Brent hesitated, waiting for Sarah to take
her seat. She looked over at him, her mouth pursed,
as if to say that he was holding her up.

When in Rome, he thought, and took his seat. She
leaned over to pour him a glass of milk, and the cotton of her sleeve brushed his bare arm.

But Sarah moved away quickly, and put more plat-
ters and bowls of food on the table.

No one said anything, so Brent just sat there. He
knew his good fortune. If Adam hadn't appeared,
Brent would never be sitting in the inner sanctum,
giving Sarah a chance to know him, to trust him.
Don't blow it, pal.

The table steamed. Various noodle and potato con-
coctions were piled in crockery bowls, and there was
shredded cabbage, apple butter, red beets. Sarah set a
platter before Adam that held an enormous glazed
pork roast, and then took her own seat.

Pork roast. *Cholesterol.* Brent could just feel it
pleasantly thickening his veins, and his stomach gave
an audible groan of anticipation, overly loud in the
still kitchen. Adam smiled at the sound, and Levi
grinned.

Brent grimaced, embarrassed, as he caught Sarah's
eye. She compressed her lips, but he could see the
incipient smile that tried to tilt the corners of her
mouth. He stared straight into her eyes, suddenly
wishing that she *would* smile. Just one smile.

Abruptly, her cheeks turned pink, and she cast her
eyes down. But not before he caught the warmth, and
a kind of...sparkle that arced from her to him. That

spark hit Brent like a punch to his midsection. He
stared at her, startled, but willing her to look at him
again, so he could see the evidence he scarcely believed, so he could confirm what for a second he'd
been certain was—

No. He was nuts. She was an Amish woman.

"Just a minute, *Vater*." Quickly, Sarah rose and
went toward the counter, where she started plunking
cookies into a basket. Her spine was straight, her
green dress fell past her knees, her hair was bound in
a knot under her prayer cap. Sarah was modesty per-
sonified.

He *was* nuts, he decided. Temporary insanity,
brought on by the changes in his life. If anything at
all had passed between them, Adam and Levi would
have noticed. And if they'd noticed, would Sarah's
father and brother be sitting around the table as
though this was an ordinary lunch?

Okay, he was lonely. He missed the office politics,
gossip, the beer or two after work as the crowd of
lawyers told war stories and showed off. He'd fit so
well into that world; being a big-city prosecutor had
fulfilled all his long-held dreams. And okay, he
missed women, too. He missed Jennifer.

Jennifer had said he would die young, eating all
that meat. Brent had laughed. He worked out at the
gym, ran a couple of days a week, and in every walk
of life, he'd been invincible.

Hell, he'd planned to live forever.

Sarah finally took her place at the table again. She
didn't seem to be avoiding his gaze, but she didn't
look at him, either. Yes, he had mistaken the whole
exchange, he thought in relief.

He'd just opened his mouth to say something, when

abruptly, everyone else bowed their heads. Quickly, Brent bowed his own.

"Would you like to say the blessing, Brent, as our guest?" Adam asked.

"Ah, no thank you. I'd like to hear an Amish blessing," he said. He wouldn't begin to know what to say, even though it was only words of thanks for food. Thanks that were unnecessary, since Levi and Adam had presumably harvested the vegetables and milked the cows, and Sarah had cooked the entire spread.

Adam went into a long monologue with God in Pennsylvania Dutch. Covertly, Brent watched Sarah. She was lovely. Surely it didn't hurt to admit that to himself. Her skin was pink and pure, and her loose clothing hinted at a body that was lush and healthy underneath. He was drawn somehow to the pristine line where her golden hair was parted.

How could a woman who was a widow, a woman who'd been raped two months ago, look so serene, possess such an unearthly beauty?

He couldn't be feeling sexual desire. Not for an Amish woman. It was simply the lure of the unusual. She simply intrigued him.

Brent favored women who were sophisticated, who had money and style and flaunted both. Women were drawn to success, to power, and it was a real high to know that the women he dated believed in him as much as he did.

His fiancée, Jennifer, had been the most beautiful, the most ambitious of them all. An attorney with one of the big firms, she knew how to tussle confidently in the courtroom, how to tussle confidently in bed. Yet she hadn't had enough faith to stick around when the Samuelson case hit.

One thing you could say about the Amish. They
had loyalty. It was a quality Brent hadn't thought
much about six months ago. He knew its value today.

He was brought abruptly back to the present when
Adam switched to English. "Bless the harvest, our
family and friends, including Norman's friend who
sits among us, and bless especially Sarah, the beloved
daughter of this house. Amen."

"Amen, " Levi said.

"Amen," Sarah said.

A beat late, Brent repeated, "Amen."

They passed him dishes and dug into the food. In
no time they were eating from plates piled high, and
Brent could see there would be little left over after
the meal.

They talked quilts and Sarah's business, and Adam
spoke of bringing in the hay. Though they'd let Sarah
serve them, both Adam and Levi kept asking Sarah
about things Brent wouldn't have guessed she'd know
about, the harvest and the current prices for beans and
corn. Her father kept urging her to eat a little more,
and Brent couldn't miss the concern in his tone.

What Brent had read of Amish society suggested
that, from the perspective of the modern American,
the women were downtrodden and subservient to
men. Looking around this sunny kitchen, Brent understood that that view wasn't quite right. There was
a kind of sharing that had nothing to do with gender.

Silently, Sarah passed him the platter of pork. He
looked down, surprised to see that his plate was
empty. He used the fork to help himself to a small
second serving before passing the plate to Adam.

A too-warm breeze blew in the open windows, re-
leasing the faint scents of starched curtains and earth

from the gardens outside, mingling with the sweeter smells of the cooling baked goods. Outside was a stillness that was more than simply rural. Up and down the road were Amish farms. The only sound was the screech, far away, of crows. This was maybe the first time he'd ever sat in a place where no noise made by mankind intruded.

He cut, took a bite, savored the plain, well-cooked food.

Sarah spoke to him for the first time since the meal began. "Good?" she asked quietly.

"Good," he agreed, his mouth too full to say more. Suddenly, he realized why he was so hungry. Somewhere in the middle of the meal, the tight muscles in his spine and chest had eased, leaving him relaxed, feeling good physically for the first time since he'd walked out of that Toledo courtroom and faced a horde of reporters. Maybe the tension had been there long before that.

He ate cherry pie for dessert.

Finally, he finished, and looked up to find Adam watching him. "You eat like an Amish man," the older man said, stroking his graying beard.

Without thinking, Brent said, "If this is how Amish men eat, I'm beginning to think I understand the faith."

For a second, more relaxed than he ever thought he'd be among the Amish, Brent wondered if he'd gone too far. The three at the table stared, and Brent was forcefully reminded of their differences. Insurmountable differences. Then Adam Stolzfus laughed, a rumbling belly laugh.

Brent joined in, relieved that his remark hadn't been taken the wrong way. Getting to know Sarah

would be impossible if he couldn't share a meal with
her family without offending someone.

After Sarah had cleared the dessert dishes, the men
rose immediately and prepared to return to the fields.
"Someday, I'd like to see the farm," Brent said. It
was one thing to order a quilt or two, with Sarah
determined to hurry him along. But if he was really
going to get to know her, he had to get to know her
family, understand her life.

Adam smiled at him. "Do you know anything
about farming?"

Brent knew better than to try to fake it. "I'm a city
kid. I don't know a thing about animals or field crops
or dairying."

"You know what you must know to survive in
your world," Adam said. "We know what we need
to survive in ours. We grow our food and sell the
surplus and do all our own building."

"Woodworking?" Brent asked. Finally, they'd
stumbled upon a subject he knew something about.

"Sure. We're building a barn at Eli Lapp's farm
next week."

Sarah carried an empty bowl to the sink. "Father
likes most farmwork, but he especially likes building
the barns."

Brent nodded, pleased that Sarah was speaking to
him in a friendly tone. Sharing a meal had helped, as
he'd hoped it would. He was coming to get to know
her. Suddenly, he wanted to do that, and not just to
get her to agree to prosecute the case. He wanted to
get to know her as a person.

As a woman.

His mind turned abruptly from the thought. "I
helped build a garage once," Brent said, giving his

full attention to Adam. "It was interesting." It had been fun, and very, very satisfying.

"Did you and your father build it?" Sarah asked from where she was rinsing a pitcher at the sink.

"No, I built it with Martin Smith, a guy my mother was...seeing." At the last minute, Brent chose the euphemism. Martin was the only one of the men his mother had "seen" who had shown any interest in a lanky, bookish and undoubtedly snotty twelve-year-old boy. Brent could still remember that summer, the quiet camaraderie, the thumps on the back, the feel of sunburn and developing muscle, the questions about girls asked and answered. In September, Martin had asked his mother to marry him, and she'd refused. She liked her freedom, and she was already restless. So Martin had gone away. Funny, Brent hadn't thought about that summer in years.

Adam frowned but asked no more questions. "Well, we had a barn raising for the new barn here on our own farm six years ago. Why don't you come on out and I'll show you the post-and-beam construction?"

"Sounds good," Brent said. He rose and followed the older man to the door. There, Adam took his wide-brimmed straw hat from a peg and put it on.

"I'll see you later, Sarah," Brent said, pushing open the screen door.

So Brent planned to hang around all day, did he?

Her father was way too trusting. With a vehemence that belied any air of gentleness, Sarah scraped plates into a bucket that Levi would later take out to the pigs.

Didn't *Vater* remember that the Amish were to be separate and apart from the world?

Some of the Amish had English neighbors. That was handy, because the English offered the Amish rides to the store in their cars and the Amish used their telephones to summon the vet or arrange for fertilizer deliveries. But on County Road 7 there were no English farmers, and hence, no casual interaction, except with tourists.

Every Amish person had to find their own way to interact with outsiders, yet live separate and apart, in the world but not *of* the world. For guidance, they had the Bible and their bishop's interpretation of biblical law.

Sarah's mouth twisted. What she ought to do was tell her father that all Brent wanted was to reopen the case that Norman—at her request—had closed two months ago. The case that the bishop said would remain forever closed. Her father would not be so cordial then. No, in his quiet but firm way, he'd take Brent to the gate of the farm and ask him never to return.

Would Brent respect that request? He hadn't respected her own feelings on the first day they'd met. That wasn't quite fair, she thought, but she didn't want to be fair! She didn't want to admit that he'd only tried to persuade her, and if she'd felt bullied it was only because what Brent was suggesting was what she secretly wanted to do herself.

Sarah ladled hot water from the vat by the stove into the dishpan. She could hear the voices of the men outside. Brent's questions sounded sincere. She liked his voice, deep and strong, like the low rumble of thunder hours after a storm had passed.

Her father's reply was lengthy. There was eagerness on both sides, one to learn, the other to explain. Her father had a quiet pride in his farm that he tried to conceal, but he couldn't quite manage it. He pointed out one gas-powered piece of equipment, and Brent's reply came again.

Now Sarah realized she was straining to hear his voice, the same way she strained at night to hear the last of the thunder, sorry that the power of the storm had passed, leaving the earth damp but unchanged. When she realized just how much she wanted to listen, she slammed the platter down on the counter.

She ought to tell her father... What? That she found Brent attractive, compelling? That this very noon, he'd looked at her the way a man looks at a woman, *only* at a woman? That that look had shocked her and scared her and...*thrilled* her as nothing else had done since Jacob had died? Heaven above, she couldn't tell her father, couldn't bear his concern—and shame— that she was attracted to an English man.

Her hand tightened around a spoon. *She couldn't bear it if he prayed for her.*

Throwing down the spoon, she left the dishes and headed up the narrow wooden staircase. In her room, she crossed the bare planks to her desk, which sat under the west window to catch the evening light.

Reaching into the drawer, she pulled out her latest drawing. It was a scene from her own world. Thick-limbed draft horses pulled a wagon. An Amish boy stood on top of the wagon, catching and smoothing down the forkfuls of hay that the man below tossed up. The man and the boy's back were to the viewer, because Sarah must always shield the Amish face.

Unbidden, her mind conjured a red car, sleek and

fast and foreign. Unbidden, she conjured a bigger
world, of cities and glitter.

Unbidden, she conjured a face. A handsome, ar-
resting face, with clear, honest eyes. Not an Amish
face.

No, she decided firmly, she would not talk to her
father about Brent. She couldn't ban him from the
farm without questions from her father and Levi,
questions she wasn't prepared to answer. So she
would ask nothing more about his past, though she
was hungry to know more about him. It shouldn't be
that hard. He was no different from any of the English
who came to her shop to buy a quilt and spend their
English money.

The Amish were her life, but they'd taken away
her freedom to handle the violation of her body. She
loved her family, she loved her friends, and she'd
received their help and support countless times. She
would be Amish until she died. But she would never,
ever ask for their help in any personal matter again.

This...whatever it was she felt for Brent, she'd
handle on her own.

THAT AFTERNOON, Sarah lingered as long as possible
in the house. Eventually, a couple of cars drove in,
and she sold a few yards of printed calico to a woman
who wanted to make her own baby quilt.

Now the woman was gone and she was alone again
with Brent.

"I enjoyed your lunch," he said as she was showing him rust and brown fabrics, plunking down bolt
after bolt onto the big table.

"Why did you enjoy it?"

"Why?" For once, he looked unsure of himself.

"Your father is right, your cooking is good. Why wouldn't I have enjoyed it?"

She'd decided how to handle him. As a challenge, if necessary. He was English; he'd expect a more direct approach than the Amish would take. Anyway, it was a relief to let some of her truer nature out, if only with an English man.

She tossed her head. "Because the English eat pizza and spicy Chinese things. You can't like my pork roast."

"You're wrong," he said quietly, looking into her eyes and making her want to drop her own gaze.

She didn't. "I know why you're here. You want me to say I'll prosecute Randy West, and I won't. So you don't have to compliment my pork roast or buy my quilts."

"Look, I just want to know why. Why won't you do it? You fought your attacker, and you cooperated with the police for a time." He hesitated. "Maybe if you'd give me a good reason this creep should still be free, I could back off. I keep getting the feeling that you want to do this, and for some reason you won't. So how can you expect me to back off?"

"Because I've decided, that's why," she snapped, getting up and going to the window. The sky had darkened. Far off in the field, she could see her father and brother getting ready to head in.

She couldn't tell Brent the real reason she wouldn't testify against Randy West. How ridiculous to the English ear it would sound to say, *My bishop won't let me. My father won't let me.* Her whole soul balked at saying those words to a determined, independent man like Brent. He wouldn't respect her. How could he know that if she defied her bishop, and therefore the community, she wouldn't be Amish anymore? If she weren't Amish, she wouldn't be anything at all.

He came up behind her and touched her lightly on the arm. She wanted to fling off his hand. She closed her eyes for a moment. God help her, she wanted to cover his hand with her own and hold it to her. She did neither. Instead, she spoke, quietly and sincerely. "I'd prefer it if you didn't touch me."

He removed his hand immediately. "Does it bother you to be touched since the...rape?" The hesitation over the word had been slight, but it had been there. He seemed so tough, so sure of himself. But that hesitation made her wonder about the man inside.

"I don't know." Amish men were undemonstrative. Aside from an awkward squeeze of her hand by Levi, no man had touched her since the rape. No man had really touched her since her gentle husband had made love to her five years ago. No one but Randy West, and his touch had not been gentle, and it had had nothing to do with making love. She only knew that she didn't shrink from Brent's touch, and that thought momentarily amazed her. And shook her.

It led her to say too much. "I loved my husband. Before he died, we...touched often." Her face flamed, and although she hadn't meant her words to conjure lovemaking, they did in both her mind and, she suspected, Brent's. She was so very aware of his presence, tall and dark and imposing.

He cleared his throat. "Of course, the rape would change your feelings. Now you have fear, where you didn't before. You had independence before, but now you have to rely on someone else to be around when you go out. It's all right to be angry and feel that something important's been taken from you. Everybody who's been raped feels those things.''

He understood, she thought. Of all the people in the world, only an English lawyer seemed to understand. Of course, he must have talked to many rape victims, put many rapists in jail. Suddenly, she admired that. He put evil men away, did what prayer could not. His quiet voice, the tense straightness of his body, told her he understood. Surely that understanding must come from within, from more than what he did for a living.

"It's hard to talk about," she said slowly. Hard, but somehow necessary. But she couldn't talk with her Amish friends or family. Maybe with a mother, but not with her self-contained father, as kind as her father had tried to be, and not with Levi, who was young and impressionable.

The whole community would pray for her, but they were also embarrassed for her. Time and time again in those early days, she'd interrupted whispered conversations. She'd caught glances of sympathy and concern, a blush or two on the face of a young wife. The Amish just didn't know how to deal with something so private and terrible. Not one of her friends had ever said, *Talk to me, I'll try to understand, and if you want to do something in the English court, I'll try to understand even that.* She'd thought about talking with her friend Rebecca, but Rebecca was an innocent, an unmarried woman.

Brent spoke. "The things is, Sarah, you're not alone.''

In this she was, and the loneliness was the worst part of all. "An Amish woman need never feel alone," she said, but she wondered who it was she was trying to convince. "We have each other. We have the faith."

"Is that enough?"

No. Yes. "Yes, it is."

"But don't you think if you testified, if you saw Randy West go to jail, it would finish that part of your life? Most rape victims feel they can't quite move on with their lives unless—"

"I'm not most rape victims. I'm Amish!" The words were vehement, and she could hear the thick note of tears in them. She'd resolved only an hour ago to keep Brent at arm's length, and now she'd told him things she'd never told anyone else, and he was about to see her cry.

Blindly, she turned from him and headed toward the door, her fist pressed to her lips. Outside, it was starting to rain, fat drops that promised a fast-moving thunderstorm.

"Sarah," he called, but she just kept going.

THAT NIGHT, Sarah couldn't sleep. She rose and lit a lamp, and in the dim, golden light, she dipped her pen in ink and drew. She worked for hours.

She drew men and women, boys and girls. With the patience she mustered for her art, she infused all her figures with Amishness, giving extra attention to the dresses, fastened only with straight pins. She spent time on the ribs of thick, black stockings, drew in every weave of a straw hat. Changing to a wide nib, she colored in the hatbands of the men, then the plain black bonnets with wide, hard brims that the Amish women wore to town. Her people were drawn with their backs to the viewer. But one woman was turned in profile. Shading in the bonnet's brim, Sarah took care to insure that it shielded the woman's face.

RANDY WEST PUT another dollar on the bar and took the glass of draft the bartender handed him. The Roadhouse had the cheapest beer in town. Swiveling on the bar stool, he looked around the crowded tavern, feeling good.

He had seen Sarah today. Riding in a buggy with her snot-faced brother and some other girl, a girl who was younger but not as pretty as Sarah. They'd pulled into Schultz's Hardware, and when Sarah had gotten out of the buggy, he'd got a good view of her legs. She had a great pair of legs, and he, Randy West, had been the one to yank off a stocking and feel her white Amish skin.

Yeah, he was feeling real good. He eyed Julie Ann O'Neal, who'd come in alone and taken a seat at a table. She must've had a fight with her boyfriend again. He'd like to talk to Julie Ann, but he never could get up the nerve. She was beautiful. He had a hard enough time talking to the ugly ones. He'd really like to brag it up with Julie Ann, tell her what he'd gotten away with, but he wasn't flamin' stupid. She might not like it, anyway.

No, he wasn't stupid at all. He'd spent enough time in juvenile detention to be scared to death of adult jail, and, at age 21, it'd definitely be the penitentiary for him this time. He was *never* going to jail again.

But he'd like to tell Julie Ann how in school they made you study the Amish, how they didn't fight in wars, how the wimpy way the Amish did stuff was somehow special. He'd tell her the precise moment it had dawned on him that the Amish wouldn't do anything if he stole from them.

He smiled, remembering how he'd tried it, filching walnut trees from Amish fencerows, selling the lumber. Daring some Amish man to catch him. When he *was* caught, the guy didn't do anything about it. So Randy had broken into a house or two.

Hell, it was so easy. The Amish would never turn him in. It was against their flamin' *religion* to call the cops on guys like him.

The Amish worked together on everything. There was a barn raising at Eli Lapp's farm next week. He'd heard all about it from a guy who worked at the factory with him.

Randy wiped the rim of the glass on his sleeve and took a sip of beer. It hadn't gone perfectly that night. He hadn't expected Sarah Yoder to punch him. Then the police had questioned him, asking how he'd gotten two black eyes, and he'd wondered for a few long minutes if she'd turned him in, after all.

The Amish bitch.

He had to lay low for a while. He was too smart to do anything right now.

He thought of the navy blue pants and suspenders he had hidden at home, and of the straw hat with the wide brim. He'd been letting his hair grow a little, and it hung over his ears now, like the Amish wore it. There would be fifty men at Eli's barn raising. They wouldn't notice one more. Yeah, for now he'd just watch.

CHAPTER FOUR

PERCHED THREE stories high, Brent crouched on the barn roof and used the back of his arm to wipe sweat from his forehead. He looked out over the wide straw hats of the crowd of men also working on the roof, and then beyond to the countryside. There, green pastures alternated with neat squares of earth so fertile it was almost black. Gravel roads punctuated the scene, and on many of them, the electric company hadn't bothered to string lines.

At least fifty men were helping Eli Lapp build his new barn. All of them were Amish except Brent. He'd worn a pair of jeans and a dark polo shirt. His soberest clothes, yet the fact he was different was obvious. His presence had caused a few raised eyebrows this morning, but no comment. Adam had simply explained Brent was a friend of the family, interested in building.

Sarah came out of the house, carrying a bucket, heading toward the pigpen. There were dozens of women in the yard and they all were similarly dressed. Even the kids looked like miniature adults, right down to the straw hats or prayer caps. If Brent stuck out in this crowd, Sarah ought to have blended right in. He ought not to be able to pick Sarah out. But he could. Easily. Thick knot of blond hair under that pristine prayer cap, from this distance the cap a glowing white. There was just something about the way she moved that was graceful and distinctly...Sarah.

"Getting tired, English man?" Brent looked up. Adam held a hammer, and his eyes were twinkling.

"No way." But in truth, Brent's neck and shoulders were feeling the strain. He'd thought he was in good shape, but he had nothing on these men who worked hard physically all day, every day. A few of the others had paused in their work and were watching him. They'd spoken English in honor of his presence, but he'd been unable to contribute much to the conversation, which centered around mastitis in dairy cows and the proper way to flush a ram for breeding. But they had accepted him at face value. That was different from his lawyer crowd, where a guy had to be aggressive, perpetually be ready to do battle in the courtroom. Brent did well in that world.

Now his pride wouldn't allow less in this utterly physical, masculine world. Under the gaze of a dozen Amish men, he pulled a nail from his tool belt and positioned it in the cedar shingle. Over the course of the morning, he had become more sure of hitting the nail the first time. So when he brought his hammer down, the nail went into the soft wood.

Adam grunted in satisfaction and bent to his own work. A few seconds later, the conversation resumed around him. Brent concentrated on the task at hand, nailing down the shingles in rows along the chalkline marker. It wouldn't suit his plan to have Adam Stolzfus guess that Brent was ogling Adam's modest daughter. And really, there wasn't much to ogle. Unlike many of the women today who went barefoot, Sarah always wore black stockings, so thick they gave no hint of the skin beneath, and heavy shoes. But if she ever took off that little prayer cap and pulled the pins from the knot of hair at her nape, that hair would be like a golden waterfall...

Well, she wasn't going to let her hair down for Brent. He really didn't want her to; it was just a fantasy. Call it a private retaliation for this morning in the Stolzfus barnyard. When Brent had shown up at dawn, those blue eyes of hers had narrowed. She'd marched past him over to the buggy, carrying a heavy crock of what smelled like baked beans. He'd tried to take it from her. She'd held it back. "Up early for an English man," she'd said.

"Adam invited me to come with all of you to help build Eli's barn."

"Oh, I bet you're looking forward to *that*."

Actually, he was looking forward to the barn raising, but Sarah obviously knew he had a double purpose in coming today. He liked her quick intelligence. He'd already discovered there was a hot temper under all that serenity, and he found he rather liked that, too. It made her more real, somehow. She was not a weak woman, and when he *did* persuade her to testify, she was going to be a hell of a witness.

"There won't be time for much private conversation today," she'd warned. "No chance to pester me about the case. The men will have this barn up in a day. You'll have blisters on your palms before dusk." She looked satisfied at the notion.

"We don't have to talk about the case today."

"We don't?" He'd obviously surprised her. *Get to know her, to understand and appreciate her point of view,* Norm had said. *Make sure she trusts you. Then ask her again.* He was taking his boss's advice, though it went against his grain to take things slowly.

"I like building," he said. "Besides, you might find out I'm tougher than I look."

She glanced toward his chest and blushed. What was it about a grown woman blushing that suddenly seemed so sexy? "Here," he said abruptly. "Let me take that crock for you." He held out his arms, prepared to be helpful, polite, gallant.

"Thank you," she said sweetly. Then she swung her arms out and let go of the heavy crock. It slammed into his midsection and he let out a breath with a whoosh. He just managed not to double over and spill every bean.

An unrepentant smile had crossed her face as she reached up and pulled herself easily, gracefully, over the high buggy seat.

Yes, he thought now, the woman could hold her own, and that notion was not what he'd expected from an Amish woman.

He started to pound another nail into yet another shingle, but his gaze was caught again by Sarah. She was coming back across the yard toward the house. He felt like a teenager who couldn't keep his mind off a girl. In disgust, Brent turned from the sight of her and pretended to stretch his neck.

Out of the corner of his eye, he noticed an Amish man coming across the fields. A latecomer, all the other men had been here for hours.

Brent put Sarah out of his mind and concentrated on the roof, pounding nails. When Mrs. Lapp finally called them for dinner, the sun had climbed in the sky and made the shingles under his knees as hot as sand on the beach. He climbed down the ladder.

"A good morning's work," Adam said quietly when they were both down on the ground. The barn was a massive frame of raw yellow wood against a cloudless sky. Brent was struck by the strong, simple beauty of the scene. Then he got in line with the other men to wash at the basin.

The men ate first, and the women served them, putting bowls of food on the tables. Sarah worked with the rest, filling plates, clearing plates then wiping down the tables as the men ate in stages. After they'd eaten, Brent followed Adam and Levi to a grassy area beneath the limbs of a maple. They lounged there, Adam with his back against the trunk, Levi lying on the grass. Brent sat beside them. Both Adam and Levi fell asleep almost instantly. All around him, the men gathered in similar small groups, and talked or napped.

Quiet settled over the barnyard. The women, Sarah among them, sat and ate and talked. They fed the children, then cleared the tables for the last time and most went inside. A couple of the teenagers watched the smaller children as a few women came and went. Then Sarah came out alone, carrying a big dishpan toward the Lapp garden.

The dishpan looked heavy. He got to his feet and headed over to her. "Let me take that for you."

She hesitated. "Sure you want to chance it?" she finally asked, a gleam of humor in her eyes.

Pleased that she apparently wasn't going to nurse her anger all day, Brent reached out and took the pan. Made of heavy steel and filled with gray dishwater, it must've weighed about ten tons.

"Thank you," she said quietly. "It was heavy."

"Yes, it is. Don't the men help you with this kind of thing?"

"We have our work, and they have theirs. Some of ours is heavy, but we get used to it."

"They should help you with the heavier tasks."

"Some of the younger men—the more modern, I guess—help their wives, especially if the woman is pregnant." As if she was a little sorry she'd spoken, she turned her head away quickly.

Brent knew she didn't have any children. He, himself, hadn't wanted them in his earlier years, didn't want to lose his focus on his career. But he imagined Sarah had always wanted children, and he knew she'd cared for her husband.

"Did your husband give you a hand with the heavy work?" He was unable to help himself; he was curious about her, what her life had been like before he got involved in her case.

"No. Jacob was very traditional. Also very devout." She slanted him a glance. "You're surprised."

"Yes," he admitted. "I'm surprised you'd fall in love with a man like that. You don't strike me as a traditional woman."

"I'm an Amish woman."

Of course she was. He couldn't forget that for a moment, and yet, something about Sarah was not traditional. Her eyes were too direct, and under all that serenity, her reactions too immediate and strong. "I guess I shouldn't be surprised about you and Jacob, though. After all, opposites attract."

"Opposites attract? What does that mean?" she asked curiously.

"It's an English saying. In matters of men and women, sometimes what attracts one person to another is mostly a sense of how different they are. A dark-haired man, for example, might go for blondes.'' He glanced at Sarah's golden hair and decided he'd given a bad example.

She let out a sound, a kind of breathless giggle. Brent was startled. Was he *flirting* with an Amish woman? If so, it was the most indirect, the most unsure-adolescent-boy-afraid-to-phone-a-girl flirting he'd ever engaged in, and he didn't like it. He was the kind of man who said what was on his mind, and he said it to women who knew the rules. Sarah couldn't know the rules. She'd be *appalled* by the rules.

They'd reached the garden gate and he paused while she swung it open.

''Did your parents arrange for you to marry Jacob?'' he asked, still so curious about their differences.

She laughed, a soft incredulous laugh. ''Of course not. What books have you been reading about us?''

He felt his mouth tighten. ''What do I do with this dishwater?'' he asked brusquely.

''I'll show you.'' She went ahead of him down the narrow dirt path between two rows of beets. At the end of the path was a rosebush, smothered in bloom. ''Emma Lapp's rosebush,'' Sarah explained. ''The vegetables are for the table, but the roses are for Emma. She wants this bush to have an extra drink of water.'' She reached out, caught the end of the dishpan and guided it while he poured. The scent of roses, powerful in the heat of the sun, wafted up and mixed with the smell of earth.

He finished pouring and stood next to her, holding the empty dishpan. Around him the entire farm seemed to snooze in the sun. Sarah's task was completed, but he found he didn't want her to go. In fact, he wished she would stand closer to him. Sturdy, crisp cotton covered every inch of her, but she managed to look so feminine, standing amid all the lush greenery. He shifted the dishpan to the other hand. A little fantasy was all right, but these thoughts were downright dangerous.

She bit her lip, hesitating, then she spoke. "Please don't misunderstand. Jacob and I chose each other, and we were happy together."

He nodded. "I believe you."

"Really, we were just like most married people. We talked, we laughed, we argued."

Get to know her. For the case. Only for the sake of the case, he repeated to himself. "What did you argue about?"

She hesitated again.

"You can tell me," he said.

"Well, it's no secret." She laughed a little, a nervous sound, and he wondered how long it had been since anyone had asked her anything personal. For a second, he was sure she was going to say it was time to get back to the others. But then she said, "We argued about my drawing. I only draw Amish scenes, and I never draw faces. However, Jacob felt I was focusing too much on the individual, by making up a scene in my mind, thinking about the human form and using my imagination to draw a figure. But I was young and I didn't want to hear it, and so I...argued with him sometimes."

Sarah acted as though she were confessing some great sin. Her face was turned from him, and all he could see was the curve of her cheek and the gathered sides and the strings of her prayer cap. His lawyer instincts kicked in suddenly. He had a sense that he was about to discover something very important about Sarah. "Did *you* think it was a sin?"

There was a long pause. "Yes," she whispered so softly that he wasn't sure at first that he'd heard right.

"A sin? To draw Amish people?"

"To focus on the individual," she explained again. He stared at her, the dishpan against his thigh.

Her hand gestured to the neat barnyard, taking in the horses hitched to the posts, and the people gathered together. "The group is what's important, it's everything to an Amish person. You can see why. How else would we have got a barn half built this morning except by cooperating?" She sounded earnest. Maybe a little *too* earnest? He could tell there was something, some strong emotion underlying her words, but he couldn't get a handle on it.

"Do you still draw?" he asked, trying to gather information.

"I didn't for a while. Sometimes I couldn't help it. I'd get a picture in my mind, and I couldn't sleep until I captured it on paper. I don't use colors, nothing so worldly as paint. Anyway, it's the lines I'm interested in, and I draw with pen and ink. It..." She paused, then, "It means more to me than it should. And lately—"

She broke off and sighed, a long, frustrated sound. "Let's just say I'm trying to curb this urge of mine, the way I try to curb my temper." She smiled, a little strained. "The way my brother, Levi, tries—on his good days—to curb his interest in cars, the way my father tries to curb his pride in his farm, the way we all curb everything about us that makes it hard to be Amish.''

"It's hard for you to be Amish?"

Her cheeks went bright red. Abruptly, she turned from him and walked back down the garden row. He followed. They got to the gate; Sarah fumbled with the latch. It stuck.

She pushed harder. Heaven above, she'd resolved to hold him at arm's length, and here she'd been talking on and on about Jacob *and* her art! Now he was asking if it was hard to be Amish, as if that made any difference. And she'd almost said...

He touched her arm. "Sarah, I didn't mean to upset you."

Her temper snapped. "Your being here upsets me. You want me to testify, and I won't, and you think if you come here under false pretenses, try to get me to talk about myself—"

"Stop. Stop right there." His hand on her arm tightened, urging her to look at him. "I do want you to testify. My motives are no secret."

Well, that was true, but...

His eyes were clear as they met hers. "I want to get to know you, for you to get to know me, because I think if that happens I'll be able to show you why your testifying is so important. But I won't abuse your trust."

She believed him. And now that she thought about it, he hadn't lied to her; he'd made it very clear from the first day what he wanted. If he secretly stirred her, that was hardly his fault. And how was he to know that reopening the case had her questioning her life when there was no point in questioning it? Her life had been set the day she'd turned nineteen and joined the church.

"I'm sorry," she said quietly, embarrassed by her show of temper. She'd been admonished about her temper for so many years, and she'd thought she was getting better at curbing it.

"Don't be sorry. I know this is hard for you."

In that instant, she truly forgave him. He really had no idea how hard it all was, but he was the first person to give her the understanding she craved. Suddenly, words just came pouring out. "I wasn't sure what I wanted when I was a teenager. The outside world seemed so big and there were so many choices in it. I prayed for guidance, but God didn't seem to speak to me clearly. Then I met Jacob, and he set an example, he made me see what I ought to do."

"But you could have left, right?"

"Before I joined the church, yes. If I'd never joined, there would be no repercussions. I could still have been around my family and friends, though, of course, I wouldn't really be part of the community. But I decided to join the church, and now I'm Amish for the rest of my life."

"If you left, you'd be shunned." He said the word with real distaste.

She looked toward the barnyard of the Lapp home, where her people were gathered, and a shiver went up her spine. "Yes. I'd be shunned," she said quietly.

"I've been reading about shunning. It's wrong," he said flatly. "It's wrong for a group to turn its back on one of its own."

She looked at him in surprise. He said those words almost as if he really had an inkling of how difficult it would be to be part of a group and then abruptly not belong. She wondered what had caused such a reaction. He might be getting to know her, but she knew very little about him. And it shook her to realize how much she wanted to know about him.

Wanting to know him, to be with him was dangerous. They'd been talking about free thinking, and the individual, all the things that were most dangerous to the Amish. Dangerous to her own peace of mind, to her place in the community. "There hasn't been a shunning in Wheatland for over twenty years," she said, using her own words to reassure herself.

She'd been leaning a little on the gate, and the latch suddenly gave way. The gate swung open, and to keep from stumbling, she took a step through the gateway. In that moment, it seemed providential. *Good. Just keep going, away from Brent and temptation.* "We need to get back," she said quickly. She started walking toward the others.

RANDY WEST WAS raging mad. He'd been watching for hours, and he was so angry. He yanked a leather harness from the wall of the old barn and threw it in the dirt, grinding with the toe of his boot until the oiled leather turned dull and gritty. He'd like to kick that dinky calf over in the far stall, but he didn't dare. He'd be discovered if the animal cried when he kicked. That made him mad, too, that he couldn't do what he wanted to a flamin' Amish cow.

Randy had been hanging around all day, in the old barn mostly. He could sure understand why they were building a new one. In this barn, the cracks in the walls were so wide you could see just about anything outside. Inside, it was sweltering, and it stank of cow and horse crap.

The starchy shirt collar chafed, and his suspenders and baggy pants made him feel like some flamin' clown. He thought longingly of the cold beer at the Roadhouse. Maybe Julie Ann would be there. Maybe she'd had a fight with her boyfriend again. Maybe tonight was the night he'd buy her a drink. Then take her home and kiss her neck and do it to her. Tonight.

He grew hard thinking about it. But instead of being at the Roadhouse, he was here, dressed up like a clown and hanging around a flamin' Amish barn all day.

Aw, hell, why not just admit to himself why he was so mad?

Sarah Yoder. The Amish bitch had given him two black eyes, and she'd *spit* on him.

But with that guy—that guy who wasn't Amish—who'd come to help build the barn, she was all smiles. She'd looked at that guy all flamin' day. They'd gone out to the garden and stood there talking, real close like, and Randy'd been waiting for him to pull her aside, maybe take her in the barn or to the tall grass by the creek and do it to her there.

And she'd like it from *him,* even though they were supposed to like it only from their own kind.

But when Randy'd done it to her, she'd spit in his face.

He'd teach her, and then he'd go to the Roadhouse, and if Julie Ann didn't want to go home with him, he'd teach *her,* too, because he was so mad he'd just flamin' teach the whole world.

One of the huge horses moved and snorted, and suddenly Randy couldn't stand being in that barn one more minute.

He pushed through the door to the outside. There

was a bunch of them by the house, talking. The
women had brought out more food. Most of the older
guys had left, he guessed to do the milking. You
could count on these stupid Amish people to do things
on time.

He didn't see Sarah. The hell with it. He headed
around back for the long, hot walk across the fields
to where his pickup was parked. Head down, he
rounded the corner of the barn.

A girl stood in his way. A young Amish woman
with a small bouquet in her hand. She looked startled.

He could hardly breathe, scared to death that up
close his Amish costume wouldn't be exactly right.
Any second now, this girl would scream. He started
to back away, suddenly recognizing her. Sarah's
friend Rebecca.

Damn. If this girl screamed, he was done for. If
they knew he was after Sarah, this time for sure she'd
go to the police.

But he wasn't stupid. His heart slamming in his
chest with the fear of a jail cell, he tipped his hat at
the girl and smiled.

She blushed again, the brick-red blush of profound
shyness.

With a wave, he went around her, out toward the
fields. He walked, though he wanted to run. For a
long time, he waited for Rebecca to call out to somebody. His body was painfully tense, his legs ready for
flight.

Nothing happened.

When he reached the edge of the trees that lined
the fields, he chanced a look back. He didn't see the
girl anywhere.

It had been a close call. Relief and elation poured

right through him. He definitely needed a beer. But hell, it would be a celebration. Rebecca had been fooled. She'd thought he was Amish. So there it was: proof he was very, very smart. Proof that he could get close, and not get caught.

CHAPTER FIVE

BRENT WAS HERE AGAIN, and he'd learned to time his visits so that she was just getting dinner on the table when he arrived. Most of the time, he claimed to be here to choose his quilt. The last two times he'd wanted Adam's advice on repairs to the house he was renting in town.

If Adam had stopped to consider how much Brent was coming to the farm, he might have been suspicious. But usually her father was out in the fields. Wheat harvest was in full swing.

The funny thing was, Sarah really liked talking to Brent, though the tension of the case was always there, unspoken, between them. She talked about chores and the things her customers had said. The simple kind of talk that said nothing special about her hopes and aspirations but felt good nonetheless. He talked about the courthouse, and his stories made the place seem real, almost as though she knew the people who worked there.

She admitted that while Brent was here, she enjoyed his visits, tried not to think too much about why he'd come. Only after he left did she deal with why, and the certainty that she was being manipulated.

Once, he'd said, "Show me your art."

"Oh, I couldn't do that."

"Why not?"

"Well, because...no one has ever seen it."

He had been incredulous. "You've never shown your drawings to anyone?"

"Never. If I showed it to someone, I'd want their opinion. I'm sure it's not really good, but..."

"What if it *is* good?"

It couldn't be good. Real artists went to school, studied drawing. But if it was good...then she'd have the sin of pride to deal with, too. It was better not to know.

He'd looked at her with an intensity that was becoming familiar. No one had ever talked about her art this way, no one even mentioned it anymore, though her father might give her a sad look if he found a purchase of a new bottle of ink. But Brent seemed genuinely interested. And because art was such a big part of her, Sarah was tempted. Oh, to show someone! To ask if she was doing what she sought to do, capturing the uniqueness of her life in her pictures. To share with someone the beauty and power of line and form. To show it to *Brent*... "I can't," she finally said softly.

But at night, when she was drawing, she would think, *Someone wants to see this.* The thrill of knowing he was interested would course right through her.

And now he was here again.

It had not been a good morning. She was just crossing the barnyard, coming from the fields, where she'd taken a heavy jug of water and a hamper heaped with sandwiches. Rain was threatening, and the men would eat in the fields. They'd have to work extra hard in order to get the wheat into the shocks before the downpour. She was sticky and she had a headache.

A customer was waiting for her on the steps to the shop. Brent was parking his car on the gravel turn-around. Sarah gave her full attention to her customer, a woman she vaguely recognized. Last week, Sarah had been unsuccessful in talking the woman into taking quilting classes, though it had been clear the customer was a beginner.

"That red fabric you sold me ran," the woman said without preamble. "Even the water in the washer was pink."

"You might remember, I did say reds have a tendency to do that," Sarah said sweetly, telling herself to calm down. "Did you soak the fabric in cool water, with no detergent, and most especially not with anything light-colored?"

"As a matter of fact, I prewashed it with that mint green," the woman said. "You should see what color that green came out! Like someone had been sick on it. Now I'll have to buy all new." She stomped up the steps past Sarah.

Sarah was *not* going to crane her neck to see around the woman, to see what Brent was up to today. She was *not* going to look him over, feeling hungry and hot; she was *not* going to check out his jeans for the tenth time, to see if they were still as tight as his skin. She already knew how tight he wore them, how they hugged lean thighs and were so immodest they left nothing to the imagination, not even... She was *not* going to get suckered into inviting him into the house. Dinner for the family was out in the fields right now. If he wanted a home-cooked meal today, he could shock wheat to earn it.

She followed her customer into the shop, and suggested again that the woman take one of her quilting classes. "Before we get started, we talk about fabric care," she explained. "Preshrinking, color-fast-ness…"

The woman was plunking bolts of fabric down on the cutting table. "I don't see why you carry all this cotton. I like polyester. You don't have to iron it."

Polyester was among the worst fabrics for a quilt. "The polyester fibers pull on your quilting thread, weakening it as you stitch," Sarah said, measuring and using her wheel to cut the yardage the customer had specified. "Worse—"

The door banged open in a sudden gust of wind and Brent came into the shop. Sarah ignored him. Why was her case so important that he'd come over on one pretext or another five times in two weeks? Not that he'd mentioned the case. Not that she was counting how many times he'd come. But it was get-ting almost routine to set an extra place at the table nowadays.

"Worse," she continued, her focus determinedly on her customer, "the polyester allows the batting to beard—to come up through the top layer of the quilt and make it look fuzzy." She smiled. "You won't want your hard work ruined by bearding. Aren't you making a baby quilt?"

The woman frowned. "No, a wedding quilt for my daughter and her fiancé, though God knows, kids nowadays…they'll probably want an electric blanket, won't appreciate all the work."

Brent was prowling the shop, in that way he had of making her shop, her kitchen, her barnyard, her whole world seem too small.

She wrote out the receipt. The customer grumbled about having to pay twice as she left. It was a measure of Sarah's frame of mind that she was actually sorry to see the woman go. She'd rather have a difficult customer than face Brent.

Yes, she would. Because Brent had to be building up to discussing her case as sure as the humidity outside was building to another summer storm. "What do you want?" she asked him abruptly.

He paused a few feet from her. "Hello to you, too, Sarah." He smiled, but his eyes were intent. They always were intent, even when he was teasing.

"You like to provoke me," she accused.

"Actually, I do. As a trial lawyer, one of my favorite strategies is to put my opponent off balance."

He could only put her off balance if she let him. "What can I sell you today?" she asked more sweetly.

He was ready with an answer. "You know that rust-colored geometric you picked out for my quilt last time?"

Sarah nodded. How could she forget? It had taken him an hour to get her advice that day, and somehow he'd managed to make his selection five minutes before noon. Her father had invited him to stay for dinner, of course. Adam liked Brent, and she suspected her otherwise careful father was letting down his guard in the glow of being asked for advice by this successful, worldly city man. The part that was harder to figure out was her sense that Brent liked her father, too, that he wanted to be here.

"Well," Brent said, "we're going to have to change it."

"It took you an hour to find that fabric!"

"Right." He was smiling a little.

She hated that smile. She liked that smile so much,

the way it quirked higher on one side than the other, as if he had a sense of humor but wasn't used to smiling that often. More than once, when she was drawing late at night, she'd draw a broad chest. Then she'd think about that half smile, and her mind would conjure the whole face. Brent's face, with honest eyes.

It scared her sometimes. Now she tried to hold on to her bad humor. But she couldn't help smiling. She was afraid of her attraction, but she liked this man. She remembered how he'd carried her heavy dishpan. She remembered how much he liked her food. She remembered how intensely he felt about his profession, how he took it as seriously as she did her art and her shop. She remembered he was the only one who seemed to understand how she felt about being raped, who'd felt—and shared—her outrage.

"You still want me to prosecute the case?" she asked, although just last night she'd told herself she wouldn't ask, would simply outwait Brent.

"Yes."

The dark clouds must be moving in; the windows went gray, the shop very, very dim. "But you never mention the case," she said. "So why do you come?" She hated how unsure her voice sounded.

He was still for a long moment.

Sarah picked up the bolt of red cotton and went to put it on the shelf. As she brushed by him, there was a bright, almost blinding flash of lightning, and then a crack of thunder. She jumped.

He took her forearm. "Are you all right? Are you afraid of storms?"

She laughed a little breathlessly. "No, of course not." He was still holding her arm. Her skin burned where he touched her. "I like storms. The world in black and white and gray." Like her drawings. *Powerful, elemental, like his hand on her.*

Nervously, she pulled her arm away. "Levi and *Vater* will come from the fields to get out of the storm, but they'll stop at the barn. The barn is closer than the house, and they'll soothe the horses and wait for the rain to let up. I don't mind the thunder, but our horses get skittish." She was rattling on, she knew. It was so dark in here. "I'm going out to the porch to watch the storm," she said abruptly. Passing him, she went out the screen door.

The rain was coming down in sheets. The afternoon sky was slate, and the rain was a wall that practically obscured the sight of the barn, though it was only a hundred feet away. Brent stood behind her, and for a moment, they both watched the storm together. Lightning flashed again. There was a startling, wrenching crack as somewhere a tree was caught and split.

"Do you like storms?" She had to raise her voice.

"I guess I've just always thought of rain as a nuisance."

She had a sudden vision of him in an elegant suit, unfurling an umbrella to cover the head of some city woman in a worldly red dress. The thought caused her chest to squeeze, a quick, painful pressure.

Sighing, she turned. There were some old kitchen chairs on the porch, and a porch swing. She took one end of the swing, and Brent took the other. She knew what she was doing, choosing the swing over one of those hard chairs. The swing was wide, but to choose this seat for two was like the teenagers playing with firecrackers—almost safe if they were careful, but not absolutely safe. There was two feet of space between them, but still she felt him...

She felt herself blushing. Jacob used to say she was pretty. She'd admonished him, but he'd insist. *You're a pretty woman, Sarah.* Did Brent think she was pretty, too?

It didn't matter.

He was English, and when he got what he wanted, he'd never be back. She took a deep breath. "Just now in my shop, you said you still want me to testify. But you didn't answer my question. Why haven't you even tried to discuss the case these past two weeks?"

He hesitated. "Because, as I told you, I want to get to know you," he said finally. "And I want you to trust me."

"You're learning about us. But how did you ever imagine I could trust you when I know nothing about you?"

He went curiously still. "I thought you knew everything about me. I'm a lawyer, a prosecutor. I want to win cases."

"Why do you want to win cases? Why is it so important?"

The rain came down even harder. Water filled the ruts the buggy wheels had made in the gravel, and then ran over to make tiny, impromptu rivers.

She was as direct as he was, Brent thought. He looked away from her, toward the wall of rain.

And he owed her an answer. He expected her to stand in a public courtroom and face a horde of strangers—strange men, maybe even reporters with pencils poised, and tell how one man had torn off her underwear and bruised her thigh and violated her.

But what was the honest answer? Did he want her

to do that so she'd be safe, or so he could save his
career?

What difference did it make? It was a win-win, he
reminded himself. Testifying would be good for
Sarah. Her faith preached pacifism, though she'd
fought Randy West. Her drawing was worldly, yet she
drew. Obviously, she was already picking and choosing among the tenets of her faith. Of course, she
would always be Amish. But it would be right for *her*
to testify, even if it wouldn't be right for other Amish
women. She could put this crime behind her, get on
with her life, the way he sensed she wanted to do.

"For years I wanted to be a lawyer," he said. "I'm
a very good one." He said it to reassure, not boast.

"I know that," she said over the sound of the rain.

"How could you know something like that?"

"I know what a lawyer does. I know how...
persistent you are." She did not smile. "And I know
that's a big part of being a lawyer."

He owed her the truth, he repeated to himself. If
his gut was tight at knowing she might not believe in
his innocence, it was only because he needed her trust
on the case. "I had trouble in Toledo," he said. "Ethical trouble on a case there." He wasn't sure if she
understood the word *ethical,* so he added, "Trouble
with honesty."

"You have honest eyes," she said.

Honest eyes? He searched her face. She was so
naive. She didn't know you could look into the face
of a man you'd caught stealing red-handed, and he'd
look you in the eye and tell you he didn't do it. Her
face was shadowed, though the rain was letting up a
little and the world was lightening. She tossed her
head, and he wondered if she was blushing, because

he knew she would be embarrassed at having said something about his appearance.

Well. "Anyway, I was prosecuting this guy, Samuelson. For a murder."

She nodded.

"I thought he was guilty. He had a long prison record for theft, he had motive and opportunity, and we had a witness who claimed to have helped Samuelson plan the killing." Brent didn't add that the witness had been a hood in a jail cell and had agreed to testify in exchange for a lighter sentence. The testimony of criminals who had something to gain was always suspect. If there hadn't been all that circumstantial evidence, Brent might have pressed further. But there had been no reason to do so.

"Sarah, what I didn't know was that there was other evidence. Samuelson didn't do it. He was a criminal, but he didn't murder anyone."

She was still watching him, and Brent wondered if she understood any of what he was telling her. He braced himself, knowing that whether or not she really understood, he was going to tell her the rest. That somehow, trust had become a two-way street.

It was hard to tell her this next part because Cavanaugh had been his best friend. It was even harder to say that he, Brent, had been a fool. That he hadn't watched his own back, that he'd made a stupid mistake. "A man named Thacker Cavanaugh was my boss. The county prosecutor. Samuelson was my case, but Cavanaugh was involved in the plea negotiations because the media was giving the case heavy coverage."

She looked a little puzzled, and it dawned on him that she didn't understand what a plea negotiation was. "The decisions, the bargaining, the strategy," he explained. "Often, if a person is charged with a certain crime, he'll plead guilty to some other crime that will get him less jail time." She nodded in understanding.

The thunder was becoming more distant, but it was still raining. Brent took a deep breath. "It turns out Samuelson was innocent, and Cavanaugh had the evidence of that innocence in his file."

"Which he didn't share with you. He let you take the case on, knowing that man was innocent."

She was smart, he thought. As unfamiliar as the court system was to her, she'd grasped what had happened right away. "Yes. Samuelson was convicted and sentenced to die in the electric chair." He couldn't look at her. "Fortunately, some kid from the law-school clinic started looking into the case. When Cavanaugh was caught with that evidence in the file, he said that since it was my file, I must have known all along. I was investigated. Since so many people— me, Cavanaugh, various clerks and secretaries had handled that file, the investigators couldn't determine who knew what. They didn't hold me responsible, but they didn't clear my name, either."

The rain was dying. Brent felt her next to him, but he stayed focused on the gray-brown water and the puddles in this Amish barnyard. He knew the risk he was taking, telling Sarah all this. If she thought he could be used so easily, why should she put her trust in him?

"So now you know how I ended up in a little town like Wheatland."

She turned to look at him. She didn't ask any questions about the case, just, "Do you miss the city so much?"

"Yes," he said simply. It wasn't the city itself, the concrete and steel. He could appreciate the beauty of the farms all around him. What he missed was the fit of his city practice, the certainty that he'd belonged. The power of belonging, of controlling his own destiny. "I'm rebuilding my reputation here, and then I'm going back." He paused, waiting for her to say something. At the same time, he told himself it didn't matter what she thought, except if it affected the case. After all, so many people—people important to his career—hadn't believed him.

But suddenly it became so hard to wait for Sarah's judgment.

She finally spoke. "That case must have been difficult for you."

"But do you think I deliberately let Samuelson be convicted?"

"Of course not."

She believed him. *She believed him.* Just because he said so. All at once he knew that he hadn't been honest with himself, that he wanted her approval, and that it was very, very personal.

"I know how important it is to belong," Sarah said softly. "I know about loss." Now she too looked at puddles in the driveway. "I know about loneliness."

He marveled at her intuitiveness. Most of the time, her world and his seemed never to touch. Now she was two feet away, and he felt closer to her than he'd felt to another human being for a long time. Something, some strong emotion shot through him. He seldom asked other people for understanding. But he'd asked Jennifer for it, the day the Samuelson case had broken. She'd said he was naive, had immediately started strategizing how to control the story. He'd said, "Do you believe me?" and impatiently, she'd replied, "What difference does it make?"

Now he'd asked an Amish woman, of all people. And Sarah gave him understanding.

He wanted her, suddenly, strongly. The power of that wanting stunned him. She was still on the swing, only two feet away. If he reached out...

He couldn't help himself; he did reach out. He lifted his hand, wanting to feel the softness of her cheek. Then he was going to put his hand on the back of her neck, close his hand around the knot of hair there and pull her toward his mouth...

His hand was in the air. Not moving a muscle, she watched it come closer. Almost there...

The big barn door opened with a roar and a screech. Adam called out some cheerful words in Pennsylvania Dutch.

Sarah jumped to her feet. She ran to the porch railing. She called something back, and her voice sounded too high, too forced.

She knew Brent had been about to kiss her. What would she have done if her father hadn't come from the barn? Maybe it was better not to know.

Brent stood. "I have to go," he said to her back. "Right now."

She didn't argue.

THE MECHANICAL alarm clock by Sarah's bed said 2:00 a.m. when she finally got up and lighted a lamp. Tiptoeing across the room to her desk, she opened the drawer and got out pen and ink. She pulled out a half-finished drawing of a quilting bee. The women were bent around a frame. Inside the frame was a center diamond quilt, one of the oldest patterns of the Pennsylvania Dutch. Her mother had brought such a quilt to her marriage bed.

Thirty-five years later, her father still had it on his bed. The big diamond was red, surrounded with a thin band of turquoise. Black set off the diamond and made it glow. But it was the quilting that made the cover truly special. Her mother had told her once that it had taken six thousand feet of thread to complete the feathery patterns.

She stared at the quilt in her drawing. She'd given it enough detail to represent her mother's quilt. Sarah had begun the drawing a week ago, thinking maybe if she drew this scene with her mother's quilt, she'd feel...Amish. It had helped. Then.

Tonight all she felt was restless.

Brent had told her something painful, asked for trust. She'd heard the note of strain in his voice telling her had been hard. He had his pride—all men did—and when they put aside their pride and told a woman the kind of things Brent had shared, sometimes that meant...

Yes, she was restless tonight. She hadn't spoken much through dinner and chores and washing-up. Thinking about that moment on the porch swing when Brent had leaned toward her. She remembered the rush of heat to her cheeks, her heartbeat that suddenly went way too fast.

This afternoon, when Brent had looked at her, hot and hungry, good memories had come back, pushing past the other ugly and painful ones. Now she remembered things from long ago with real clarity: waiting for her husband in bed, how Jacob would use a rough palm to softly brush her nightgown up. Jacob had kissed her hard sometimes, and she'd wanted it that way. She'd never been afraid of Jacob because even hard was gentle with a man you loved.

What would Brent's mouth feel like, meeting her own?

She sighed, sat down at the desk and dunked her pen in ink. She knew she might never feel the touch of a man again. She didn't want any of the Amish men who'd offered to court her.

She couldn't let Brent kiss her. He was an English man. He'd said right out loud what his plans were, and when he got his reputation back, he wouldn't even be in town, much less in her life. He'd go on to prosecute murders again and live a glamorous, worldly life, the very life the Amish rejected.

She pushed too hard on the nib of her pen suddenly. Ink flooded the picture she'd spent ten hours drawing. Sarah bit her lip to keep from whispering something profane.

Clearly, she didn't have the patience tonight for her work.

She folded the drawing in half and tossed it in the wastebasket at her feet. But she still itched to draw, to do something to forget how she'd felt waiting for an English man's kiss.

Opening the drawer again, she pulled out another piece of paper and a piece of charcoal pencil. All right, she thought. Something simpler then, something she could complete tonight. She closed her eyes against the image that formed.

Not him!

Okay, a man then. An Amish man, of course. No face. *No face,* she told herself firmly. She sketched the head, the column of neck, the breadth of the chest—very clearly a man's torso.

And now the face. She hurried before she could change her mind. Some extra work on the eyes because the eyes said so much about a person...the nose... Now she was hurrying...faster...and faster... Hands quivering a little, sketching in the details that took that face from generic to very, very specific.

God help her. A part of her had known what she was going to do. The image wasn't even remotely Amish.

She'd drawn *his* face. She felt suddenly hot, then cold. She'd drawn a face, the first time in her life she'd ever done so.

But it was only an English face.

It wasn't a sin, she told herself. It was only a sin to draw *Amish* faces. Surely she'd never heard the bishop forbid drawing a nonbeliever.

Of course, she knew the bishop wouldn't forbid drawing an English face. Because it would never occur to him that any Amish would want to do such a thing.

Brent's image, his honest eyes, intent expression, his mouth hard and somehow passionate, stared up at her, flickering in the glow of the lamp. Quickly she opened the desk drawer and put the drawing inside. She pulled a couple of other drawings on top of it and shut the drawer.

It wasn't a sin, she repeated to herself. But oh, it surely felt like one.

CHAPTER SIX

SARAH LADLED warm water into a bucket and added ammonia. She'd got out of bed at four-thirty this morning, strained the milk, made breakfast and mopped the floor. Now if she hurried, she'd have enough time to clean Levi's room before the shop opened for the day.

She felt tired after her sleepless night, but knew the best thing to do was to keep busy. Idle hands did the devil's work. She smiled grimly, remembering her busy hands of the night before.

But thoughts of Brent felt good. They felt right. That was the nature of temptation, she reminded herself. Humming one of the sternest hymns she knew, she climbed the stairs, bucket in hand.

Through the open window in Levi's room, she could smell the earthy scent of the farm, so familiar she seldom noticed. Today she was consciously taking comfort in the familiar.

The wooden floor was bare. There were no curtains on the windows, no pictures on the walls. The quilt on the bed was one of the plainest patterns, called Bars. Electric-blue stripes against a black border, with a binding of bright red.

Levi's trousers were in a heap on the floor. She never could get him to take them to the hamper.

Nothing changed here. People were born, lived,

died Amish. The land never really changed. When she was a child, she'd longed for change, longed for the world to be bigger than County Road 7.

Now she told herself she was glad some things didn't change. Things like the love of her family, her friends, the pleasant routine of her shop. This was her world, and as an adult, she'd learned to appreciate it, even treasure it. There were worse things than routine.

She started to strip Levi's bed, yanking off the top sheet. The bottom sheet was fitted, and she put her hand on the corner to dislodge it. Her fingertips touched a flashlight tucked between the mattress and box springs. She smiled.

She knew all about Levi's flashlight and autoracing magazine. Forbidden. But not the end of the world. Her brother liked to talk cars with Brent. Levi, of course, was attracted to Brent and his glamorous, worldly lifestyle. She understood.

Wasn't Sarah herself drawn, not to the speed, but to the freedom that red car represented?

She balled up the sheet and tossed it to the floor. The magazine fell out with the sheet, and Sarah picked it up, ready to tuck it back in its hiding place.

She flipped it over and stopped short. Heat blasted her cheeks until they felt red-hot. It wasn't an autoracing magazine.

A naked woman stared up at the viewer, her expression so provocative that even her face seemed obscene. She smiled, beckoned.

Hands shaking, Sarah sat down on the bed, the magazine in her lap. She knew such magazines were for sale, but she'd never seen one. Once, some girls had whispered that the druggist in Wheatland had immodest magazines under the counter, and the English men would buy them.

She paged through the magazine, hardly daring to look. The inside was worse than the cover. There were lots of pictures, women touching their breasts, their most private parts, too, as if inviting a man to touch them there. She shut the magazine with a snap.

What was she going to do? Someone should talk to Levi. He had feelings, she knew, all people had urges...

Telling her father would be the sensible, safe, Amish thing to do. But she hated to tell her father. He was kind, but he could be stern. His sternness had hurt her a couple of months ago; she'd hardly been able to bear it.

For a second, she thought of trying to talk to Levi herself. After all, she was a widow, not a shy virgin. But she quickly rejected the idea. How could she convince him that she understood his feelings, but that this kind of thing was wrong?

Or she could do nothing. She stood, hesitating, then slipped the magazine back into its hiding place. Who was she to chastise her brother? After all, Levi hardly had a monopoly on sin.

The drawing of Brent's face that she'd shut in the drawer came back to her. She picked up the bucket and went to the window. Squeezing out a rag, she began to wash the glass. If allowing Brent into her life was bad for her, it was bad for Levi, too. That magazine was proof that Levi had gone farther in sowing his wild oats than anyone suspected.

This—whatever it was with Brent—would have to end. If he came to the farm again, she would tell him so. She'd just say firmly that she'd made her decision.

About testifying. About her place in the community, about her intention to become Amish in her soul.

BRENT LOOKED toward the witness-box as he waited for his elderly witness to continue. Bob Kay said, "Well, I told him if he had a contract, I'd sign it. He had a nice truck and, like I told you, he seemed like an honest businessman."

"Did you actually sign a contract?" Brent made a note on his legal pad. Lyle Davis had come to town promising to install replacement windows on some of the old houses, and he'd absconded with thousands of dollars from innocent people. Davis had been caught, but in the way these things usually went, the money was probably gone forever.

Brent could put Davis away in prison—planned to—with this witness and a number of others, but that wouldn't get the people their money back. The law had its limitations, and those limitations could be frustrating at times.

The old man studied his hands. "I did sign that contract. I was supposed to put down two thousand dollars for a deposit, but I thought, why not just pay for the whole thing, not have a bill later, and I says to the guy—to Mr. Davis, I mean…why not just let me pay you cash…" His words were slowing. "He said, real honest-sounding, you don't have to do that…but…I…"

"Did you pay him cash?" Brent asked.

"Yeah."

"How much cash?"

The witness twisted his hands. "Everything I had. Eight thousand dollars."

There was an audible gasp from one of the jurors.

"What happened on the date Mr. Davis was to show up to actually install your windows?" Brent pressed on. His witness's voice had gone rough and quiet as the old man told the familiar, sad story of trying to track down a man who was good at covering his tracks. The witness was effective, and the case was solid. In Toledo, Brent hadn't been assigned these routine theft cases for a long time. Things were different in Wheatland; except for Sarah's case, this was as high-profile as it got.

But he felt strongly about this case he was prosecuting today. The depth of his anger at Davis, the two-bit con man, was actually a little surprising, considering how routine the work was. But the people of Wheatland were decent, hardworking, and they deserved justice.

To his right, he could see the jury leaning forward to hear the witness's quiet answers. Brent had them listening, and Davis was going to go to jail. That felt pretty good.

Six people had been caught in the scam. He could have just used Bob Kay as his witness. But because Brent wanted a conviction on multiple counts, he was bringing all six in to testify. When the judge called a break, Brent left the courtroom. He joked with the teenager who was working at the concession stand and poured himself a cup of coffee. Needing a few minutes of quiet, he took his cup and headed down one of the private hallways of the old courthouse.

"Brent!" It was Norm, coming around the corner, puffing from moving so fast.

"Norm," Brent acknowledged, starting toward his boss. Something must be wrong to get Norm moving like that. "What's up?"

"Bertram Snow is what's up. The guy hasn't had a scoop in years. I thought he'd stopped trying and just concentrated on stuff like the Rotary float." As he got close to Brent, Norm waved a folded newspaper. "But he has a scoop now, a damn rotten scoop."

Surprised by his boss's unexpected profanity, Brent reached for the newspaper. "Here, let me see that." He snapped open the paper.

The world tilted under his feet.

Alleged Rapist Loose In Wheatland, the headline read. Then, under it, Amish Woman Alleged Victim, Won't Testify. An Exclusive by Bertram Snow, *Wheatland Post* Editor.

Sarah. His gut tightened. Brent knew how this kind of thing worked. Sarah's story would now be fodder for public scrutiny and gossip. He scanned the story rapidly. The paper quoted "unnamed sources" at the police department and referred to Sarah only as "the Amish widow." It wouldn't be hard to figure out who the unnamed source was. There were only about 20 cops in Wheatland, and Brent knew them all.

"They don't know her name," Norm said next to him.

"Maybe they're saving that for tomorrow night's exclusive," Brent said from between clenched teeth.

Norm put a hand on his arm. "No. If they had it, they'd use it. They must not have Randy West's name, either."

Brent didn't care about West's privacy, but he cared very much about Sarah's. There were so many Amish in Wheatland County that no one—provided no one else did any talking—would guess Sarah's identity. Still…

Very evenly, Brent said, "I'm going to throttle Bertram Snow, and then I'm going down to the police department and find out who gave Mr. Snow his exclusive, and then I'm going to commit a felony."

"Don't tip your hand," Norm said. "If you do, I'll have to have you arrested for menacing."

Brent looked up quickly, his hand fisting around the paper.

"Okay, bad joke," Norm said quickly. "Look, I don't like this, either. I'm the one who said don't cause a scandal, remember? I like Sarah. I respect her, you know that."

Brent nodded. He was shell-shocked. He'd thought he had plenty of time to convince Sarah before the media got involved.

But he'd waited too long, and he knew without a shadow of a doubt why.

He'd waited too long because, like Norm, he'd come to like and respect Sarah and her feelings.

He'd waited too long because he liked spending time with her, and if he'd pushed too hard he wouldn't have an excuse to see her.

He'd waited too long because he wanted to kiss her.

He'd waited too long because he wanted to do a lot more than kiss her.

He'd been a fool. He'd known what needed to be done and he'd lost focus. Brent McCade was not the kind of man to be a fool twice.

The rage, the disgrace in Toledo rolled right through him, mingling with his feelings for Sarah, an innocent victim who was now the titillating subject of a newspaper article.

Norm stroked his mustache. "The Amish don't always read the newspapers, but they hear things. Sarah will learn about this article. Do you want to talk to her, or should I?''

"I'll do it.''

"Just tell her we didn't contribute to the article, and we sympathize.''

Brent exploded. "For God's sake, Norm, that's not all you expect me to tell her, is it?''

The bailiff came to the head of the hallway, motioned for Brent. Impatiently, Brent held up a hand to indicate he'd be there in a minute.

"It's still her choice about testifying," Norm reminded him.

Brent didn't like it. He had never liked it. But it was Sarah's choice not to testify. If he could only feel in his gut that it really was her choice, her free choice. Ever since he'd learned how she'd once considered giving up her Amish roots—

"But she's Amish now," he mused aloud.

"Yes. And I can tell you're starting to understand—*really* understand—what that means.''

"Mr. McCade, the judge is retaking the bench," the bailiff called.

"Coming," Brent called back, but he didn't move.

"Go. You have a case to do.''

"I won't be out of here until tonight. Then I'll go talk to Sarah." And say what? That she had the prosecutor's sympathy?

When he got to the courtroom, he saw that the bailiff had been premature. The jury box was empty and the judge hadn't yet retaken the bench.

He slapped the folded newspaper on his counsel table, headline down.

"Did you read the article about the Amish

woman?'' Steve Townshend, the public defender who was representing Davis, stood next to him and nodded at the paper.

"Yes," Brent said shortly.

Steve let out a low whistle. "I've been here four years, and we never had a rapist on the loose. Wonder what my wife will say? Fortunately, she's from the city originally. At our house, we lock our doors at night. We're still in the habit of thinking safe."

Safe. The word troubled Brent. Did this article make any difference to Sarah's safety? He'd never really thought she was safe, but as time passed he'd wondered if West had decided he'd had his thrill.

Brent had checked out Randy West ages ago. The guy was a loner who had a job but hung out in some dive every night, hardly speaking to anybody. He had a juvenile record. But with the exception of Sarah's rape, he hadn't done anything illegal since he'd turned eighteen three years ago, so apparently he was able to exercise some control over his behavior. The question was how much.

Brent didn't like not knowing the answer. A conviction was the only sure thing.

Steve shook his head. "Wonder why she won't do anything against whoever did it."

"She's Amish. And you know what a rape trial's like."

"The pits for the woman," Steve agreed. "But she'd make a great witness. Those baggy dresses, and that little hat thing they always wear. An Amish woman would make a better witness than a nun." He grinned.

"This is a rape case. You think there's something funny about that?"

"Hey, lighten up. What's eating at you?"

Brent was saved from an answer by the appearance of the judge.

"All rise."

Brent stood as Steve hurried back to his own table.

Brent would talk to Sarah, but he had a trial to finish first. In his world, that had to come first.

But he couldn't shake a sense of foreboding. Now that the case had hit the newspapers, would Sarah be safe?

Would any woman in Wheatland County be safe?

"NOT SO MUCH MINT, Sarah!" Laughing, Rebecca Bontrager grabbed Sarah's hand just as she was about to add another handful of chopped mint to the pitcher of lemonade.

"Anna always makes it too sweet. The mint helps cut all that sweetness." Sarah hadn't tasted the lemonade, but she knew all the recipes the women used. She knew, for example, that the raisin cookies would be cakelike confections, so carefully baked there wouldn't be even a hint of browning around the edges. Emma Lapp had made them. Sarah knew the coffee cake would have very brown edges because it had been baked by Sadie Hershburger. She knew that Martha Miller had bought the marshmallow cream at the store, because Martha's arthritis made it hard for her to bake.

Sarah felt a rush of genuine contentment. It was good to hear the low voices and laughter of the women gathered around the quilting frame in the living room. It was good that Sarah could bring this work to them. Not only did it help them support their families, it also gave them a chance to visit on a hot evening. It was good to roll her eyes at Rebecca, smile a little more broadly and dump all the mint into the pitcher.

Since that morning a week ago when she'd found that magazine in Levi's room, Sarah had known she had a decision to make. She was going to try to be Amish in her heart, and if nothing else, set an example for Levi. Soon she'd pull that drawing of Brent from her drawer and throw it away.

Sarah stirred the lemonade while Rebecca loaded a tray with refreshments.

"Two whole jars of marshmallow cream," Rebecca said. "But we only have one jar of peanut butter and one loaf of store-bought bread."

"Just enough for Anna." They looked at each other and laughed.

Anna Troyer's sweet tooth was legendary even among people who loved sweet things. Anna's favorite was a sandwich made of marshmallow cream, peanut butter and the softest store-bought white bread.

"I don't know why anyone likes this," Sarah said, opening the jar and sticking a knife into the white mass inside.

"Too sweet," Rebecca agreed. Suddenly, she stood on tiptoe to see out the window over the sink. "Speaking of sweet…"

Sarah glanced out the window. Amos Troyer, Anna's oldest son, was coming across the barnyard carrying a basket of vegetables.

"He's sweet on you," Rebecca noted.

Sarah felt herself blush. Amos was a widower with two grown children. Over the past couple of years, he'd become the most determined of her suitors. He was a good man.

Absolutely nothing about him interested her.

"You should marry again," Rebecca said, her eyes on the window. "Amos is nice."

"Nice and boring," Sarah muttered. "Sorry, Rebecca, but I'm not interested."

"But don't you want a husband? Children?"

There was a long pause. Family meant everything to the Amish. Of course Sarah wanted a husband. In the first years after Jacob's death, she'd missed him keenly. She'd always wanted children. But if she married again and raised a family, she'd have to give up her quilt shop. A married woman with children didn't run a shop. No sensible Amish husband would let her work so hard, dissipate her energies so widely.

English women had both jobs and children, but they had a lot more conveniences than the Amish. And their men, she'd heard, often helped with chores and children. English women... Well, what did it matter? She wasn't an English woman. She was an Amish woman who'd come to cherish a bit of independence.

Of course, if she loved the man...

"Amos isn't boring," Rebecca said. "There's no one better with the sheep. He advises the other men on their flocks."

Sarah was not interested in sheep.

Rebecca liked sheep. She was strong enough to set a hundred-and-fifty-pound ewe on its rear for shearing, one of the hardest tasks on a farm. She could discuss the endless diseases the beasts fell prey to, and the flocking instinct that could send the lot of them into danger much like lemmings going off a cliff. Rebecca, Sarah knew, had never had a moment's hesitation about her Amishness. It was amazing how lonely that thought made her feel.

Rebecca hadn't taken her eyes from the window. "You could do worse than Amos. Besides, there's worse than boring."

Sarah's hands tightened on the pitcher.

"Oh, I didn't mean…"

Sarah looked up to find her friend hovering, distress in her eyes. She knew what Rebecca was thinking—that Sarah was remembering Randy West.

But it wasn't Randy West who caused Sarah's hands to quiver as she picked up the pitcher. Forbidden was worse, a lot worse than boring. With Brent she was never bored. Instead, she was intrigued, restless, breathless. "Don't worry about it," Sarah said gently. "I know you didn't mean anything."

Rebecca looked relieved. They'd never talked about Sarah's rape, except for a few oblique references. Rebecca had always been shy and naive even for an Amish woman. Sturdily built, she was pleasantly plain-featured. Talkative with the women, she was utterly tongue-tied with the men. Rebecca was twenty-two years old, old for an Amish woman not to have married. Some in the community were beginning to quietly consider her a spinster.

"There's always Amos for *you*," Sarah teased as they started through the kitchen doors.

"Oh, come on! When Amos looks at you, he looks like Bossie the cow. How would I compete with that?" She blushed.

Ah, thought Sarah.

"Who looks like Bossie the cow?" Anna Troyer, Amos's mother, said, looking up from the frame as the younger women came into the living room.

"We have a jar of marshmallow cream," Sarah

said brightly, managing not to look at Rebecca as she set the pitcher of lemonade on the table.

Anna squealed. "What do you say, everyone? Should we break now or keep sewing?"

Practically en masse, the women rose. Only Emma Lapp kept sewing serenely, her thimble working the needle in and out of the quilt stretched on the frame. Her thread and scissors stood ready at hand.

Emma never stitched less than ten stitches per inch, even on the tourists' quilts. She never overcooked a dish, even on a temperamental woodstove. She'd raised ten children, and she could be up making noodles at 5:00 a.m. Emma was perfect. Sarah would be like Emma, she resolved. Good at everything required of her in her world.

Emma finished her length of thread, then took off her thimble and eyeglasses and stood. "Food is better if it's earned with work, and best of all when it's shared with friends," she said, helping herself to a piece of bread and waiting her turn for the peanut butter.

"Quilting going well?"

At the new voice, the women turned. Amos Troyer stood in the doorway, still in his barn clothes. He'd taken off his boots, and for some reason, his stocking feet annoyed Sarah. Or maybe it was his expression, intent on her face. Bossie the...

Ashamed of her uncharitable thoughts, Sarah put her head down, grabbed a cookie and set it on a napkin. "Do you want a snack?" When she looked up, she smiled brightly in contrition.

Too brightly, apparently, because Amos just stood there for a moment. Finally, visibly gathering himself, he said, "No, I only came in to get a dose of anti-biotic. I've got a ewe lamb with scours."

A ewe was especially valuable. "Rebecca could help you," Sarah suggested.

Rebecca flushed brick red.

"She's good at using the bolus gun," Sarah added. Getting a pill down the throat of an animal was easier with a helper, especially one as strong and willing as Rebecca.

"Really?" Amos finally glanced over at Rebecca.

Rebecca didn't say a word, and her face was redder than ever.

"There's not much Rebecca doesn't know about the stock," Sarah said. Every woman nodded. "She likes sheep."

Amos looked longer at Rebecca. She ducked her head. "Well, then," he said a trifle impatiently, "come on if you're willing. I've got a coverall in the barn you can use." He turned and left the doorway.

With one panicky look Sarah's way, Rebecca followed.

As soon as the pair was out of earshot, Mary Miller giggled. "That man certainly had eyes for you, Sarah. Perhaps Adam should have set out lots of celery plants in the garden this spring."

Celery was the traditional wedding dish. A long row of celery in the garden was tantamount to a wedding announcement. "He's a nice man," Sarah said lamely. "But you know me. I'm sort of a spinster now."

There were heartwarming sounds of protest.

"Surely, Sarah, with a good man like my Amos, you could be happy," Anna said with a touch of sternness. "He'd be a good partner to you, and he's a good father. Look how well he took care of his boys when he was widowed."

Amos would take one look at her art and be horrified, Sarah knew. And after experiencing real love and sharing with Jacob, she couldn't bring herself to marry for anything less.

"You should give him a chance." Anna put down her sandwich. "Sometimes independence is merely another form of pride, and a woman shouldn't be alone if there's a man wishing to take care of her. It's the natural way of things."

Sarah gritted her teeth. She'd heard such words since childhood. But surely there ought to be something more. What Anna was suggesting made women sound as if they were incapable of taking care of themselves.

Anna added, "Amos would court you if you'd give him a bit of encouragement. It's not immodest to let him know you wouldn't be adverse if he came calling—"

"Sarah never has liked sheep, have you, Sarah?" Emma interrupted in a gentle voice.

"No," Sarah said, "I've never liked sheep."

"What's sheep got to do with any—"

"Rebecca likes sheep," Emma continued in a conversational tone. "Rebecca is a hard worker, a good woman. I've always thought that things go better between men and women if they have something in common. Like an interest in sheep, for example. Something to talk about."

"Well, of course," Anna agreed.

"And did you see that girl blush? Why, I'd guess she thinks your son is the handsomest man she's ever seen."

"What difference does it make how a man looks? It's how hard a man works and how devout he is that are important. What nonsense you speak, Emma." Anna pursed her lips, trying to hold on to her frown.

A couple of the other women smiled at each other. If Anna noticed, she pretended not to. The talk turned to when there would be enough tomatoes in the gardens to get out the canning kettles, and Sarah shot Emma a grateful glance. Emma didn't seem to notice, just sat calmly sipping her lemonade.

Thank you, Sarah thought. She didn't want to hurt Anna's feelings, or Amos's. Perhaps Anna was right, that Sarah had not taken the time to really get to know her son. But he didn't stir her, and that was the long and short of it.

In seven years, only one man had stirred her. One man who was forbidden.

THE JURY had deliberated for two hours before asking for a dinner break. Brent had elected to grab a hot dog from the concession stand.

That was a mistake.

Most of the courthouse personnel had left about forty-five minutes before, but there were still stragglers coming down the marble steps past him. They all had an opinion about the newspaper article.

"That poor Amish woman," one of the secretaries had said as she rummaged in her purse for her keys. "Can't you do something, Brent?"

"I can't *make* her testify."

"Well, why won't she?"

"She's Amish."

"I know, but..."

Later, it was two women, asking Brent if they'd be safe. A question he couldn't answer.

Marlene Ward was the last straw. A sour-faced woman who worked in the filing department, she stood blocking his way to his office.

"What are you going to do?" Marlene asked without preamble.

"About what?" Brent asked, though he knew what was on Marlene's mind.

"About what! About this Amish girl who won't go to the cops. These Amish are trouble." She wagged her finger for emphasis. "You haven't lived here long enough to know how hard they make things for the rest of us folks. They put on those silly clothes for the tourists. Oh, they make money out of that, all right. And those tourists spoil town all summer."

"A lot of other people make money because the tourists come to see the Amish," Brent said, trying to be reasonable.

Marlene's mouth went tight. "Well, it's just that they flaunt it."

Brent tried not to show his annoyance. "The Amish go about their business without paying much attention to the rest of the world. It's the tourists and everybody else who've made a three-ring circus out of watching them."

"Well." She huffed. "They get in the way out on the highway with those slow buggies of theirs. Last Sunday one of my boys almost hit one of them!"

Marlene's oldest boy had been in juvenile traffic court more than once. But Brent wasn't about to get into that. "If you'll excuse me—"

"Brent, the woman was *raped!*" She managed to make the word sound both dreadful and titillating, and

Brent clenched his fists at his sudden surge of anger. He often felt impatient with Marlene, but the sheer force of his reaction stunned him. Of course, sex crimes had always upset him. But this was more. This was Sarah, a woman with a special integrity, that they were talking about.

"Marlene—"

"That Amish woman has made it dangerous to walk the streets! There's a rapist out there, and he'll certainly take one of us over an Amish if he gets the chance. Those holier-than-thou Amish, they think they aren't in our way but they are, they think they're better than us, but they're not..."

With deliberate rudeness, Brent walked around her.

Her voice followed him. "I know Norman Bauer is really the prosecutor, but you've been doing most of the cases and you'll be a pushover in this town if you let that Amish woman get away with..."

He reached his office. How dare Marlene suggest he wasn't doing his job? He was the only one who hadn't accepted Sarah's refusal to testify. Besides, Marlene had worked long enough in the courthouse to know how hard a rape trial was for the victim; it wouldn't have killed her to have shown some sympathy for Sarah's plight.

But she was right about one thing. As long as Sarah didn't testify, there was a perpetrator of violent crime out there. He could understand the feelings of every woman who'd sought him out. But the implication that he wasn't doing his job rankled. When the phone rang, he couldn't keep the anger out of voice. "Brent McCade."

"Mr. McCade? This is Bertram Snow, with the *Wheatland Post*. I'm working on the story of the

Amish widow who was allegedly raped. Have you seen the story? Would you like to comment?''

Brent's lawyer instincts kicked in. "What would I know about any rape?''

"Are you denying a rape took place in Wheatland three months ago and that the victim was an Amish woman?''

Careful, Brent thought. These people were bottom feeders; they wouldn't care anything about Sarah's feelings. "If you want to pursue a crime story, why not go to the police?'' He knew the answer. Snow had already been to the police and they hadn't given him Sarah's name.

Snow let out a sigh of frustration. "They won't tell me any more.''

He sounded so like a whiny little boy that under other circumstances, Brent might have smiled. "Well, I guess you have a problem. Maybe you'll have to stick to stories about the cheese festival and the bass-fishing tournament.''

There was an indignant pause, which Brent found himself enjoying. "She won't testify, I hear,'' Snow finally said doggedly.

"Really. You know, I have a jury out on a theft case. I'm afraid I'll have to cut this conversation short.'' He felt deep satisfaction. In Toledo, the media had never let him rest. During the height of the scandal, the news crews had camped out in the front yard of his condo. Every day was like running a gauntlet. Bertram Snow wasn't going to get a thing out of Brent McCade. Once, in Toledo, Brent had given an interview to the press, hoping to quell a rumor. When the story came out, his words had been taken grossly out of context, distorting the story.

Snow whined again. "It's your job to put guys like this away."

"Tell me something I don't know. See you later." He was just about to hang up, when Snow said, "Wait. Wait! Do you have a comment on allegations you aren't doing your job?"

Brent went cold.

There was a long silence. Then Snow said, "You're the prosecutor. You could take a case like this without the cooperation of the witness."

"If a crime has been committed in Wheatland, we prosecute it. Assuming we have the evidence," Brent said between clenched teeth.

"Witnesses are your evidence. Why haven't you persuaded this witness?"

Brent was silent.

"Wouldn't you like to comment, Mr. McCade? You could be an unnamed source—"

Brent quietly hung up the phone. The day he'd participate as an "unnamed source" was the day he was dead.

He sat there for a moment. Rage wasn't the word for what he felt, it was an anger deeper than rage, more all-encompassing, yet less impetuous than rage.

Sarah may find it difficult to live the life she'd chosen, but she was living it with integrity. No matter what, he wouldn't let her story, her life, her private sorrow be for sale for the price of a newspaper.

Once before he hadn't been able to control a scandal.

And he would do his job just as he'd been doing every day for ten years.

The *Post* was a small-town newspaper, Brent reminded himself, and Bertram Snow had probably bought a cop a beer and stumbled onto the biggest story of his career. With luck, the story wouldn't go any farther.

But it was a warning; it was time to act. It was time for Sarah to trust him.

CHAPTER SEVEN

SARAH SAW BRENT pull in and came out onto the porch. Her throat was tight and stiff with the effort of holding back tears. Levi had told her about the article in the *Wheatland Post*. Levi was upstairs in his room, but he probably wouldn't come down. He wouldn't want Brent to know he'd been crying.

Brent sprang from the car, a newspaper in his hand. So he had seen the story, too. Long ago, she'd resolved not to be ashamed of what had happened. Angry, yes. Frightened, surely. But not ashamed. But this newspaper article made her feel both ashamed and guilty.

Brent came up the steps toward her, still in a suit and tie. He seemed elegant and out of place in her barnyard in the hazy twilight. But he also seemed...invincible.

"Sarah, there's been an article in the paper," he said without preamble.

She swallowed hard. "I know."

"You know?"

"Yes. Levi was in town and heard, but he was..." She stopped and governed her voice. "He was upset and didn't think to buy a copy of the paper before he came home. My father went out a few minutes ago because I wanted a copy." She paused. "*Vater* isn't sure it's the right thing to do, to bring that English newspaper home, but I insisted. It's worldly of me to care what they're saying—"

"Damn it!" he snapped. "Of course you care! Who wouldn't care?"

Sarah looked down at her dress. Her apron was splotched because she'd helped with the dishes at the Troyers'. There had been so many helpers, it had been a messy job.

It had been a happy job. Sarah had felt genuine contentment.

Until she'd come home to find Levi waiting. The sight of his reddened eyes had scared her. After she'd found out about the newspaper article, she'd felt weary, discouraged, wondering if what had happened three months ago would ever really be over for any of them. Now, seeing Brent's tense face, looking up into his eyes, she was somehow comforted that this powerful English man had come to her. It was suddenly hard to keep from crying. Her lip wobbled and her voice was high and halting. "It doesn't change...anything, but I don't...like that everyone knows—"

He reached out and pulled her into his arms.

The shock of it—that he would do such a thing—raced through her body. Then came other shocks, one right after another. The feel of being held against a man's hard chest, the smell of a man, that earthy, distinctively compelling smell, coupled with a scent of some sharp, spicy cologne.

She was crying then. He had both arms wrapped around her. His hand was making circles on her back. The sheer comfort of being held, of having another human being accepting her, simply undid her.

Not just any human touch. *His.*

She cried, long, wrenching sobs of loss and pain.

"Ah, Sarah," Brent said, and his voice was so low and rough that it broke something inside her, something that had been there since that night. The tears flowed out of that place, too. Those sobs were painful because they came out of her throat with such force. She clung to his shoulders, afraid for a moment that he'd be disgusted by her display, might let her go, and she couldn't bear it if he didn't hold her.

She needn't have worried. He held on to her as if he would never release her. Time stood still as the hot breeze stirred the evening and the cows lowed from the pasture and the sun went slowly down.

Her sobs lessened, then died altogether. The tightness in her throat had eased, but there was tightness in the skin of her cheeks where her tears had dried.

She pulled back slightly, and he let her go immediately.

Scrubbing a fist against her eye, she was suddenly embarrassed. "Goodness, I didn't mean to fall apart like that," she whispered, "what you must think of me..."

He reached out, grasped her chin, gently forced her head up. "What I think," he said slowly, "is that you're a very brave woman."

Heat flooded her. She wasn't brave at all, but Brent thought so. He admired her. He'd held her, and suddenly she needed to feel that again, needed it as she'd never needed anything in her life.

Abruptly, so that she didn't have to think about what she was doing, she threw her arms around his neck. And she kissed him, a passion rising in her that was so powerful it reached every part of her body, like the summer lightning that lit the whole sky. Sarah

Yoder, Amish woman, did what she'd wanted to do since the day she'd met him. She kissed the English man with all her heart.

She felt him start—the stiffening of his spine mirrored her own a few moments before. Then his mouth hardened, and for a second she feared he was going to push her away.

But no, his mouth kissed hers, molded to hers, moved but did not withdraw. She felt his day's growth of beard, scratchy against her cheeks and chin. Married Amish men wore beards, and now she felt the difference in Brent's face. That difference should have stopped her. It didn't.

Instead, she reveled in the difference. A whimper came from her throat. The spicy, citrus scent of him that had seemed so foreign a few moments ago, quickly became familiar. The scent heightened her desire as it mingled with the smell of the hay fields. She touched the back of his neck, felt the starched cloth of his collar, the impossibly crisp line of his barber-styled hair. She sensed the breadth of his shoulders and the long leanness of muscle. Her breasts became heavy, and the nipples ached where they were pressed to his chest.

She opened her mouth for his tongue. He explored gently, but with purpose. With passion. He took, and in taking he gave, sensation so strong and so compelling that she started to tremble.

His hands slid from her back, lower, to come to rest on her hips. He groaned and pulled her to him. There was no mistaking his desire.

Thrill and fear slammed into her as one emotion. She pulled back.

"Ah, Sarah, don't stop me—" But he let go. Sarah

swayed, so caught in the thrall of the kiss and the fear
that her legs went weak. There was a breathless pause.
Then Sarah looked up, needing to see his expression.
But he turned and took a few steps toward the porch
railing. He put both hands on it and stood, gazing out.

Sarah backed up to the wall of the shop and rested
her spine against it. She was having trouble steadying
her breathing. Her thighs felt weak.

She stared at his back in a charged silence. Heaven
above, she had kissed an English man! And there had
been nothing chaste about those kisses, they had been
real and fierce and she'd initiated them, hadn't been
coaxed into sin at all.

And sin it surely was. She had deliberately encouraged Brent's passion—she had felt it, *there.* It
had been powerful, bold, and that had frightened her,
but it had brought her to her senses, too. She thanked
God for that momentary fear because it had enabled
her to stop.

But at the same time—oh, at the same time, the
knowledge that she could cause such a reaction in an
English man like Brent made her still want to—

She looked at his broad back, his hands resting on
either side of him, a big man's hands grasping the
porch railing. Finally, she took a deep breath. "Look,
I don't want you to think I encouraged you, that I
wanted—" She stopped, because she very much *did*
want. And she had definitely encouraged him. Her
lips were swollen and tender. Her body was hot, a
flame that was lively and glorious. If she'd felt fear
for a moment in his arms as she'd sensed the power
of his arousal, the fear was waning.

Finally, he said, "I'm sorry. This was a mistake."

"I started it," she said, and the words came out sounding childish. Amish-girl naive.

He turned to look at her finally. "Does it matter? I finished it. And scared you in the process."

There was no mistaking the self-reproach in his voice. He was so powerful, yet so gentle. Her heart squeezed. "You didn't really scare me. For a moment there, I got a little frightened, but it wasn't anything like…"

He swore then, one brief, blasphemous syllable.

The sun had truly set now. The porch was becoming shadowy. Her father would return soon and Levi could decide to join them at any moment.

What on earth had she been thinking, to go into the arms of this English man?

"I'm sorry, too," she said abruptly. "We did wrong."

His head shot up then, and he stared at her with a familiar intensity. "Do you think we did wrong, Sarah? A mistake, yes. But in your heart, do you really think we did wrong?"

She didn't, not in her heart, and the thought stunned her. Confused, she wanted to look down. Instead, she forced herself to look at him. Of course kissing him was wrong. It had to be, because if it wasn't…

"Yes," she said in as firm a tone as possible. "It was wrong."

Even in the darkness, she could see the breath he let out. He said, "Well, that about covers it, doesn't it?"

She lifted her hands, made a gesture that seemed fluttery and silly, even to her.

Brent saw that gesture, that tiny, feminine and futile movement, and for the first time since taking her into his arms, he felt angry. If she thought it was wrong, why had she kissed him? Curiosity, to see if an English man would respond to her?

Ridiculous. She was Amish, she wouldn't deliberately taunt him; she didn't have it in her. That lack of sophistication and artifice was one of her chief attractions. So why?

His own motives were muddled. He'd come out here one last time, to persuade her. Instead, he hadn't been able to bear her distress.

And he hadn't known how to comfort her. He knew from experience that he could put on a clean trial, he could win, and that winning would be healing for her—as it had been for the women in other rape cases he'd handled. But he couldn't offer comfort, a promise that with the right man it would be different. The law that was so important to him had its limits. He'd always accepted that.

He was becoming way too involved in Wheatland. With Sarah. He'd spent way too many sleepless nights imagining pulling that starchy prayer cap from her hair, dislodging her bun and feeling the mass of silk spill over his fingers. When he'd kissed her, he'd felt the straight pins that were the only thing holding her modest dress together; Amish women wore nothing so worldly as buttons.

All he had to do was tug gently on her dress and...

Everything would be out of control.

When he spoke, his voice was harsh. "It's best, then, if I don't come out here anymore."

By the wall of the porch, she nodded. "I agree. I'd decided, even before—" In the gathering darkness, the white of her cap stood out boldly, emphasizing her Amishness.

He couldn't want her. Wanting her went against every grain of his being, of the man he wanted to be. Anyway, he could never have her. Suddenly, his reputation seemed more important than ever. He had a plan that was not going to be derailed by an Amish woman who smelled like soap and cinnamon.

He wasn't coming back to this place. It was dangerous here. So he'd better say what was on his mind and say it well enough to persuade her.

He could still taste her on his lips as he spoke. "We need to remember why I first came here."

"When you first came here, you wanted me to testify." Her words sounded weary, resigned. "Now, even after you've seen who we are and what we believe, you're still pushing for the same thing. Don't you understand why I can't testify?"

"I do. But I know that the newspaper article hurt you, and I know that the only way to make that hurt go away is to testify, Sarah." He took a few steps toward her.

Almost warily, she watched him approach.

"The people in town are talking about you." He almost winced at the need to hurt her. "The women are afraid, and you're putting them at risk."

"I hate that part," she admitted.

He heard the sorrow in her voice. If she were truly Amish, deep down, would she care much about women outside the circle of her faith? "You said once that you had thought about not joining the church when you came of age. And many things about you don't seem Amish to me."

"What things?" Her voice rang with suspicion...and maybe fear?

He hated the thought of that. That kiss had changed everything. He couldn't pretend now that he didn't care about her.

But he wasn't coming back, this was his last chance to persuade her. "Your eyes are too direct. I've seen other Amish women, I was around them that day of the barn raising. Believe me, you're different."

She looked stricken. "Why are you doing this?"

"I understand you're Amish now. But you told me you didn't want to join the church at first, so that alone makes you at least a little bit different. Then there's your drawing, your wanting to do something the Amish don't condone." He saw her wince, but he couldn't—wouldn't stop. "Maybe testifying wouldn't help the average Amish woman. But it would help you. Admit it. What happened to you three months ago doesn't seem finished."

"All right! I'm different! It's wrong to be different, but I am different!"

That sense of triumph left him suddenly, and he felt like what he was. A bully. The need to pull her back into his arms was strong. But he had to press on, to make her see. "Can you see that nothing's finished until you testify?"

"No!" She looked at him as though he were the devil himself. "I admit it was Jacob who persuaded me to join the church. I was young and in love. Now I'm older. I might be confused. I might not be a pure Amish woman, but for my self-respect I can never let a man dictate to me again. Jacob wanted me to join the faith. You want me to go against it. Well, I can't let you persuade me. I can't let a man take away my self-respect. Not anymore. Not after—''

She cut herself off, then came across the porch, her sturdy shoes ringing on the wooden floorboards. He reached out, but she threw off his arm and stormed past him.

He followed her onto the dust of the gravel driveway. His stride was longer, and he caught up with her and whirled her around.

She jerked her arm away. ''We were sheltered on the porch, our kiss witnessed only by God. Do you want Levi to see you now? Don't you think my little brother has had enough to deal with these last three months?''

Abruptly, he let her go. ''Goddamn it, Sarah—''

''Don't take the Lord's name in vain!'' she snapped.

They stared at each other. He was making things hard for Sarah. A part of him knew that, but he was so sure that this was right.

But if he respected her...

He heard the clop of horseshoes on the road leading to the farm. The buggy, with Adam in it, turned in at the gate.

He felt an almost desperate urge to speak his mind before Sarah's father was within earshot. ''Look, Sarah, I...care about you.'' Why were those simple words so hard to say?

She swiped a hand across her forehead. ''I care for you, too, Brent. You've become a friend to me.'' She swallowed. ''Despite what you said, I know you're trying to do the right thing. But we need to stay in our own worlds, where we both belong.''

His throat felt tight. Of course she was right.

This—this whatever it was between them, was only about friendship. One human being's life had simply touched another's.

They both watched as Adam slowed the buggy, spoke a quiet word to the horse. He got down and looped the reins around the hitching post in the barnyard. He looked old, Brent thought suddenly. Brent had seen Adam do the work of a young man. But tonight he stooped slightly as he walked toward them. When he reached them, Brent saw that the man's face was etched into rough lines and his eyes seemed almost sunken.

"Hello, Brent," Adam said quietly. "I didn't think we'd see you out here tonight. It's long past mealtime."

"I saw the newspaper article and came," Brent said.

Adam nodded. "Thank you."

Brent felt bitter laughter well in him. *Adam, I came out here so your daughter could save my career. I know she's been through a lot, though, so I kissed her, and Sarah stirred me the way no woman has before...* Thank him? Good God. He looked into Adam's eyes and for the first time in years felt himself flush.

Adam didn't appear to notice. "Did Brent show this to you?" he asked Sarah, indicating the newspaper he held.

She shook her head, holding out her hand for the paper.

Adam hesitated, then gave it to her. "I can't see what earthly good it will do to read this. I've heard even many of the English don't believe everything the newspapers say." He turned to Brent for confirmation.

Brent nodded. "That's so."

They were both quiet as Sarah finished reading. Now she looked up. "But this article isn't lies, *Vater*," she said quietly. "They say here in this newspaper that an Amish woman was raped and she won't testify. What they're writing about me is the truth."

Adam grunted. "It doesn't matter what outsiders think."

She hesitated, nodded.

Adam turned to Brent. "Is there any way this could affect Sarah, hurt her again somehow?"

Brent couldn't miss the love and caring in the grave tone. "I don't know," he admitted. He sensed that Adam could be an ally, but he also knew Adam wouldn't respond to exaggeration. "Most of the women in town don't believe Sarah is right to let this pass. I'm afraid of repercussions against the Amish."

Sarah gave a tiny cry of protest.

Adam turned to her immediately, but he didn't touch her. Brent longed to soothe her, but to do so, he now knew, would be a mistake.

Adam said, "Our people have been persecuted before. There are some good people in town who don't judge others because they're different. I don't worry about the people who do pass judgment, and you shouldn't either, Sarah. You're not responsible for anything but following your faith."

Brent knew her father had meant to comfort, but he suspected that Adam's words fell far short of what Sarah needed tonight. Adam didn't give Sarah's hand even a quick squeeze, much less give his daughter a hug. Brent thought suddenly of Sarah's art, and her husband admonishing her, and he wondered again if she'd ever got complete understanding from any of her people.

Hell, he decided, of course she hadn't. Who in the world, Amish or English, ever got real understanding from others? But maybe Adam could be made to see reason.

"I'm concerned about Sarah's safety," Brent said softly.

Adam's gaze went to his, suddenly sharp. "How so, Brent?"

"I don't want to alarm either of you, but I've always wondered why Randy West has never done anything...else. Sarah has never seen him, not since that night." He cast a quick look at Sarah. Her mouth was set, her chin up. "No other women that we know of have been molested. But I never count on a criminal's good behavior, and you shouldn't, either. This newspaper article—well, people are talking. You don't know how he's going to react."

Sarah's eyes had gone wide.

Anger gripped him. Nobody should have to live with being the target of a violent criminal. If something happened to Sarah...

He looked Adam right in the eye. "So far, Sarah has told me she won't testify. So now I'm asking your help as her father. Persuade her to go to the police. If she does that tonight, I can have an indictment filed in the morning."

He waited. Sarah was still, and in the hot night, not a breeze stirred even the light strings of her prayer cap. Adam, too, remained deep in thought. "Adam, if you love your daughter—"

"No," Adam said. Then, more slowly he added,

"I can keep my daughter safest by keeping her Amish."

Brent just barely bit back an expletive.

Adam nodded decisively. "You don't know what this man will do. Nobody but God can know."

"I can predict—"

"Brent." Sarah cut him off, her voice quiet but firm. "I've already told you my decision." Her eyes were frightened but her spine was straight.

"You're wrong," he said flatly to Sarah, and then with a nod of his head he took in Adam. "This is too big for the community. The law in America is for everyone."

"You're our friend, but you aren't Amish. We don't expect you to understand, so we forgive your ignorance."

Brent knew Adam thought he was being magnanimous, generous. Damn, he thought. He couldn't take on both of them. His only hope was getting Sarah alone again, to finally make her see reason. *It was dangerous to be alone with her.* But he had to do it. For her sake and his own. "I'll go then."

He reached out, grasped Adam by the shoulder.

Adam looked at him, surprised. "Keep her safe," Brent said, and his voice came out rough, gravelly. "Don't let her be alone, not ever. Do you understand?"

"I understand, English man, and I agree."

"Sarah. I want your promise you won't go anywhere alone."

"I won't," she said readily. "I haven't, not since that night."

He got in the car a few minutes later. He should feel better for having got their promises, but they were all so trusting. Would they—could they—really protect Sarah?

He drove out of the barnyard onto the county road. With no electric lights to mark the location of the farms, it was very dark.

Sarah had been raped on this road, just after dusk, when she'd been out picking wild asparagus by the ditch.

Suddenly, with complete certainty, he knew if Randy West hurt Sarah again, Brent would kill him.

CHAPTER EIGHT

RANDY WEST wanted to cut out the article and save it, but he didn't. A smart person never left any evidence.

The police weren't after him. That article was proof that Sarah really hadn't changed her mind, *wouldn't* change her mind. He was really smart to have figured out this flamin' Amish thing.

He put on a new pair of jeans, got into his truck and went to the Roadhouse. Inside, he ordered a beer, feeling good enough to say to the bartender, "And how about washing the glass first, why don'tcha?"

He swallowed a few mouthfuls of beer and waited for Julie Ann O'Neal to come in. She got paid on Friday nights and always came in after she cashed her check. The Roadhouse was crowded. A noisy game of pool was going on in the back.

When Julie Ann came in, he caught his breath. She had that fluffy blond hair and her lips were frosted in pink. She seemed pure somehow, even though that tank top was always so tight. Sexy and pure, too. Way too pure for her boyfriend, Mel; Mel was a whiskery pig who scratched his armpits when he played pool.

Tonight Randy was going to talk to Julie Ann. He really was. He took a long slug of beer for courage and remembered that newspaper article. He watched her open her purse and take out a cigarette case. He didn't like it that she smoked, but he always studied her lips when she did it. Yeah, tonight was the night he'd get to know her. He left the bar and walked over to her table.

"Yo," he said, putting his beer down on the table-top, sticky with rings from other glasses. His hand was shaking, so he shoved it in his pocket.

"Yes?" she asked, looking up as prissy as could be. It angered him that she said yes that way, as if she'd never noticed him before.

"Have a fight with your boyfriend?"

She shrugged. "We always make up."

"Buy you a beer?" Randy said then, real casual-like. He knew he didn't show it, but his heart was hammering.

She stopped, her cigarette in one hand, her lighter in the other, and looked up finally. Really saw him. But hell, she *knew* him. He sat in this crummy bar every flamin' night. How could she not know him?

He smiled.

She frowned. "Mel wouldn't like someone buying me a drink."

"To hell with Mel. I can handle Mel." Mel was huge and had a reputation for liking a good fight. Randy suddenly had to go to the john.

There was a pause. "I don't think so," she said finally.

A white-hot rage went through him. The bitch wouldn't even let him buy her a drink. His hand, still in his pocket, tightened into a fist.

"Me and Mel will make up," Julie Ann repeated. "Mel's the jealous type, you know? No sense my getting a pop in the mouth for a free beer." She sighed, then smiled. "No hard feelings, okay?"

"Oh. Okay." Randy swallowed. His rage ebbed. Mel was a bastard, and of course she didn't want to get hit. Randy had been hit plenty by his old man and a couple of older kids in the neighborhood, and he really couldn't blame Julie Ann for not wanting to get smacked.

Only...only couldn't she see how he'd treat her right? Take better care of her than Mel and not hit her at all? So he was still mad when he went back to the bar.

He drained his beer and motioned to the bartender for a refill. The guy grinned at Randy. "Struck out, huh?"

Randy felt rage again, just like that. He never talked to the bartender. The guy had tried to make conversation a time or two, but by now he knew Randy liked to be left alone. At least, you'd think the stupid guy would know. "Who gives a damn about Julie Ann O'Neal," he said, when he really wanted to tell the bastard to mind his own flamin' business.

The guy laughed and went on to serve another customer.

Randy watched Julie Ann. She was sipping a rum and cola, her frosted lips touching the glass in a way that turned him on. He could give it a try another night. Now that he thought about it, he did think she'd smiled at him in a small, secret way.

In the meantime... God, it had been so long since he'd been with a girl. He needed it a lot. He really wanted it when he was low, and he wanted it more when he was happy. Those times when he knew he was so, so smart.

Sarah had made him feel strong and smart. She might have fought, but he'd had his way. That newspaper was proof that he could have any one of them he wanted.

Any of them. So, maybe not Sarah this time. After all, he already knew what it felt like to have her. There was that flamin' Amish girl he'd seen at the barn raising. He'd fooled her that day into thinking he was Amish.

Rebecca. She wasn't as pretty as Sarah, but she was bustier, more like Julie Ann. He remembered how she blushed when he'd seen her at the Lapps' barn raising.

Rebecca. He didn't know if she was a virgin or not, and he thought about that and decided that the way she'd acted, she probably was. When he began to think of the things he'd make her do, he forgot about the cheap beer and the dirty Roadhouse.

Rebecca. It was getting harder and harder to lay low.

IN THE NEXT TWO WEEKS, Brent learned something about small towns. If the people liked you, they tended to let things ride. Bertram Snow had written one more newspaper article about Sarah. It suggested that Assistant Prosecutor McCade could put together a case if he wanted to, Sarah's testimony or no. Then Snow had gone back to the cheese-festival and bass-fishing stories. Not a soul had said anything to Brent about Snow's assertion that Brent wasn't doing his job.

His conviction rate was excellent—approaching a hundred percent, in fact. Of course, the cases were easy. Smaller. But they were good cases and he gave them the time they needed. Here people appreciated that. They thanked him for doing his job.

When no other women were molested, Brent allowed himself to relax slightly. Nothing had happened as a result of the article. He was just too big-city cynical about crime, he guessed.

He stood in the coffee area of the prosecutor's office and spooned some cream into his cup. He liked his coffee strong enough to be lethal, and there was always one pot of the really thick stuff on the warming burner.

"Brent?" He turned to see Kelly, his secretary, standing behind him. Her voice was hesitant.

"What's up?" he asked.

"Jeremy, believe it or not."

"Jeremy?" he asked in some surprise. "Don't tell me he's getting into trouble." Jeremy was her seventeen-year-old son.

"I know, I know. I've always said he's a mother's dream of a teenager."

Kelly was a nice woman, efficient and genuinely kind. She and her husband had divorced when Jeremy was twelve. Kelly always talked about how responsible her son was. Brent had met the kid a time or two and thought he was shy and nice, like his mom.

"He's been charged with a crime," Kelly said in a rush, her cheeks pink.

Brent set down his cup. "Oh no. What's he charged with?"

"A traffic violation." She averted her eyes.

Brent willed himself not to smile. He put a light hand on her arm. "Come into my office and tell me about it." He ushered her into his office and shut the door. He persuaded her to sit down and took the seat next to her.

Kelly took a breath, seeming a little less embarrassed now. "Jeremy borrowed his father's motor-cycle, which is bad enough. But he wasn't wearing a helmet. And Herb Farmington picked him up."

"The law against riding without a helmet has been repealed."

"Herb cited him for driving recklessly, but the only thing he really said, according to Jeremy, was about the helmet."

"Let me call the chief and see what I can do," he said.

Kelly's hand flew to her mouth. "I don't expect you to get him out of it. That's not why I told you, I just wanted to know what to expect when we go to court. How much the fine is likely to be. I don't want to use my position for gain," she added solemnly.

"You've got a good kid. We really have enough to do without prosecuting the good ones," Brent said gently. "Besides, I'd do it for any kid like Jeremy."

"But he's got to learn something from this, too."

Brent thought again. He'd handled enough juvenile cases to know that there had to be consequences for kids, and those consequences had to be something they understood. There was no point in the judge assessing a fine that the boy's mother would end up paying.

"How about I talk to the chief, and Jeremy works out his fine by doing some volunteer service, maybe in the Wheatland animal shelter." He'd often seen Jeremy riding his bike, a big black dog running beside him.

Kelly's eyes sparkled. "A good lesson, a good deed or two. Sounds great. Can you really do this?"

Brent pushed the buttons on his phone. "I think so." He was on good terms with the chief, and when the other man came on the line, it only took a couple of minutes to get him to agree. "The chief and I will talk to the judge. He'll go along with our solution, I'm sure."

Kelly stood up. "Thanks, Brent."

He waved aside her thanks.

She was almost at the door, when she paused. "The only reason I let you do this for me," she said, "is because I really did know that you'd do it for anybody else's kid."

He nodded.

"The thing is...this was the perfect solution for Jeremy, and you knew things about him, like how much he likes animals." She paused. "You really fit in here, don't you? It's almost like you were born in Wheatland."

For a moment he was too astonished to speak. He knew he'd just been paid a supreme compliment. But fit in here in Wheatland? Sure, it was a nice town, if you had a family.

If you wanted a certain kind of life.

"Where you live is none of my business, of course." The hesitant note was in her voice, before she added more briskly, "Well, I'd best get to work."

Even after Kelly had gone, Brent sat, thinking. He'd come to Wheatland for one reason. He still planned to go after a year or so. And he still had his goals to accomplish while he was here.

He eyed Sarah's file, which he always had out on his desk. He'd heard nothing more from Sarah. He hadn't gone out to the Stolzfus farm because until he came up with some argument that was more persuasive than the ones he'd used so far, there was no point.

Over the past two weeks, he'd almost convinced himself that the passion in their kiss had come entirely from his side. Sarah had needed comfort.

He felt like a heel. He'd gone out there to save his career. He'd taken advantage of her pain and fear.

After all, she couldn't possibly know that he lay awake on hot nights with his ceiling fan cooling the air, and imagined her with her hair unbound, spread across his pillow, her fair skin almost as white as the bedding.

But it was only a fantasy. An Amish woman wouldn't consider an affair. With them, it was marriage—to an Amish man—and kids or nothing.

He wasn't opposed to marriage. In Toledo, he'd felt ready; he'd had a career that could comfortably support a family. But he'd always contemplated marriage with a woman who understood him.

Sarah understood him. Maybe too well.

Brent almost swore aloud.

"Hey, Brent." Norm paused in the doorway. "You've got a call on line one. I was passing so I picked up the phone."

"Thanks," Brent said. "Who is it?"

Norm looked pained. "I forgot to ask."

Brent chuckled as Norm turned away.

"By the way," the older man called. "Jessie said to tell you, with your manners, you can come over anytime. She keeps asking why *I* never bring home flowers."

Brent had been invited to dinner at the Bauers' last Saturday night. He'd taken wine and flowers. Most of the guests were couples, the small businessmen of the town. There had also been the obligatory single female, a pleasant divorcée. They'd talked, but both had tacitly agreed that they didn't strike any sparks.

Brent punched the button for his line. The evening had been remarkably enjoyable and stress-free. No pushing him for free legal advice. No showing off. Just a nice dinner with friends. Wheatland was like that.

"Hello, this is Brent McCade," he said into the receiver.

"Hey, what kind of operation you got going down there. Some old geezer answering the phone, claiming he's the prosecutor."

"That was Norm Bauer. And he *is* the prosecutor," Brent explained, trying to place the voice.

"You don't know who this is, do you?"

Ah, hell, he was caught. He was supposed to know, he figured. The voice was familiar, he just couldn't...

"Your mind going to mush in that godforsaken town or what? This is Teddy Forman."

"Hey, Teddy, how are you," Brent said quickly. "You know how it is, man." He chuckled. "I'll try a blind call on you some time and see if *you* can place the voice." Teddy had been one of his pals in the city, one of a group of lawyers that hung out together. The guy was okay, just a little pompous. The only one in their circle to smoke a pipe, Teddy was fond of waving the thing in the air while telling how he'd wowed a jury. He'd just made junior partner in a huge private law firm. "You must be doing great," Brent added, trying not to show any envy. Congratulations." Brent hadn't wanted a partnership; private practice didn't really interest him. It was only that Teddy's career was on track, while Brent's...

A familiar dissatisfaction gripped him. He'd just

been thinking he was getting used to Wheatland, and all it took was one phone call to bring an acid gut craving for his old life.

"Anyway," Teddy went on, "a couple of us have been talking about you."

"I thought by now I'd be yesterday's news," Brent said, knowing he still sounded bitter.

"The thing is, some of us have been wondering if you didn't get sucker punched over that Samuelson deal."

"The finest minds in the Midwest, and you're just now figuring that out?"

"Some of us thought at the time you were maybe innocent," Teddy said quietly. "However, you had a fire in your belly none of the rest of us had, and some people thought your ambition just got the better of you. But even before the investigation was over, quite a few of us thought maybe you'd been had. That you were naive. And you know as well as I do that sometimes naive is just as bad as guilty."

Brent understood. A lawyer couldn't afford to be naive. It was a fundamental flaw.

"So, anyway," Teddy added, "I think you're a damn fine trial lawyer."

Brent felt his mouth tighten. He knew he was a good lawyer. His weakness always had been needing people to acknowledge the fact. "Thanks."

"Our firm has an opening. Insurance defense work. Interested?"

Brent was silent for a moment. Once, insurance defense work would have seemed purposeless and boring. Now he understood he was being offered another chance. A real chance.

A couple of months ago he would have jumped at it.

"Look," Teddy said, "this is big-client, high-profile stuff. You do a good job on these cases, you get noticed, and you make partner in a few years."

The offer was tempting. Damn tempting. Prestige. Excellent money. A chance to rebuild his reputation. It was more than Norm Bauer had been able to offer, by a long shot.

Norm. Oh, hell. "I promised Norm a year in this job."

"Come on. He'll understand. He's a lawyer. He knows you've got to follow the money trail."

Norm might not have much to offer him, but he'd given Brent a job when nobody—including Teddy Forman—had even been willing to be seen with Brent at lunch. "I'll think about it." He'd talk it over with Norm. If Norm was willing, Brent would help recruit his replacement before he left. Of course, Norm wouldn't hold him back. Being a genuinely nice guy was Norm's weakness. Now, Brent thought, feeling more cynical than he had in years, he was about to take advantage of a nice guy's inability to say no.

"Don't think about it too long," Teddy said. "I've gotten the other partners to agree to give you a month to decide, but I don't know if I'd wait that long if I were you. There's been some talk."

Brent straightened, pressing the receiver more tightly to his ear. "What have you heard?"

"Nothing really. Just that you've had some trouble down there."

"Trouble?"

"Over that Amish woman."

Brent went cold. "How the hell would you have heard about that?"

"I'd just won a big case. The Allured case, and the reporters were in court. The one from the regional paper said he goes through some of the small-town papers, surfing for stories he can use. Said he saw a story about an Amish woman, and some reporter down there saying you're not doing your job."

Brent swore, one syllable, low. "She won't testify. I prosecute cases when I have the evidence."

"I know that. Hey, people were ready to believe you let Samuelson hang because you were too diligent, not the other way around. I told the guy from the paper that you were always gung ho. He's thinking about writing some crap like 'Prosecutor McCade in Trouble Again.' You know these guys. What you need to do is get that case prosecuted and come home. You know what I'm saying?"

"Yes." Brent knew exactly what the other man was saying. That Brent McCade had been thrown a bone and didn't have too many chances left.

This story of Sarah's was going to get out of control, just as Norm had predicted. "I appreciate the offer," he said. The offer, the show of support, had come quite a few months too late, but it had come. Apparently, ten years of hard work wasn't that easy to ignore.

He could have his old life back. If he could just convince Sarah to testify, the stories would end, she would go back to her quilt shop and he could take this offer. As for kissing Sarah, as for wanting her, being strangely drawn into that quiet world of easy acceptance and horse-drawn buggies... If he went to

Sarah's again, he'd be playing with fire. But the sooner he did as Teddy suggested, the better.

SARAH HAD NOT EXPECTED to see Brent again. Oh, maybe she'd run into him at the store or something when Levi took her to town in the buggy. But he was never coming back to the farm. He'd said as much. Now here he was. He got out of his red sports car, and on cue, Levi came in from the barn to inspect it. Looking at them both from the door of the quilt shop, Sarah felt a contradictory pang. Brent was good with Levi. The teenager was so eager to hear about the car, and Brent explained things to Levi in a quiet manner, without fanfare. But Brent was bad for the boy, too, just because of who he was.

Sarah stepped into the driveway. Brent was explaining something to Levi about "torque." He stopped abruptly and turned his head to look at her.

She stopped, too. She couldn't look away. The thought that she might not see him again up close had her hungering for every detail—the straight line of nose, those honest gray eyes...

He stared back. Her palms went damp as she recognized the same hunger in him.

"Hey, Brent," Levi said, "don't you know this stuff, after all? Cool car like this, I'd know everything about it."

Brent's mouth tightened. Her own fists clenched. Swiftly, he turned to her brother. "I do know about it. The same as you know about your buggy."

Sarah wondered if Brent had deliberately used the comparison to remind himself of the differences between their worlds.

Levi waved his hand in dismissal. "This baby's

lower than the buggy. Faster. And red. Why don't you take me for a ride?''

"Levi!" Sarah exclaimed. "You don't ask things like that!"

"That's all right, Sarah," Brent said. To Levi, he added, "I'll take you for a ride sometime."

"*Okay.*" Levi held his palm up, slapped Brent's.

Brent looked startled. "You also do high fives?"

Levi flushed a vivid red.

Sarah was confused. She had no idea what a high five was, and she asked Brent to explain.

"Just a sort of handshake," he said, still looking with speculation at Levi.

He must mean the English did this handshake. "Have you been spending a lot of time with English children?" Sarah asked quickly.

"They're not children," Levi said.

"You have been spending a lot of time with English boys? With English girls?" Her own problems suddenly faded in the memory of that magazine she'd found in Levi's room. She'd never been sure she'd done the right thing in keeping Levi's possession of that magazine a secret from their father.

"What if I have been spending time with some new kids? With some English." Levi looked at her with a rare defiance. "They aren't bad kids, they just like to laugh and have fun."

"And drive cars and go to all kinds of places, and their parents have no idea where or what they're doing." Anxiety laced her words. She appealed to Brent. "Isn't that true?"

He watched her carefully. "Not for most. Most kids don't get in any real trouble."

"But some do. Levi, I don't think you should

spend so much time with the English. What about your other friends? I haven't seen Isaac over in so long—''

"Isaac's boring. His idea of fun is to play a little rock music on his transistor radio.'' He used the toe of his boot to rub a line in the gravel, then turned to face her. "There's a whole big world out there, Sarah. People go places in their cars, places you'll never see outside the buggy window. Out there are mountains that almost touch the sky. The English kids said there's a roller coaster that sends you down a hill until you smash into the water. There's a whole park like that, right here in Ohio, where they have rides and roller coasters.'' His voice had gone high and tight, picked up speed. "There's so much out there—dancing, and girls who smell like flowers—'' He stopped abruptly.

An appalled silence hung over the barnyard. Sarah thought again of that magazine in Levi's room and felt herself blush deeply.

Brent finally said, "Levi, maybe you should listen to Sarah's point of view.''

Levi ignored him, still focused on Sarah. "You and Father, you're so sure we're better because we're different. Separate and apart.'' He kicked at the gravel and raised dust. "Maybe I don't want to be separate or apart. Maybe I don't want to be different.'' He stood, straight and tall, and looked her directly in the eye.

Heaven above, Sarah thought, now what? "You'd better not let *Vater* hear you talk this way,'' she warned.

Levi didn't move a muscle. "I don't care if he knows.''

"He could punish you," Sarah said in a low voice.

"Well, maybe I won't let him. I'm stronger and quicker than him." Sarah stared, at a loss for words at Levi's disrespect. "Oh, *hell*," Levi added, his voice harsh and vehement. Grabbing his hat by the brim, he threw it into the dust. He turned and strode off.

"Levi!" Sarah called. He didn't turn. "Levi!"

Brent touched her arm. "Let him go. He's a teenager. He needs to let off steam."

"How would you know what's right for him?" Sarah snapped.

"I know," he said quietly. "I was a teenage boy once. And if anybody had threatened to punish me, I think I'd have said worse than Levi."

"He's Amish!"

"He's a boy, about to become a man."

Sarah bit her lip. "That's why I worry."

"Maybe he won't join the church."

"Yes, I worry about that, too."

"But maybe that's the best thing for Levi."

She shook her head and started to walk back toward the porch. He fell into step beside her.

She tried to keep her voice steady. "If Levi wasn't Amish, he'd lose most of his ties to the community. They wouldn't shun him if he hadn't yet joined the church, but he wouldn't be one of them, either. One of us," she added hastily. Brent gave her an assessing glance that irritated her. "Our children are trained only to be Amish. If he left, he'd have a hard time making a living. Levi knows farming, but nobody nowadays can just go out and buy an expensive farm."

Brent nodded. "So you do have a reason to worry."

"Thank you," she said quietly, stopping in front of the porch steps.

"For what?"

She hesitated. "For trying to understand, I guess."

"I have tried to understand."

He was talking about more than Levi, Sarah knew. He had been understanding about her feelings about the rape. He was relentless in pursuit of the case, but he did try to understand. She...liked him for that. She cared about him deeply.

Oh, heaven above. She couldn't care for this man. She should never have kissed him. Maybe then, at night, she wouldn't remember his lips on hers and feel cheated of his presence.

A shiver went up her spine, because she knew in that instant that she could, with only the slightest provocation, cross that forbidden line and love him.

Brent must never know how she felt. No one could know.

He took her gently by the elbow and turned her to face him. "You didn't expect me to come out here again, did you?"

She shook her head.

"The thing is, I've tried to understand you." There was a pause. "Have you tried to understand me?"

I've taken pen and ink and paper and I've drawn your likeness. I think about you all the time. "Yes," she said. "I've tried to understand you. I know enough about you to know we aren't a good mix, the Amish and English. I'm thinking there's a good reason our bishops stress our separation from the world."

"I'm a bad influence." He said it as a statement of fact, as she imagined a lawyer would state it in court.

"Yes." She smiled and tried for a lightness she didn't feel. "Because it's the middle of the afternoon and I haven't finished my inventory for the shop, and now Levi isn't working, either. My father is out harvesting with the hired men in the hot sun and I'm loafing in the driveway with you."

"That's not why you think I'm a bad influence." He wasn't going to let her get away with keeping it light, she thought. His stare was intense and direct.

"Something's happened," she said. "Hasn't it?"

"Not really. It's just that—" He stopped and shoved his hands in the pockets of his suit pants. He'd taken off his jacket and tie, and his white shirt glistened in the afternoon sun. He'd unbuttoned the top couple of buttons, and a bit of gleaming dark hair curled in the V at his throat. "I've got a job offer," he said, and his voice was almost curt. "In Toledo."

Shock washed over her. Profound disappointment. But she shouldn't be surprised. He was powerful in his world.

It was for the best, she told herself firmly. Maybe God was finally done testing her and would demonstrate His approval by removing Brent's tempting presence for good. "Well, that's what you've wanted all along." She swallowed hard. "When are you leaving?"

"I don't know. I've got to talk things over with Norm. Maybe in a month or so."

A month. In relief she thought, *A whole month.* But after that month, there was the rest of her life without him in it. Of course, he'd never really been *in* her life anyway. She forced herself to say, "I'm happy you're getting what you want."

She was looking into his eyes, and she read the split second of hesitation there.

"It's what I'm good at," he said finally.

His words were puzzling because there was no excitement, no exhilaration behind them. "But...you do want to go back?"

"Yes. I need to go back."

He was always honest. So she must have imagined that momentary reluctance. "Then I wish you well." Turning, she went up the porch steps, across the rough wood of the flooring and opened the screen door to the kitchen.

"Sarah," he called, his voice husky. "Back there is who I am. It's where I belong."

"I know," she said, not facing him. "I know you came here to prove yourself, and then you planned to go back. You told me, remember? So go...and be happy." With that, she walked into the kitchen, her back straight, the tears welling in her throat.

CHAPTER NINE

HE FOLLOWED HER. He was relentless that way.

In the kitchen, she went to the sink and picked up
a pitcher. Reaching up, she watered the sweet-potato
plant on the windowsill. She heard him come to a
stop by the kitchen table, and she sensed him watching her.

"I... This...whatever that's been between us. I
didn't plan to kiss you," he said finally.

"It was a mistake, you said."

"*You* were the one who said it was wrong."

She reached up once more and watered her hanging
parsley ball. "I said it was wrong, but it didn't feel
wrong." Out of the corner of her eye, she saw him
stiffen. But he was going away, so this time she said
what she wanted to say.

He didn't move. "I care about you, Sarah. But
surely you know we have no future together."

A little honesty was one thing, but for him to say
it so directly, when maybe at night she'd been pretending a little... She turned and looked at him. He
was watching her, his eyes narrowed. She felt the jolt
of that gaze even in the slightly dim kitchen, and she
just missed dropping the pitcher from suddenly nerve-
less fingers. She may have been imagining some
things, but not this. She hadn't imagined his arousal

that night, had not imagined his desire for her. "So you're going back."

"I have a future there. I have a job offer. I won't be working for the state of Ohio anymore. I won't prosecute criminals. I'll work in a law firm, representing insurance companies."

"But you have a passion for what you do. This new job—it sounds so pointless."

"Why do you do this to me, Sarah?" he asked abruptly. "Why do you make me doubt who I am?"

Did she do that? She hadn't thought about it. All she knew was that he was the one who made her doubt herself and her life. She set the pitcher down. "You can be anything you want."

He gave a harsh chuckle. "Not really. You know I wanted my prosecutor's job in Toledo, but I was robbed of it. Now I have a chance to go back. It's a chance I have to take, but I need you to help me take that chance."

Help him go back to Toledo? She shook her head. It made no sense. "I can't help you."

"Oh yes you can, but you won't."

"How can I—" Realization dawned. "My case has something to do with your going back to Toledo."

He smiled grimly. "An old friend got me that job on the strength of his own reputation. But a few people in Toledo, reporters and the people in my new law firm, have heard about a case here that I haven't been able to prosecute. Your case, Sarah. They're wondering if I can do my job, after all. If I want to come to Toledo as anything more than a beggar, I have to take a big win with me."

"My case."

"Yes." The word was hard. She looked into his

eyes and now saw only toughness and ambition. How could this be the same man who had held her so sweetly a couple of weeks ago? It was beyond understanding, and it hurt terribly.

"Well, it's too bad you can't be somebody important in Toledo." She wanted to throw something suddenly, but such a display would be unseemly. Instead, she pulled a bowl from the shelf and thumped it onto the counter. She yanked the lid off a canister and plopped flour from it into the bowl. She had eggs to use up, so she'd make noodles for supper. She'd best forget this selfish English man and get on with it.

She picked up an egg and whacked it on the side of the bowl. Pieces of eggshell fell into the bowl.

"Sarah." He had come up to her and now put a hand on her forearm. "Try to understand." A moment ago, there might have been hardness in his eyes, but there was an ache in his voice, a vulnerability that stunned her. Slowly, she turned toward him.

"I...care about you," he repeated. It was amazing how much she needed to hear those words again. "I want the right thing for you. I really do."

She wasn't sure who reached out first, but they were together suddenly. She grabbed his shoulders, getting egg and flour on his shirt. He held her, and she smelled the starch of his shirt. His worldly buttons pressed against her cheek.

"I'm sorry," she whispered. "I'm sorry I can't do what you want."

He moved his hand to caress her cheek, keeping her head cradled against his chest. She listened to the beat of his heart. She took a deep breath. "Why is going back so important? Norman needs you, and here you could have a good life, an ordinary life but a good life.''

He held her closer. "Ordinary isn't good enough.''

"Tell me why,'' she said softly.

"I've had big plans for my life since I was fourteen.''

She waited but he said nothing more. Finally she touched his cheek, leaving her mark on him in flour. "Tell me why this is so important to you.''

He looked away.

"Tell me,'' she urged again.

"Ah, Sarah,'' was all he said at first. Then, "I didn't have much growing up. There was just my mother and me.''

"Where was your father?''

He looked past her, toward the window. "I don't even know my father's name.'' Sarah couldn't help a stiffening of her body.

"Yeah,'' he said softly. "I knew it would shock you. When I first came here, I thought the Amish didn't have a single thing I wanted. But you have roots.''

"So your mother didn't marry your father—''

"No,'' he cut in curtly. "My mother wasn't the marrying kind. She had a hard time staying with one man. In most ways, she wasn't a bad mother,'' he added slowly. "She worked as a secretary, but she couldn't hold a job for very long. Yet she made sure I had okay clothes and the things I needed for school. She was happy. She laughed a lot.''

"Oh.'' Sarah had no idea what to say.

"She liked to go out, have a good time. The neighbors called her a floozy, and sometimes they weren't too careful who was in earshot when they said it.''

The bitterness in his voice was bone deep. He rested both hands on the counter. The kitchen was so still she could hear the hallway clock ticking.

"I didn't plan to give you the long version of this story."

"Just tell me," she urged.

"I never told anybody before."

"Tell me. I'm just an Amish woman. I don't know anyone to gossip with, and I'm a very good listener."

He paused, then said, "When I was fourteen, everything changed. My mom had a job for six months, and the pay was very good. Then her boss…touched her."

"Touched her?" Sarah thought and then said, "Oh, *touched* her. But I thought it was okay with her if—" She bit her lip.

He gave another harsh chuckle. "Yes, you and the rest of the world thought the same. That she'd had so many men, she must want it from her boss. But she didn't. Not from that man."

His hands had been resting on the edge of the counter. Now they fisted. "Oh, Brent," she said softly, ashamed of her first reaction. "I'm sorry. How foolish of me."

"Forget it."

"No, really. What if I'd been…with a lot of men? I wouldn't have wanted Randy West to touch me, no matter how many men I'd…been with. I can understand why she didn't like it."

He turned slowly to face her. His eyes were dark and very shiny. Intent. "How amazing that an Amish woman can see what twelve jurors had such a hard time grasping."

"So her case went to court."

"Yes, finally. You see, her boss kept after her. For some reason, she got stubborn. She was determined to keep her job, and get her boss to leave her alone." He took a deep breath. "She hired a lawyer. In our neighborhood, going to a lawyer for something would be like going to the moon. A lawyer was so important, so…"

"So powerful. Like lawyers seem to us."

He smiled tightly. "We shouldn't understand each other. We shouldn't have any common ground."

"But we do." Her chest felt tight with the responsibility—and the gift—of his trust. "Is that when you decided to become a lawyer?"

"Yes. When my mom came home all starry-eyed, talking about the lawyer's office in the high-rise and how she was going to sue her boss. That her boss would never be able to do to another woman what he did to her. And then I thought, I could have a high-rise office and make sure women didn't have to be scared going to work. The thing is, even by that time, I was…ashamed of what my mother was. But somehow, hearing her cry at night, I couldn't—" He stopped and swallowed.

"You're a good man," she said softly.

"Not really. But some people do realize I'm rather idealistic about certain things. In my line of work, that's considered a fault."

She must have shown her surprise, because he added, "Caring about your cases can cloud your judgment."

"But surely, to care about your cases—"

He shook his head with a grim smile.

"What happened to your mother's case?"

"The trial was long. But I'd see those lawyers talking and hanging around in the courthouse, and it seemed like they belonged to something big, you know? At the end of the day, they'd clap each other on the back, even if they'd been arguing against each other in court. They belonged. I don't know any other way to put it.''

''But...did you want to belong so much?''

''Of course,'' he said simply. ''In my neighborhood, I was different. Nobody read books. Nobody in the neighborhood went to college. They had no respect for anybody who didn't go to work as soon as they were out of high school. Add to that the fact that my mom went out a lot, and you get the picture. I was a lonely kid.''

Only the slightest breeze stirred the dish towel folded over the hand pump. Sarah knew that telling her these things was difficult for Brent. She felt closer to him than she ever had before.

She looked down, overwhelmed by his nearness. ''Your mother must have been really happy when she won her case.''

''But she didn't,'' Brent said.

She looked up. ''But I thought her boss—''

''He did. But my mother was the neighborhood floozy, remember? The lawyer her employer hired made her look like the neighborhood whore.''

She gasped.

''Oh, yes, Sarah, I sat in that courtroom and listened to all the neighbors testify about how she went out with men, how she came home giggling and tipsy. The other lawyer made it seem like she instigated everything. That bastard made her cry in front of the jury, and still he never let up.''

Sarah was silent, imagining the shame of it.

"She changed after that trial, Sarah. After she lost the case, she lost her job, and she never went out again. I don't think I heard her laugh after that, and she'd had a nice laugh. I didn't like what she was, but I...missed hearing her laugh."

She didn't say anything. There was nothing to say because she heard in the depths of his voice so much sorrow and pain. She reached out and covered his fist with her hand. She looked down, at her hand, small, work-worn and floury, curling over his knuckles. His hand was big and masculine, touched here and there with shining curly dark hair. That hand looked strong and invincible. "What happened to her? Does she still live in Toledo?"

"She died when I was in my last year of law school." His voice went low and fierce. "I swore I'd be the best lawyer in the state. I'd be part of the group, but nobody would be more skilled, nobody would ever be able to make a client of mine look bad, make my client feel ashamed. I swore that nobody would ever go through what my mother had."

Outside, there were sounds of an approaching wagon, the squeak of harness, the low voice of her father, saying something to the horses.

"So now you know the story of Brent McCade," he said, his voice harsh and almost self-mocking.

"Yes." She longed to give him comfort, but the stiffness of his spine suggested that any offer now would be interpreted as pity. "The thing is, Brent," she said carefully, "you do your best, and I'm sure you've helped a lot of people. But you can't fix everything for everybody."

"I can if they let me," he said, knowing immediately that she was referring to her own case. "We call

a situation like yours and mine a win-win. We both
get what we need."

"I can't," she said, feeling a touch of panic.

He said, "You can."

Those honest, intent eyes. If she ever did testify,
she was certain she'd be in good hands. And sometimes, she really did want to testify...*needed* to testify. Sighing, she wiped her hands on a dish towel.

His hand came out and covered hers. "Do you trust
me?"

"Yes," she said softly.

"If you trust me, you can testify."

She hesitated. "I can't," she said finally.

"I know I've never heard exactly why you won't
testify. I know you've always held something back."

She flushed and suddenly flung the dish towel onto
the counter. "The bishop has forbidden me to testify.
To cooperate with the English legal system in any
way." There, she thought, she'd said it at last. She'd
been guilty of the sin of pride, because all along,
she'd wanted Brent to think this was her decision
alone. English women were so much more independent. She'd known he would think less of her for
allowing the bishop to make this decision, and her
pride couldn't bear it.

"The *bishop* forbids it?" Brent looked stunned.
"What's the bishop got to do with your case?"

"By this time you should know enough about us
to realize the bishop rules in church matters."

"In church matters, maybe, but this is about you,
Sarah, and only you."

Outside, it had grown still. The cheerful voices and
noise of horse and wagon had faded in the distance.
The men must have returned to the fields. Brent was

waiting for her response, his body leaning forward slightly.

Sudden tears filled her eyes. The rape had been hers to endure, but everyone thought they had a say in what she ought to do about it. "Any contact with the outside world is a church matter."

"He can't make you do something you don't think is right. Tell me the truth, Sarah." He looked her in the eye. "If it were just up to you, would you testify?"

She shouldn't answer him. After all, he'd always had his own motives for trying to persuade her. Still she said, "Yes, I think I would." For a second, that felt good, to say exactly what she wanted.

"Good for you, Sarah. Good for you." He looked into her eyes for a brief second, and the genuine admiration she saw there left her momentarily breathless. For a second she thought he was going to touch her, but he didn't. Instead, he paced. "Okay. It'll be hard for you to testify, I know that. But I'll prepare you well. You don't have to worry—"

"Brent, I'm not testifying," she said to his back.

"I know the bishop's disapproval makes it tough for you. But after all—"

"I *can't*."

He'd reached the end of the kitchen, and now he turned. "If you don't, then you're not the woman I've come to know, a strong and brave woman. Strong and brave women make their own decisions."

She hadn't expected him to understand, but still, his lack of understanding made her heart ache with loneliness. "If I go against an express order of the bishop, there's a good chance I'll be shunned."

He stopped on his forward pace and stared.

She took a deep breath. "I'd be—" despite her best efforts, her voice cracked "—alone."

The word rang in the kitchen. Sarah watched Brent's face, watched the enormity of it sink in.

"Shunned. Forever?"

"Maybe." She had to struggle to keep the tears from clogging her voice, just at the thought of it. "I'd be shunned until I confessed that I did wrong. If I couldn't sincerely confess, the shunning would... never end."

"Have you been threatened? Has he—your bishop—threatened to shun you?" Brent stopped pacing a few feet from her, and his hand clenched in a fist by his side.

"No, because I've been following his directive."

He swore.

She said, "Don't swear, Brent. Shunning is hard, but it's the right thing to do. We Amish have so many things going against us. The outside world is so tempting. We need church leaders to lay down laws for us, just like you need laws in the English world."

"For God's sake," he snapped. "You make being Amish sound like some kind of cult!"

Anger swept her. She'd listened to him, tried to understand him. She'd been starting to fall in love with him. Now he mocked her way of life.

She could ask him to leave. She didn't have to stand here and explain all the nuances of being Amish to a man who didn't want to understand. But she said, "The bishop isn't some evil cult leader. He's Jacob's father, and I love him."

"That does complicate things, but—"

"To be chosen bishop is a great burden." She sighed, suddenly tired of explaining, of being pulled so hard in two directions. She made one last try to make him understand. "One night long ago, Daniel—our bishop—told Jacob and me how he hadn't wanted to be bishop, how hard he'd prayed not to be chosen. But when he *was* chosen, he prayed just as hard for wisdom. All his life, he's sacrificed for the community."

She paused, then spoke again. "That's what it means to be Amish. To sacrifice your own worldly desires for the sake of the group. So before you start on free will and make comments about Daniel being a cult leader, think about that man. A man with eight little children and a farm to run, praying his heart out that he wouldn't be chosen to lead us."

Brent spoke softly. "If he loves you, he wouldn't shun you." He took a step toward her. "They wouldn't do that to you, not to you, the victim of a crime, Sarah. Not to you, a caring, kind intelligent woman."

If she'd gone all cold inside at the thought of shunning, his words warmed her, a small and steady flame.

His gaze was intent. "Surely if you'd testify, you'd disappoint Daniel, but your community would realize what you went through and not out and out shun you."

"Maybe," she acknowledged. Her heart gave a little surge of hope. Daniel had never used the actual word *shun* when he'd forbidden her to use the English court for English justice. Her father could talk to Daniel, explain how hard it had been for her these last months... It was tempting, and that scared her very much.

"How can I take the risk?" she whispered. "Maybe for myself I could take the risk, but for my family to have to risk the ban— You saw Levi today, heard him. He needs me. He needs me to be Amish.''

''Sometimes you have to take risks,'' Brent said, his gaze never leaving hers. ''This is right for you, Sarah.'' His voice rang with conviction.

Yet he'd said himself that his mother had not got justice in the English court. He himself had lost his reputation there.

''Listen to me,'' he said. ''No matter what beliefs you espouse, you aren't the kind of woman to let a man tell you what to do. A man who knows nothing of what you went through.''

Once she'd let a man influence her greatly. If she hadn't loved Jacob, would she have joined the church? Jacob had been devout, had only led her by example, by the gentlest of persuasion. There was no reason to feel this sudden resentment. ''Well, Brent, you're a man, and you're trying to do the same thing. And you probably understand me less than Daniel does.'' It was a lie, and that shook her, that she would lie. Because she did think Brent understood so much. But she had to forestall him somehow. She allowed her anger to take over. ''What's so great about the English court? It failed your mother. Your lawyer friends rejected you on the basis of a rumor. At least I have a family. People to care for. *That's* what you don't understand, how important a family is. How we all need someone to love and care for. *That's* what you want me to put at risk.''

''Sarah, listen—''

''Will you never quit? What do you have that's more important than family?'' Her voice rose. ''What do you have except winning cases and being alone?''

He brought his fist down on the table, hard. ''Damn

it, Sarah! Don't lecture me on how to live my life!
Not while you're still listening to your daddy and
your bishop and sneaking around just to draw and
wearing that little white cap that says you won't join
the rest of the world!''

The sting of his words reached way deep inside her,
and she wanted to cry the kind of tears a person cried
when they were too angry for words.

There was a long, ugly pause. Then abruptly, he
turned to go.

He was almost at the door when she found her
voice. "I care about my family, and I'm not ashamed
to admit it! I *am* making my own decision. I won't
do it. How's that for independence, Brent McCade!''
She was shaking all over as he went out the door.

SHE HAD SINNED.

Sarah rolled onto her back in her narrow widow's
bed and looked at the moon-washed ceiling. She had
said cruel things in anger; she'd let a good man goad
her into saying them. He'd been angry and said too
much, but she'd done wrong too.

She had committed the sin of pride, to care so
much what a man—an English man!—thought of her
ability to make her own decisions.

She still believed Brent thought he was doing the
right thing when he urged her to testify. That he
wanted her to heal. So what if he got something out
of winning her case too? What had he called it? A
win-win situation.

Right, Sarah thought grimly, reaching behind her
to flip her pillow over so that the cooler side was
against her neck. Brent wins. Sarah wins. Maybe. And

her family loses. Her people lose. And then Brent goes away.

She sat bolt upright in bed, wide-awake. When was she going to be able to sleep peacefully at night again? The moon was a full, orange-gold ball. Its light made the room brighter than she was used to. In fact, it was almost as light as when she lit her lamp to draw.

She wasn't going to draw tonight. Lately, drawing seemed to make her more restless than ever.

She thought about right and wrong way more than she should have to as an Amish woman. Her fingers itched to draw, and she was already lonely because an English man who'd hurt her today was going away.

She'd had more excitement, more...everything since Brent had come to the farm. She'd had a taste of the outside world and now she craved it. A part of her had always wanted to know what was out there. Now she wanted to see the world Brent lived in, to taste the freedom.

Throwing off the covers, she got up and went to the window. Brent would be back in Toledo in a month, and he'd wonder whatever had possessed him to kiss a modest Amish widow.

Her paper was in the drawer. She'd been trying not to draw ever since she'd drawn Brent's likeness. She looked out the window. A tiny cloud raced across the moon, so fast that if she'd blinked, she would have missed it. Life was like that, fleeting images that she longed to grasp and put on paper.

Her hands were surprisingly steady as she opened her desk drawer and took out a sheet of paper, as white as a prayer cap. Next, her nibs and her ink.

She'd draw the women. Amish women around the quilting frame. This time she wouldn't show much background; it was the people she wanted to capture. But it was a sin to draw Amish faces.

It was a sin to fall in love with Brent McCade.

It was a sin to want to testify.

She had to do something or go mad. So which would be the smallest sin? Which would cause the least hardship to those she loved?

She made her decision and she took her time. She drew in perfect Emma, and no-nonsense Anna Troyer, and she drew in the sturdy, square figure of her friend Rebecca. She started on aprons, and caps. She did the faces last. All of them. All of those forbidden faces.

She managed to finish the whole drawing before her hands started to shake. There was a place where she'd got the ink a little too heavy and the paper had puckered. It reminded her of the oldest quilts, when the Amish quilter would deliberately make a mistake in the pattern. A quilt couldn't be perfect, because only God was allowed perfection.

Then she slowly put away the drawing and got back into bed. She told herself she had sinned. But—defiant, maybe—she fell asleep easily and slept soundly.

CHAPTER TEN

"HE DOESN'T HAVE any fire," Norm complained mildly about Timothy Smith, the young attorney they'd just interviewed. "He's a nice guy, but there's no drive."

"You like nice guys," Brent reminded him. They were sitting in Brent's office, a high-ceilinged, paneled room. "Smith doesn't have much experience, but he should do okay after he gets his feet wet. Besides, you like the negotiator-type lawyer, the ones who don't cause trouble."

"I changed my mind." Norm glanced down at his legal pad. On it was a remarkably short list of candidates to fill Brent's post, and most were just out of law school. Wheatland's off-the-beaten-path location wasn't any more attractive than it had been when Brent had taken the job.

Brent grimaced. Norm had found fault with every person they'd interviewed. Guilt made Brent's stomach turn acid.

After a short pause, Brent spoke. "Look, Norm. I know you said my leaving was okay with you, but if you really don't want to train somebody new, I'll stay." The words had been hard, but saying them, Brent felt unexpectedly better.

Norm sighed. "It's a good opportunity. I won't

hold you back. Let's bring Tim in for another interview."

"Got it. I'll have Kelly set something up." Brent put down his pen, leaned back and rubbed the bridge of his nose.

Norm got up slowly from his chair. "Man, I feel stiff today," he said, but the words were more conversation than complaint. He lumbered over to the window. "My wife's going to miss you. She had a list going of every single woman within fifty miles."

Except for a few hundred Amish women, Brent thought without humor. Except for one woman. Sarah.

"She was determined to marry you off."

Brent forced a grin, though Norm didn't turn to see it. "A man likes to run his own life."

Norm turned from the window. "That gets lonely, Brent."

Brent shrugged. He stood and picked up a legal pad. "I'll just give this to Kelly now."

"Running away from our discussion, are you?"

"Damn it, Norm!" Brent said angrily. "I'm not running from anything."

"Aren't you?"

"I belong there," he said simply.

Norm smiled. "You may be right about that. You do have a tad too much energy for a small town. The secretaries gossip about you, you know. You come in every morning, yank your stuff out of your in-box as though you had fifty arraignments to do by noon, then you sit on the edge of your desk to read your mail."

Brent shook his head. The pace of Wheatland could be seductive, but he'd never really learned to slow down. Maybe if he'd spent a year or two here...

Norm turned again to the window, and stood gazing out. "You know, belonging is a funny thing," he said reflectively. "Just the other day Kelly said you got her kid out of some traffic violation, let him work off what would have been his fine by doing some volunteer activity."

"It just took a few minutes. And then I talked to her son, put a little fear and respect for the law in him. And lectured him on the importance of using a helmet."

"Then there was Frank Operheimer over at the pharmacy. Said you advised him about the latest shoplifting laws."

"I was buying aspirin anyway. What's your point?"

"Then, of course, there's Bob Kay, that guy who was swindled in the replacement-window scam. I understand you helped him out last week by reading over his homeowners' insurance contract. I also heard he's been in about twice a week since the trial, with one problem after another, and that he always wants to see you."

Brent had been a trial lawyer long enough to know when he was being manipulated. "He came into the office, and I wasn't busy. The guy lost every cent he had in that scam, so now he worries that everybody's taking him. And I always have time. It isn't exactly the Manhattan Superior Court around here."

"True."

There was a little silence. Brent knew this game, too, the silences that were hard for your opponent to resist filling. "Ah, hell, Norm, I know what you're trying to say. That I belong here. But here I'll never have a big case, and I've trained myself for those."

"But you're going to be doing insurance work," Norm said.

Brent's teeth ground together so hard they ached. "I might make partner someday."

Norm finally turned from the window. He crossed to the desk and took the pad from Brent. "Well, all I know is that for a guy who's so hell-bent to get out of town, a lot of people are going to remember you. You were a real success."

A bark of laughter erupted from Brent's throat. "There was only one big case here, and I never got to prosecute it."

"Ah," Norm said.

"No ah about it. Sarah's case was going to be the making of me again and I failed there. The only good thing about the whole damn mess is that Randy West has apparently decided to leave her alone."

Though he'd never admit it to Norm, had tried not to admit it to himself, Brent felt surprisingly warm toward Wheatland, and surprisingly unenthusiastic about his job in Toledo. But he told himself that the moment he picked up the strings of his old life, he'd look upon his months in Wheatland as just one of life's bizarre twists.

Norm stroked his mustache. "You spent quite a bit of time with Sarah, I hear."

"You hear more gossip than an old lady. Look, Norm, I know you mean well, but I do actually have a case or two to prepare this afternoon."

"Okay, okay, I'm going," Norm grumbled. "You're pretty persuasive. I just thought you might have got her to go along with what you wanted to do."

"She's stubborn." And beautiful, and her yielding,

lush woman's flesh had excited him as nothing else
had ever done. Of all the women in the world, it was
her hair he imagined running through his fingers, *her*
mouth pressed to his own.

He needed sex, he decided. Friendly sex with a nice
woman in a place where people wouldn't gossip about
it in the morning.

If what he felt for Sarah was more than sexual...
Even more than friendship...

It couldn't be. It was a crazy interlude at a time
when his life was in a shambles. He wasn't even going to see her again. He just needed to get out of
town.

Norm opened the door on the way out of the office,
and left it open. A moment later Kelly came in. "I've
got a phone call for you." She held out the pink message slip. "It came in while you were interviewing
Timothy Smith. You're supposed to call some kid
named Levi Stolzfus."

Brent's head shot up.

"Levi Stolzfus sounds like an Amish name," Kelly
said cheerfully. "But that can't be, because he says
he's been arrested. He's calling you from the police
station."

SARAH WAS out in the vegetable garden, so she saw
Brent's car from a long way off. Now what did he
want? It had been a week since she'd seen him last,
so that made three until he was gone for good. Her
heart quickened its pace as she stood and used a hand
to shield her eyes. She would keep working; she had
tomatoes to pick.

She'd thought he wouldn't be back; she had resolved to have nothing more to do with him. Their

last conversation had had a ring of finality, and over this past week she'd come to terms with the fact that it was all over.

She did not need Brent with his car and clothes, his manners, all that reminded her there was a whole world out there, bustling cities she'd never seen, and the roller coaster Levi talked about that roared down a hill and smashed into the water.

She didn't need excitement; she needed serenity.

Brent never brought serenity. He brought choices and stirred things up and made her long for his touch. Sarah bent resolutely to her task. One more bushel, and she could start the canning.

She heard the thwack of the car door, then another. "Sarah!" Brent called.

She wouldn't look up. She wouldn't! She pushed aside a big tomato leaf and got its yellow-green sap on her hand.

"Sarah!" Nearer now, and it was hard to keep her body from leaning toward the sound.

An overripe tomato squished when she squeezed too hard. The gate squeaked and Sarah finally looked up.

Brent was here, in the elegant suit that was as out of place in an Amish barnyard as an apron would be at a ball. Levi was with him. *Levi?*

"What's going on?" she asked, standing quickly.

Levi's face was brick red, and he wouldn't meet her eyes.

"Levi's in some trouble with the law." Brent's expression was very grim. "Where's your father?"

"In the barn," Sarah said, pushing down a flash of alarm. "I'll go get him." She started to pick up the basket of tomatoes, but Brent said curtly, "Leave the tomatoes. We'll all go find Adam."

As they started down the path to the barnyard, Sarah asked, "What kind of trouble?"

"Traffic trouble, pretty serious."

"Nobody got hurt," Levi said in a high voice.

"Save it for your father," Brent said sternly.

Sarah bit her lip to keep from asking more. Brent was right; her father needed to hear this.

Even though she was concerned for Levi, awareness of Brent penetrated. She felt him, big and dark, a little behind her as she led the way. *"Vater,"* she called as they neared the barn, and then asked him to come out in Pennsylvania Dutch.

"Please speak English," Brent said.

Her father came to the door of the barn. "What is it?"

"We have to speak English," Sarah explained.

Her father noticed Brent and smiled a greeting. "Well, here we are between meals, and still you've come."

Brent didn't smile back. "Adam, there's been trouble in town with Levi. He caused an auto accident today."

Sarah gasped. "With the buggy?"

"No, he was driving a car," Brent said grimly. Levi stood next to him. There had been a shaky defiance in her brother's expression, but he couldn't hold it. He looked down.

Her father didn't say a word, just wiped his greasy hands on a rag. Finally, he said, "Let's go in the house."

The four of them sat in the Stolzfus kitchen. Her father asked Brent to explain. "Levi apparently decided to try driving. He has some English friend, Scott Graber. Scott's not normally a troublemaker. Anyway, he has a temporary driver's permit, but isn't supposed to drive without a licensed driver present. But he was, and Levi persuaded Scott to let him drive. Scott was in the passenger seat, giving a lesson.''

Brent smiled grimly. ''Apparently, Levi has a heavy foot. Before they knew it, he was going very fast. Several witnesses said they saw the car narrowly miss a busful of tourists, hit a parking meter and finally crash into a parked Cadillac. Scott has a bruised nose, but no one was really hurt. In that, Levi was lucky. The way that car was going from side to side down the street, it's a wonder someone wasn't killed. Levi, too, could have been seriously hurt.''

There was silence. A moment later, her father asked in a stern voice, ''Levi, is this true?''

Levi had taken off his hat when he'd come indoors. Now, head down, he nodded. ''I was wearing a seat belt,'' he said in a small voice.

Her father made a noise—one syllable—that managed to convey utter disgust. Then he said, ''I'm saddened and angered by your behavior.'' The coldness in his voice gave Sarah a pang. Her father meant well, but when he chastised, you knew you'd done very, very wrong. In fact, he could sound so stern that if Sarah had not found him crying in the barn four months ago, she might have missed the slightly thickened note in his voice.

Her father turned to Brent. ''Will Levi go to jail?''

''He could have. As it is, he has a court appearance in a month, and he'll have a large fine to pay. Not to mention the damage to the Cadillac, which he's responsible for.'' Brent paused. ''He could be in jail now, Adam. Fortunately, he called me. When I got to the police station, I found out from the chief that Levi has been driving his buggy recklessly, and almost caused an accident last week. Apparently, he and his non-Amish friends have also been warned about noise from playing their boom boxes along Main Street. I had to make some serious promises to be allowed to bring Levi home.

"I took responsibility for bringing him home today and also for his driving and conduct until his court appearance. A jail is no place for a kid like Levi. Juvenile hall is full of rough kids." He paused. "I don't want him to get hurt."

There was silence. Sarah twisted her hands in her lap. Her father stood slowly and held out his hand, a gesture that looked absurd coming from an Amish man. But no one smiled. Instead, Brent also stood, took her father's hand and shook it.

"Thank you," Adam said simply. Then he added, "I'm so angry at Levi, so disappointed. But you've given me a chance to deal with him as an Amish son, and for that I thank you."

Sarah got a lump in her throat. From the beginning, there had been an odd camaraderie between her father and Brent. Now she sensed the true bond of friendship between the two.

She couldn't do what Brent wanted, and she'd said some harsh words about his values the other day. But he'd taken time out of his life to help an Amish boy who was on the wrong path, and to bring him home.

Who could not love such a man? Sarah loved him, deeply and with all the truth she acknowledged in her heart.

She took a deep breath. Everything she'd been

taught said it was wrong to love an English man. But her heart sang. It didn't feel wrong. It felt right and good and powerful and full and bright and...

Swiftly, she tried to school her expression, to regain control. Brent—no one—must ever know her feelings. Her father respected Brent, but Adam would never accept his daughter loving an English man.

Besides, Brent was going away, back to a world he was convinced he wanted. She knew he *should* go away, because if he didn't, someday he might discover how she felt. Sarah clenched her hands in her lap against the loneliness of his going and her need to shout that she loved him.

Adam stroked his beard. "Levi, your sin is almost too grave to contemplate. We're the most peaceful of people, yet you could have killed someone today."

Levi kept his head down. "I didn't mean for anyone to get hurt," he said softly. "I just wanted to know what it would feel like to go fast."

"That's no excuse," her father said sternly. "I'll pray for guidance. For now, you are not to leave the farm. You'll work from sunup to sunset, and you won't drive the buggy to town for so much as more kerosene for the lamps. Do you understand?"

"Yes," Levi said almost inaudibly. His shoulders were hunched, and despite Sarah's knowledge that he had to be dealt with severely, her heart hurt for him. She looked into Brent's eyes, but he looked away immediately.

"But, *Vater?*" Levi looked up then. "The sing on Sunday night—"

"You won't be going to any sing."

"But I'm to drive Katie and Mary Hershburger, and their parents can't take them. I'm to help the

Schultzes set up for the sing, and I told Benjamin Schultz I'd help move the barn beams beforehand.''

Adam nodded slowly. "Because of your obligations to others, you may go. But you won't sing. You'll sit off to the side, and after the sing you'll come straight home." He paused. "In other words, you won't need the courting buggy."

Levi nodded, his face red.

Brent cleared his throat. "Ah, Adam, I promised the chief that I would be responsible for Levi. He can't even drive the buggy unless I'm there."

"You could come to the sing, Brent," Levi urged.

Brent shot Sarah a glance so quick that if she hadn't been focused on his face, she would have missed it.

"Do you have time for a foolish boy, Brent?" her father asked. "I don't like the idea of letting him off from his obligations to others. I could take him, but I've got a mare due to foal—"

"Adam, even you can't supervise. Not in the buggy. Levi is up for a serious charge." There was a long pause. "I'll go along to the sing."

"*Vater,* surely Brent is busy," Sarah cut in. Her father was treating Brent almost like an Amish man; the Amish didn't hesitate to ask favors from one another and didn't think much about what the other person might have going on.

To her surprise, Brent flushed a little. "It's a Sunday night. I don't have anything to do. I'll take Levi."

THAT NIGHT Randy West heard the official word; the bartender was in a talkative mood. The guy put his elbows on the bar as he dried a tumbler. "So I heard Julie Ann really did throw Mel out. Mel just couldn't keep his pants zipped around any good-looking chick, you know?''

Excitement gripped Randy, though he looked right through the bartender as if the guy wasn't there. The bartender shrugged. "Just thought you'd want to know. You were carrying a torch for old Julie Ann, I thought." When Randy still didn't answer, the bartender moved off.

The last three times Julie Ann had been in the bar, she'd been alone. So, Randy thought, what he'd suspected was really true. She'd broken up with Mel for good.

He knew she'd be in tonight because it was Friday. But she was late, and he'd had to have one more beer than he was used to, just waiting for Julie Ann. Well, the beer would loosen his tongue and help him make conversation, even if it did make him need to piss all the time.

When she came in, he hardly waited for her to sit down before going over to her table. He certainly didn't wait for her to take out her cigarette. Randy didn't like smokers, and when Julie Ann was really his girlfriend, she'd quit.

He pulled out a chair, turned it around and straddled it, the way he'd seen James Caan do in some old movie. "Hi," he said.

She looked irritated. "I want to be alone."

Randy nodded, pleased with this confirmation of her single status. "You have to be alone because you broke up with Mel for good."

She narrowed her eyes. "What of it?" She took out her cigarette case. He put his hand out to stop her.

"Hey," she said, pulling her arm away.

He let go but leaned over the table. "Let me buy

you a beer.'' His heart was pounding, but he didn't show it.

"No thanks."

"I know what kind you drink."—He signaled to the bartender. Oh, man, this was just like the movies.

"No. I don't want a beer. Really, I don't want you hanging around, okay?"

"You broke up with your boyfriend," he reminded her. That was the only reason she'd turned him down the last time.

She gave a laugh that sounded weird, sort of nervous. "Maybe I just like being single."

"Look, Julie Ann, you don't know me very well—"

"I don't know you at all."

He swallowed. This conversation wasn't going how he'd planned, and he willed down a touch of desperation. "I know you," he insisted. "I know you like to wear red or white, you have new white slacks with a little label on the pocket that has embroidery on it, you smoke two different brands of cigarettes—that's very unusual, by the way. You have a straw purse that has a broken strap that you mended with—"

"Stop! " She shrieked the word. Then she put her hands over her ears. "Stop telling me this stuff. I've seen you watching me and I don't like it!" She took a couple of breaths. "I don't want you hanging around me, so leave me alone!"

The blood pounded in Randy's ears; he hardly heard the last of what she'd said. She didn't want to get to know him? Was she crazy, or what? How could she not see—

"You got trouble?" A big, beefcake kind of guy

stopped by the table, a cue stick in hand, and was addressing Julie Ann.

"I don't know," she said, looking across the table with a wariness that made Randy so mad he could have spit. "I just want this guy to leave me alone."

Mr. Beef turned toward Randy. "You heard the lady. You gonna leave her alone, or do I gotta ruin a good cue stick?"

"All *right*," Randy said, and he got up and shrugged. His belly was quivering with rage, but he managed to grin at the slob. "You can't blame a guy for trying."

The guy relaxed, grinned too. He looked Julie Ann over good. "No, you sure can't blame a guy for trying."

Randy turned toward the bar, but from behind him, he heard Julie Ann invite the guy to sit down. A guy like that with a greasy ponytail and a mesh shirt worn way too tight. Prissy Julie Ann had turned down Randy, a guy who'd treat her right, for a pig like Mr. Beef.

When he got to the bar, Randy ordered a shot of whiskey. The bitch! The bartender set the glass in front of him. Randy gulped. The whiskey burned his throat; he never drank hard stuff. He coughed and sputtered.

Somebody laughed.

Something snapped in Randy then; he could almost hear the sound. He threw the shot glass toward the back wall of the bar. A mirror shattered.

"Hey," the bartender said, starting to walk over to him.

The blood was roaring in his ears, like that snap had been a big vein bursting somewhere in his body. The roaring made it hard to think. All Randy could come up with was one word. *Soon.*

CHAPTER ELEVEN

BRENT WISHED he hadn't agreed to come to the Stolz-fuses tonight. Why on earth had he volunteered to accompany a bunch of Amish teenagers to a sing in a buggy? Well, he'd have an interesting story to tell in Toledo.

He knocked, figuring that with any luck, Sarah would be in her shop or up in her room. He had no intention of seeing her any more than necessary. In less than three weeks, good case or no, he'd be back where he belonged.

Adam opened the door. "Brent." He stood aside without an invitation to enter, but Brent, by now used to the Amish way, stepped inside.

Sarah was there, after all. The house was dim; they needed to light a lamp. The white of her prayer cap gleamed, and her golden hair shone. He'd remember her this way, he knew suddenly. Golden hair and white cap. The knowledge that he'd remember her for a long time made him impatient.

"Levi, are you ready?" he asked more curtly than he'd intended.

Levi's face and neck were pink from scrubbing, and his straw hat looked new. "I'm ready."

Adam glanced at his son. "I don't think you need your new hat," he said. "I told you, you won't be courting tonight."

Levi looked away.

Adam sighed, clearly exasperated. "Fine. Wear the hat. Brent, I've asked Sarah to accompany you tonight."

Sarah? Going with them? Oh, hell, he thought. When he'd agreed to help out, he'd never guessed that he'd be spending the evening with Sarah. Brent glanced over at her. She was retying the strings of her prayer cap, and then she made what seemed to him like an unnecessarily big production of repinning her apron. Apparently, like him, she too was uncomfortable about the evening's plans.

Adam spoke. "Levi and I have had some words this week. I've talked, I've chastised, but Levi doesn't seem much in the mood to respond. So I've asked Sarah to go. You don't know our ways. You need to keep an eye on his driving for the court, but Sarah needs to keep an eye on *him*."

Brent knew there was no way to refuse. After all, what could he say? *I'm sorry, Adam, but when I'm alone with your daughter, I want to kiss her. I want to push off her prayer cap and pull the pins from her bun and slide my fingers into her hair. It's really not Levi who bears watching tonight.* Hell. He was good and trapped into spending the evening with Sarah.

They took the covered buggy, though the night was warm. Brent handed Sarah up to the buggy, touching crisp cotton. As she scrambled in, he got a good look at her calf in her dutiful black stockings. She had a nice calf, sturdy and dainty at the same time... His mind turned abruptly from the thought.

They picked up Mary and Katie Hershburger. Katie, who was about Levi's age, sat in the front with Levi. Mary, who looked a few years younger, got into the rear seat, forcing Sarah—in the middle—to squeeze against Brent.

"Sorry," Sarah said, a little husky, breathless note in her voice as her body pressed against his side. Her voice sent his awareness of her up another notch. He looked at her profile; she stared straight ahead. If he hadn't heard that breathlessness, he'd have thought she wasn't at all conscious of their bodies so close.

The buggy ride was rough, the buggy's uncushioned wheels making it bounce along the road. A big bump threw Sarah against him. He put his arm around her shoulders to steady her. When she gave a little shrug, he remembered he shouldn't be touching her and took his arm away.

The reins jingled and the horses snorted. From behind, Brent heard a car come up, then roar around the buggy.

In the front seat, Levi was in high spirits. He spoke English for Brent's benefit. Around his father, Levi had been quiet, contrite. Out here, he talked and joked with Katie.

"Hungry?" Levi asked Katie.

"Yes, a little," she said shyly.

Levi turned into the parking lot of the local McDonald's. Sarah said sharply, "We don't need to stop here. You aren't going to the sing for fun, Levi."

"What *Vater* doesn't know won't hurt anything. Besides, Katie's hungry."

Sarah cast Brent a look as if he was supposed to say something. But what was he supposed to do? It was true that Levi was in serious trouble. Trouble, Brent thought now, that he might not have been in if his natural urge for freedom hadn't been curtailed.

So he said nothing when Levi took the buggy to a

parking space. The teenager leaped down and found a tree to hitch the horses to.

Inside the brightly lit restaurant, the patrons stared. Brent didn't know any of them, so he took his cue from his companions and paid no attention. After a while, people looked away and their conversation resumed. Brent placed his order, then he tried to pay, but Levi wouldn't let him. "I brought money," Levi said with a touch of defiance.

Katie and Levi were laughing as they sat down at the table. Brent noticed that Katie was careful to keep a good distance from Levi.

"Tell us about Toledo," Levi urged Brent. "What's it like?"

Brent said, "Well, it's small, as cities go, about four hundred thousand people."

Katie gasped. She and Mary had treated him with exaggerated respect, and now she looked at him with openmouthed envy. "Lake Erie is probably the most imposing thing about Toledo," he added, a little amused at their expressions.

"What's the lake like?" Levi again.

"Brent, don't encourage him," Sarah said. But she was leaning forward slightly herself, as if she too wanted to know what it was like.

"Well, there are a lot of islands, and they're tree-covered and green. Some of them have docks where boats tie up, and places to shop for shells or souvenirs. There are places where you can't see across to the other shoreline, the lake is so large. Almost like the ocean. In fact, when there's a storm and the waves crash in, it definitely reminds you of the ocean."

He could have sworn he saw longing in Sarah's eyes. He wasn't an artist like her; he didn't have any particular appreciation for nature. But he was good with words. Suddenly, he wanted her to see the things he'd seen, to share his world with her the way she'd ended up sharing hers with him.

"On a clear day, the water looks navy blue," he began. "But if you're out on the lake in a boat, you can see the individual waves with the sun behind them, and then they're green. The breeze smells like fish and seaweed. Some of the sailboats have sails that look like rainbows, and there are yachts so lean and sleek they just cut through the water."

He stopped speaking and looked at his audience. There was a short silence. Then Mary said in a wistful voice, "I'd like to see that lake that's almost as big as an ocean."

"I," Levi said, "would like to see the lake and the city too. I'd like to see the train station, and take a ride on a jet."

Brent looked at Sarah, wondering if Levi's words would cause her worry. But her eyes were dreamy, faraway. She was beautiful. Even the loose-fitting clothes and the unflattering hairstyle couldn't hide that fact. Suddenly, Brent found himself far away, too, but he wasn't focused on water or planes.

Instead, he could see Sarah in his world, her hair flowing around her shoulders. Her shoulders would be bare, he decided, her dress strapless and red. No stockings to cover her lovely legs—just a pair of little gold sandals that would bare her toes. He felt a surge of desire.

He stared at Sarah. He knew he was showing what he felt, that the desire—almost pain-sharp in his groin—would show in his eyes. He willed her to look up, to acknowledge what was between them.

Slowly, her eyes met his. In them was a hunger he couldn't mistake, a hunger as keen as his own. Sarah might be naive, but she wasn't innocent. She'd been a married woman. There was passion under all that cotton. And she wanted him. He knew it as certainly as he knew his own name and that he had created his own destiny.

She spoke. "All the Amish sometimes want to see the faraway places. Wanting to do that is natural." Her voice had gone a little tight. The others turned to look at her. "Wanting something you can't have is—is natural," she repeated, a deep blush staining her cheeks.

"I could show the city to you." Brent sensed the others watching, and so he included them in his gaze, though he meant his words only for Sarah. "In Toledo, I have tickets to the symphony, to the opera. Have you ever heard opera? There's so much glitter, such a richness of song that it's unlike anything you've ever heard."

Nobody moved or spoke for a long second. Then Sarah gave a quick shake of her head. "What nonsense we're speaking! Eat up, or Levi will be too late to help Benjamin."

As if a spell had been broken, the young people ate. Sarah picked up a French fry, set it down, picked it up again. Brent felt suddenly ashamed. It wasn't right to dangle his life in front of her when, despite his fantasies, she would never be a part of it.

"I'm going for some coffee," he said abruptly, leaving them alone at the table, three young Amish who confessed to sometimes wanting to see the world. And a woman with golden hair who drew pictures and ran a quilt shop and wore a prayer cap that was like a beacon that said, *Don't touch. Don't touch.*

AT THE SCHULTZES', Brent joined the other men and boys in helping Benjamin Schultz lift a heavy beam onto the skeleton framework of his shed. Wearing tight jeans and knit shirt, he stood out from the other men. She'd have to be careful, Sarah thought. If Levi and the girls hadn't been so young and naive, they would certainly have been able to read the underlying message in her and Brent's words. What an example she'd set tonight! She had to do better. She hadn't wanted to come, but there'd been no way to refuse without questions from her father.

She went into the barn. The large cattle-loafing area had been hosed down. Fresh sawdust had been spread, and it gave off a clean, piney smell. A long table was set up in the middle of the space. Some boards and concrete blocks made benches. Around the perimeter, more chairs had been set up.

Brent came up beside her, and the sense of him there caused the skin of her forearms to prickle. Neither spoke. Before long, people began to troop into the barn. Rebecca was there, and Sarah introduced her friend to Brent. Rebecca and Sarah exchanged a few words in Pennsylvania Dutch. Benjamin shut the big double doors and opened the smaller door, the one that ran along the shady path to the house kitchen. As darkness fell, lanterns were lit and hung on the beams until the sawdust on the floor glowed gold.

Too shy to look at Brent, much less talk to him, Rebecca kept focused on Sarah. "Are you going to join in the singing?" Rebecca asked, still in Pennsylvania Dutch.

"I don't think so," Sarah said. "I'm chaperoning Levi tonight. He's in the doghouse with Father."

Rebecca looked sympathetic. "What happened?"

"An accident with a car. Levi was driving."

Rebecca gasped. "That makes Jeremiah's behavior seem mild." They both looked over to where Rebecca's younger brother, Jeremiah, was talking with Mary Hannah. Rebecca's father had planted celery in the garden this spring, and everybody knew whose wedding was planned. "I know Jeremiah didn't want me in the courting buggy tonight."

"You couldn't beg off?" Sarah asked. Once, she had loved the sings, and going home in Jacob's open courting buggy after. Now a sing usually made her feel old, as if life was passing her by. But she didn't feel that way tonight, she realized with a start. Instead, she felt…aware, her senses on alert. The reason, she knew, was the presence of the silent English man by her side.

"I didn't have to come. I just decided I would at the last minute, with Jeremiah," Rebecca said, and Sarah had to struggle to recall what she'd asked her friend.

Sarah nodded.

"It's just that…" Rebecca blushed and lowered her voice. "Amos Troyer came over last Sunday afternoon. I thought maybe he'd come about a problem with his flock. That day I helped him with the bolus gun, we had a good talk about sheep diseases. Then— Oh, Sarah." Her voice dropped. "Amos asked me to come to the sing. He was going to bring me in his buggy."

"The courting buggy," Sarah said, feeling a leap of pleasure for her friend.

"Oh, no! He'd only take the open buggy because it would be unseemly for a single man to be seen in a closed buggy with a single woman. He wouldn't use it as a courting buggy."

Sarah wasn't fooled. "But you didn't come with him?"

"I couldn't," Rebecca's voice had a note of panic in it. She gave Brent a sidelong glance, even though he couldn't understand a word of the conversation. "What would we talk about, driving all that way by ourselves?"

"Sheep?" Sarah suggested gently.

"As soon as he offered to drive me to the sing, I forgot everything I ever knew about sheep!"

Sarah reached out and squeezed her friend's hand. The place had filled up until there were over thirty people in the barn. Though the door was open, the lanterns and the crowd made the area hot. Next to her, Brent mopped his forehead.

Rebecca spoke again. "So I didn't plan to come, but at the last minute I just wanted..." Her voice trailed off. "Amos probably won't come tonight anyway. Ever since I got here, I've been praying he won't."

At that moment, Amos Troyer stepped into the barn.

Rebecca let out a squeak and stood even closer to Sarah. Amos looked toward Rebecca, and Rebecca said quickly, "I'll just help Deborah with the refreshments." She fled to where Deborah, Benjamin's wife, was setting out pies.

Sarah explained the situation to Brent. "Later, I'll have to figure out how to get those two to spend some time together. On her own, Rebecca will never be able to handle things.'' A sudden impulse made her add, ''A sing is where the Amish court.''

''I know,'' Brent said in a deep, husky voice.

Mentioning courtship had been a bad idea, Sarah thought. She concentrated on explaining the ritual of the sing to Brent. ''The boys sit on one side of the table and the girls on the other.''

''I thought this was courtship.''

''It is. Before. After. Not during. The sing is just an excuse for the boys to get out their open buggies and take the girls for a ride at night.''

''Oh.''

She wondered if he was remembering the ride over, when their bodies had been pressed together.

She took a deep breath. ''One of the boys will lead in the first hymn.'' Across the room, Amos had been approached by Benjamin Schultz and was deep in conversation.

The first hymn was short by Amish standards, but Brent shifted restlessly.

''I know the music seems odd to outsiders,'' Sarah whispered sympathetically. ''There's no musical accompaniment, and once, an English girl said we sing rather slowly.'' He nodded.

After a second hymn, the teenagers rose and mingled. Deborah had set up refreshments on a couple of boards placed on sawhorses. Outside, true night had fallen, and the mosquitoes were beginning to find their way into the barn. Swarms of moths circled the lanterns overhead.

''Want some marshmallow cream?'' Sarah asked with a smile. Brent grimaced and her smile became a laugh. He was leaving town soon. But what was the harm in pretending a little tonight? To love, even if she couldn't really show how she felt.

Sarah and Brent headed to the refreshment table. There, Deborah spread marshmallow cream an inch thick on a slice of white bread and plunked it, without asking, onto Brent's plate. Another giggle bubbled out of Sarah's throat. Suddenly she felt almost giddy.

She led Brent to a stack of straw bales and sat down. "Now, I want you to eat every bite," she said. "You don't want Deborah to think the English man isn't being polite."

Brent took a bite. "I never imagined you Amish would eat this stuff," he said as soon as he'd swallowed.

"You probably didn't imagine a whole lot of things about us," Sarah said flippantly.

He looked at her a long moment, suddenly serious. "No, I didn't."

A sudden hurt stabbed her, and she wasn't sure why, except maybe the knowledge that he'd never given a thought to the Amish before coming to Wheatland. For some reason, the thought made her feel almost excruciatingly lonely.

She saw Rebecca standing alone with a plate of food in her hand. "Rebecca," Sarah called, motioning her friend over. It would be better to have her friends close tonight; it would help her ignore the pull of this man next to her, the one with a touch of marshmallow cream on his lower lip. She was done pretending; pretending was dangerous.

Rebecca came over right away. "Did you have one of Emma's cookies?" she asked. Before Sarah could reply, Rebecca's face went white. "Oh, no, he's coming," she wailed.

Amos Troyer was indeed walking through the throng with obvious purpose.

Rebecca fled. Amos started to turn her way, and she veered and went right out the barn door.

Amos reached them. "If this isn't the most ridiculous... All I was going to do was talk to her..."

"I'll make sure everything's okay." Sarah got up quickly and followed Rebecca out into the night.

Once outside, she blinked to get used to the darkness. She saw the gleam of Rebecca's prayer cap, about ten feet in front of her on the path to the house. She started forward, and was almost upon her friend when an Amish man stepped into the path just ahead of Rebecca and took a step toward her.

Sarah started and looked over Rebecca's shoulder toward the man.

She recognized his face.

Randy West.

Shock ran through her whole body. For a frozen moment, they stared at each other. Even in the low light, she caught the crazy gleam in his eyes. Something she remembered well...

A scream started in her throat. It came out a wavering squeak. Randy West took another step toward them.

Hot terror washed over her. Her knees went weak. *Run!* she told herself. Feeling as if she was moving in slow motion, as if everything was moving in slow motion, she started to turn.

But Rebecca—

Sarah yelled, at the same time grabbing her friend by the apron strap that went over one shoulder.

Rebecca was just turning in surprise when she felt the tug and stumbled.

"Come on," Sarah yelled. Her heart was pounding and her legs wouldn't work right.

Dear God, it was just like that night.

"Come on come on come on," she said, her breathing coming in gasps as she hauled Rebecca back down the path.

At the doorway to the barn, she ran smack into a man's chest. She let go of Rebecca and her knees gave out as she stumbled and almost fell.

Brent caught her. "I heard somebody yell—what's wrong, Sarah?"

She was still gasping. He held her tightly and tipped her face to his. "What happened? Did something scare you?"

"Randy West," she gasped. "He was here, Brent! He was dressed as an Amish man and he stepped out in front of me on the path and Rebecca didn't move so I grabbed her and we ran—"

He cursed. Then his hands moved to cradle her cheeks. "Are you all right?"

"Yes, he...he never got a chance to touch—"

He engulfed her in a brief, fierce hug, almost tight enough to crack her bones. Then he turned her toward the door. "Go inside. Right now."

Amos appeared in the doorway. "Take Sarah and Rebecca inside," Brent said curtly. "I'm going after the bastard."

Sarah started to protest, but he was gone. Amos and Rebecca pulled her into the barn.

Rebecca was crying, loud, choking sobs. A little knot of people had formed around her and Sarah.

Sarah grabbed Amos's arm. "Brent could get hurt. Take some of the others and help him."

Amos hesitated, and Sarah wanted to scream with

impatience. This was no time to be passive! A couple of the younger men exchanged uneasy, indecisive glances. Amos said, "Perhaps we could do something..."

The night he'd accosted Sarah by the side of the road, Randy had had a knife. Brent was unarmed.

Sarah pushed through the protective circle that had formed around her and Rebecca. Rebecca called out to her as she ran through the barn entrance.

Brent was coming back down the path. Alone.

"Damn it," Brent said as he came closer and saw her on the path. "I thought I told you to stay inside."

"I was afraid for you." Her voice was shaking again. She took one long look at Brent, assuring herself he was safe, and then promptly burst into tears.

"Shh," Brent soothed. "You were brave, Sarah, to drag Rebecca back, and then to come looking for me. But you should have stayed inside."

With Amos in the lead, several people had belatedly followed Sarah out onto the path.

"He's gone, then?" Amos asked Sarah in Pennsylvania Dutch.

"Where did he go?" Sarah asked Brent.

"I don't know," Brent replied grimly. "I never did see him. When I came around the corner of the house, I heard a truck start up down the road. There's a thicket of trees just off the road, he must have hidden his truck there." He gripped Sarah by the shoulders again, harder this time. "*Now* are you ready to see this creep go to jail?" He didn't wait for an answer. "He's dangerous, Sarah, like I always said. Now he's playing with you."

She shuddered.

"He's an animal," Brent said grimly.

No he's not, Sarah thought. An animal hunts for food, does what instinct prompts. Randy West was simply evil.

Brent looked her in the eye. "Now he's dressing up like an Amish man, watching you. I hate to scare you, but you've got to understand. What he's doing is called stalking, and he'll make your life a living hell if you don't do something about him. Do you understand me?"

He was gripping her shoulders so hard. She looked around at the other faces, all Amish, all trained from the cradle to be passive, to turn the other cheek. Deborah handed her a glass of cider. Sarah stared at the glass. A stalker was after her, and Deborah was bringing her cider. She relearned a hard truth in that moment. To stop Randy West, to protect herself, she'd need more help than her people were prepared to give her. They hadn't even responded quickly enough to help Brent a few moments before.

Brent could help her.

"I...I don't know what's best," she whispered. Her brain felt like mush. She needed time to calm down and think.

"Drink," Deborah said kindly. "It'll make you feel better."

Levi was there suddenly, coming through the knot of people to her side. "Sarah, what happened?"

"Where were you?" she asked, after taking a dutiful sip of the cider that didn't make her feel one whit better.

"Around," Levi said vaguely. He turned to Brent, who explained what had happened. Levi put an awkward arm around her shoulder. In a loud voice, he said, "You don't have to worry anymore. I'll fight him."

At his words, there was a collective gasp, then complete silence.

"No, Levi," Katie said in a small voice. "You must not think such things. We must all pray for Sarah."

Brent shook his head in disgust. Then he touched Levi's shoulder. "Let's go home."

CHAPTER TWELVE

THE DAMN BUGGY was too slow, that was the long and short of it. Levi drove, and Katie sat in front with him, and Mary sat in the back with Brent and Sarah. Nobody spoke much. Brent would have liked to hold Sarah, to reassure himself that she was safe, but he didn't dare with Mary so close.

He asked her once if she was all right, and she said a quiet yes. It was hard to believe she was still hesitating about testifying. But she was. Why? Randy West was a violent criminal and now he was dressing up as an Amish man. Brent could hardly imagine the horror of that for Sarah.

He was so frustrated, sitting in the back of the slow, bouncing buggy. All she had to do was let him do his job!

After they dropped off Katie and Mary, he did put his arm around Sarah's shoulders for the short ride to the Stolzfus farm. Her body was stiff, her shoulders tight. She stared straight ahead.

At the farm, Levi let them off by the door and went to see to the horse. In the driveway, Brent gripped her arm. "Well, Sarah," he said, and his voice was harsher than he intended. "What's it going to be?"

She looked up at him and said, "You saw them tonight. You heard them. We're taught to turn the other cheek." She reached up and touched a finger to his lips when he would have spoken. "I shouldn't have gone out alone. I know better."

"Is that the way you want to live the rest of your life?"

She hesitated for the longest moment. He felt suspended, waiting. He knew her next words were important, but he resisted the urge to add words of his own, persuasive words. He knew with every lawyer instinct he possessed that sometimes you had to let silence work for you.

"I'm changing," she said softly. "I'm different from the woman Randy West raped. Knowing you—" She cut herself off.

What had she been about to say? That she had feelings for him that were more than friendship? With more effort than he should have required, he forced his thoughts to the issue at hand. *Keep thinking about her as a potential witness, because that's all she'll ever be. It's all you want, it's all you can hope for. At least then you can go away knowing she's safe.*

In the barn, he could see the light of the lantern; Levi was inside, grooming the horse. Sarah looked up at him. "I've been drawing," she said abruptly.

Drawing? What the hell did drawing have to do with— Sudden excitement gripped him. "What have you been drawing, Sarah?" he asked. "Tell me."

"Amish faces," she said so softly he wasn't sure at first that he'd heard her correctly.

"That's forbidden, right?"

"Yes. But I feel that I *have* to draw them, and draw them fast. I know that doesn't make much sense, but... Except that I've changed. I'm not exactly Amish because I really don't know if I can turn the other cheek on this."

"Sarah," he said, and it was all he could do not to pull her into his arms.

She took an audible breath. "I might have to give up all that I am in order to be safe."

"We'll talk to your father." Brent was still convinced that she could get her people to accept her decision. After all, she'd been one of them from birth. And if she couldn't explain things, her father could.

They went up the walk to the house. "I know I'm different," Sarah said sadly, "that I'll always be different, but I don't think I'm ready to give up everything I've ever known."

Brent's mind was already on the task of convincing Adam. Sarah had no choice, so it didn't matter anymore what she was ready for. The thing to do was to explain it so that Adam would be on her side.

They had to wake Adam. He came down in a plain cotton nightshirt. Sarah warmed coffee on a little propane camping stove. Nobody drank it.

Levi came in from the barn, and without being invited, sat too at the table. Brent did most of the explaining.

Finally, Adam said, "What do you want to do, Sarah?"

She took a deep breath. "It will be hard to face strangers, *Vater*. But what Brent says about the stalking—"

"We'll keep you safe," her father said gruffly.

Brent said on a surge of anger, "There was a whole barnful of people tonight. It wasn't enough."

Adam sat lost in thought. Finally he said, "If this man is still after my daughter, maybe even an Amish man can't turn the other cheek." He looked over at Sarah, and even in the low glow of the one lamp,

Brent couldn't mistake the love that shone in his eyes.
"I'll talk to Daniel. Then perhaps Sarah can testify
without repercussions."

"Don't take too long," Brent warned. "West may
be scared off for the moment, but don't wait too
long."

"No." Adam stroked his beard. "From now on,
Levi, you don't work in the fields. You stay with
Sarah in the shop, help her with customers." Levi
nodded. "She's never to be alone, even on the farm."

The relief that flowed through Brent was pure and
powerful. He wanted safety for Sarah more than he'd
ever wanted anything in his life.

A few minutes later, she walked with him to his
car. He said, "I'm going to watch you go back to the
house."

She nodded.

"Are you still scared?"

"Yes," she said simply. Then she added, "But I'll
be all right. I'm glad in a way that things are hap-
pening finally. For these last months, I've felt as if
I've been in some kind of nightmare. You know the
kind where you try to run and land up going nowhere."

"Oh, Sarah." He took a step toward her, and as if
helplessly drawn, she closed the gap. And then he was
kissing her. She wasn't his witness yet, he thought,
and that was good, because he needed to kiss her as
much as he needed to breathe.

She grabbed for him too, pulled his head down and
held the back of it so that he could press his lips to
hers. If she'd resisted, if she'd whispered one word
of protest, he might have been able to pull away. But
she made little whimpering sounds, as if she was as

frantic for his touch as he was for hers. Her hands went down his back and she held him tight.

His tongue was in her mouth, utterly possessive, and she sucked on his tongue until it ached. His hands fisted over her prayer cap, and he tugged. It came free with a slide of organdy ties. And then there was only her hair, and his hand closed over the knot. If he could just see her once with her hair down...

God, what was he doing?

They both broke away in the same instant. He stood mere inches from her, and he could hear the rasp of breath in his own throat. He could see the rapid rise and fall of her breasts.

"Your father, Levi—" He cut himself off because there was no need to say what she must know. They'd left the door open; only the screen door separated them from discovery.

"Brent," she said, and there was a low note of pain in her voice. "I'm not the woman you need. Even if I'm changing, even if I weren't Amish, we're different. I'm happy to live quietly, with my shop and my friends, and a family to love." She squared her shoulders. "You've always wanted something more... tangible out of life."

It was true, he thought. All the time, he'd been thinking, *I can't care about her because she's Amish.* But it was a whole lot more than Amishness that separated them. A few hours ago, he'd been imagining her in a red dress that bared her shoulders and a good portion of her breasts. Sarah would never in a million years wear something like that, in her world or his.

He wanted something tangible, she said. She'd used kind words to describe his overriding ambition.

He needed to be somebody, and he needed a woman whose status reflected his own.

But he didn't want to be that selfish, didn't like the thought that he'd been that man all his life.

"Go inside, Sarah," he said roughly. He pulled on her prayer cap, trying to bring it back into place. She pushed his hands away, and set it in place herself. She didn't look at him as she retied the strings.

"Sarah, are you all right?" Adam opened the screen door.

It had been a close call. Brent could still taste her on his lips, could still feel the imprint of her body.

She'd been through hell tonight, but her voice was steady. "I'm fine, *Vater*." She turned without a backward glance, and Brent waited until they closed the door.

She was brave and strong and wise and good. He didn't deserve her and he would never have her and he knew that was for the best.

But that didn't stop him from wanting her and it didn't relieve the ache in his heart.

"I CAN'T COME for a while, Teddy," Brent said into the phone. "That rape case might be coming up for trial soon."

"Hey, you're supposed to be here. Why wait now?" his friend asked. "It's good to bring a big win with you, but you don't want to make it look like you're dragging your feet. The partners want eagerness and enthusiasm in new employees. Remember? Gung ho, all for one, work your fingers to the bone for the greater glory of the firm."

Brent didn't reply, just used the silence to convey his intent.

"Okay, when can you come?" Teddy finally asked with resignation. "We've got a guy who didn't make partner here, and he's out the door in a couple of weeks."

"But he can stay on longer if necessary."

Teddy sighed. "If he doesn't find another job right away, I guess he'll be glad for the paycheck. How're things going on your end? Got your replacement yet?"

"Yeah, the kid's coming on board in two weeks." Norm had asked Brent to make the call to Timothy Smith. That call had been surprisingly hard to make. Telling the secretaries he was leaving and hearing them say they'd miss him had been hard, too,

It was almost time to move on. Tonight he was going to Sarah's because Adam was meeting with the bishop to explain Sarah's situation. Brent didn't anticipate any problems, given what had happened last Sunday at the sing.

His gut clenched at the memory of Sarah running into Randy West. Brent was going to thoroughly enjoy nailing the son of a bitch.

And then what? The question popped out of nowhere, insistent. *And then what?* Why, he'd go back to where he belonged. He'd remember her, sure, but he hadn't been that involved. He hadn't slept with her, and he was thankful for that.

He threw his pencil across the room in disgust. Everybody talked to themselves. It was only when you started answering yourself that you knew you were crazy.

Brent smiled grimly to himself and pulled the heavy law book toward him. *Prosecuting Sex Crimes,*

Third Edition. He was reading up, because Sarah was counting on him.

SARAH MET HIM in the driveway. That was becoming almost routine.

"Are you okay?" he asked. Her face was paler than usual and the skin under her eyes looked puffy. "Hey," he added, touching the pad of his thumb to one of those spots. "Have you been crying?"

She shook her head, her eyes on his. "No. I'm just not sleeping very well."

"Me neither," he admitted.

A little blush stained her cheeks. "I've been drawing."

"I envy that. A stress releaser."

She blushed even more furiously. "My drawing isn't any good, but maybe it's good as a—a 'stress reliever.'"

"Will you show me your work? I'd really like to see it."

"Oh, I couldn't. It doesn't matter. Drawing's just always made me feel better."

Suddenly, he felt awkward, standing there in the barnyard. The reminder of holding her in his arms assaulted him with real force, as if he could feel her body and skin against his.

She looked away quickly, and he wondered if she was feeling the same pull. "Daniel Yoder is in the house," she explained. "He brought some of the men who advise him in spiritual matters. They've been talking with my father for a while now."

"What's to talk about?" Brent asked, almost instantly angry. "The creep is after you. End of story."

"Not to us," she said, and he heard weariness but

also defensiveness in her voice. She might have had to make decisions that no woman—and certainly no Amish woman—should have to make, but she was still one of them. She still had pride and a need to make him understand.

"When will we know their advice?" Brent refused to call it a decision.

"Soon, I think."

They sat on the porch to wait. Sarah asked Brent about his cases. He discussed the office a bit, though he knew her mind was elsewhere.

"Sarah." Adam came to the door. "Can you come in?"

Brent rose to follow her.

In Sarah's kitchen three men sat around the table. Adam made introductions. Brent watched the men carefully as each was introduced. Finally, he was introduced to Daniel Yoder. A man of about sixty, he had a careworn face and a very long beard.

Daniel nodded gravely, then said, "Adam, I have reservations about an English man being present."

Adam's spine stiffened slightly. "He's my friend, and he could answer any questions you have about the procedure Sarah would have to face."

Daniel looked Brent right in the eye; Brent looked back. When Daniel broke eye contact, Brent brought over two more kitchen chairs and he and Sarah sat down. For a moment, nobody said anything. There was a lamp lit in the center of the table, and it had just grown dark enough to need one.

Sarah sat with her back straight and her hands folded in her lap.

"Adam has explained what happened at the sing,"

Daniel said. "I prayed for you last night with special fervor, daughter."

"Thank you, Daniel," Sarah said, and Brent couldn't mistake the warmth in her voice.

"But what the English want you to do—it would be so immodest. Adam says that this hearing, this trial, would have to be public."

Brent spoke up. "The grand jury part is private. And one of our judges would be very sympathetic to Sarah. He wouldn't allow much in the way of press coverage." Judge Whalen was a fair and decent man. Brent hoped that he'd be the judge assigned to the case. Judge Jonathan Jones, the other county judge, was newer on the bench, less sure of his rulings and, perversely, more cocky. Judge Jones had also been heard to complain about the Amish and their slow buggies. Brent had no control over which of the two judges was assigned the case.

Daniel was looking at him shrewdly. "So there are *two* of these hearings?" the older man asked.

Reluctantly, Brent said, "Yes. Sarah would have to testify twice. First in the closed jury hearing, where we'd get an indictment. After that would be the trial."

"The public trial," Daniel again. "And one of the judges might not be kind to Sarah, appreciative of all she's gone through?"

Brent nodded. "That's not what I anticipate. But it's possible." He looked around. The lamplight brought out the features of the men in high relief, and all seemed troubled. Sarah gave him a quick look, as if she herself hadn't anticipated this difficulty with the courts.

"There are no guarantees," Daniel observed. No

one contradicted him. After a moment, he said, "Yet you want to do this, Sarah. Why?"

"I don't think I'll be safe unless Randy West goes to jail," Sarah said in a fine, clear voice. Only her hands, tight in her lap, betrayed her nervousness.

"But you don't mind telling this story of what happened to you to strangers?"

"Of course I do! But he has to go to jail!"

Daniel shook his head. "I've been talking to a few people who've seen these trials on television or read about them in the newspapers. There was a man in California who was found innocent, but everybody thought he was guilty. The judgment of men can be flawed." He turned to Brent. "That's one of the reasons we leave judgment up to God."

"Juries usually come to the right decision." Brent leaned forward. "Also, I have experience with sex crimes and I usually win my cases. I promise you, Sarah's case won't be lost on a legal technicality."

Daniel nodded, accepting his word without question. Brent was relieved.

"We can keep you safe, Sarah." This time it was one of the other men who spoke.

"You didn't keep her safe at the sing." Brent was losing patience.

There was a long silence. Finally, Daniel said, "But he surely wouldn't do anything in front of witnesses."

"What if he's figured out how reluctant you are to use the courts? What if he knows you don't like to testify, so he figures he has nothing to lose if there are a hundred witnesses to his crimes, as long as they're all Amish?" *Think of these men as a jury,* Brent thought. *Show them your expertise and your sincerity*. That last wasn't hard. He wanted their approval. Their approval mattered to Sarah, to her life, and this trial would be hard enough for her.

There was a long silence. Finally, Daniel said, "You make a compelling argument. I think if this Randy West is ever around any of our women, we should escort him to the roadway and make sure he goes away."

"With force?" Adam asked incredulously.

Daniel stroked his beard. "It would not be force if we collectively took hold of him and took him bodily to where he can't harm one of our own. We wouldn't fight. All we have to do is be around Sarah all the time."

Did they really think they could handle a vicious criminal that way? Brent thought, suddenly overcome by a sense of foreboding. He'd hardly slept for two days, worrying about Randy West. He'd asked a couple of cops he was friendly with to keep an eye on the guy. Randy had gone to work and gone to the Roadhouse, and then he'd gone home. Just as he'd done every day except last Sunday, when he'd shown up at an Amish sing. What had brought the guy out that night?

"So there's no need for this testifying," Daniel said firmly.

There was a gasp from Sarah. "You can't mean that," Brent said. "Sarah is a grown woman, surely she has the right to do what she thinks best."

Daniel's eyes went flinty. "For nearly forty years I've kept this community Amish. I've done that with the help of God and with the understanding of the brethren that they aren't completely free. The most basic tenet of our faith is to keep separate and apart from the outside world.''

Brent brought a fist down on the table. The lamp rocked and one of the men reached quickly to steady it. ''Nobody in this community has gone through what Sarah has.''

''That's what has made this decision so difficult.'' Daniel still spoke in a controlled voice, and now he looked around the table. The other men nodded. ''At first I thought we must do as Sarah wanted, in order to keep her safe. But now that she can be made safe—''

Sarah jumped up. ''Do you think that's the way I want to live, Daniel? Always looking over my shoulder? Always having to have the others around to protect me?''

Adam put out his hand, said, ''Sarah—''

''You don't understand,'' Sarah said. ''None of you had your stockings torn off and a hand clamped over your mouth. None of you had to yield something precious to an evil man, and none of you had to feel dirty afterward!''

Her hands were shaking but her voice held fire and power. Brent wanted nothing so much as to take her in his arms, to soothe her, to offer any comfort he could. In this house, he couldn't do that, and the knowledge made him boiling mad. Only the certainty that he would make things a whole lot worse for Sarah kept him from taking one of Daniel's suspenders in each hand and shaking some sense into the man.

The door to the kitchen flew open in that moment, and Levi stalked in. ''How can you make the decision when this is Sarah's choice?'' the boy said.

Adam rose and put a hand on his son's shoulder. "Levi, you're making this worse for Sarah."

"*They're* making it worse. *You're* making it worse. Don't you remember how she cried?" He burst into tears. Angrily, he swiped them away. *"This is Sarah's choice!"*

Daniel folded his hands on the table. "Don't you see, Sarah, that what you're asking is already tearing your family apart? It could tear the community apart." His voice went low and husky. "We don't say this kind of thing often, but surely you know I love you. You were my daughter-in-law. You're my sister in the faith. I'm trying to do what's best for you."

"Daniel." Sarah came to stand beside the older man. "This isn't just about my being safe. The thing is, I can't really be Amish with this hanging over me. It distracts me from my duties, interferes with my search for peace. It..." She hesitated, then went on. "It makes me angry that the men of my community don't understand me, and that makes me feel that I'm not a good Amish woman, to harbor those feelings. If I could just testify, then I could go on and be Amish again. Do you understand?"

Daniel looked up into her eyes. "No. I don't understand how being part of the large world will keep you Amish. Have a care, Sarah. Have a care in your thoughts, because these words of yours worry me greatly."

"Oh, Christ," Levi cried.

There was an appalled silence. Adam said, "Apologize. Now."

At almost the same time, Brent said, "Levi, you aren't helping Sarah." He started to rise, intent on putting a supporting hand on the teenager's shoulder, but Levi turned and stormed from the room.

Daniel wiped a weary hand over his forehead. For a moment, no one spoke. Then Daniel said, "Adam, it's your duty to hold your family together."

"Don't you think I know that?" Adam asked in the hardest voice Brent had ever heard him use.

Sarah said quietly, "Daniel, if I testify, what will happen to me?"

"We would have to decide then. Please don't push me into anything."

Adam put his hand on Sarah's shoulder. "Just know something, Daniel. This is my only daughter, and she's been through what no woman ought to be asked to deal with. If she's shunned, I really don't think I could..." His voice was suddenly barely audible. "I don't think I could bear it."

Daniel sighed heavily. "None of us knows what we can bear until the Lord gives it to us to bear. Think hard, Sarah."

She nodded. She said quietly to Brent, "I'll walk you to your car."

He was incredulous. "That's it? This—whatever kind of meeting is over?"

"Yes. As Daniel says, I have decisions to make."

He waited until they were almost at his car. "For God's sake, Sarah! They have no right—"

"They have every right."

"Then you have the right to decide whether or not to follow them."

"Yes, I do. I can decide if my self-respect is worth my being shunned by the whole community."

That word *shunned* stopped him. "Maybe they

won't do it," he said, knowing the words to be lame but having no other.

"And maybe they will," she countered. "I'll tell you what I've decided in the morning."

He was losing her; he could feel her withdrawal. He didn't know what to say. He'd said it all before. There was only one more thing he could add. *Don't be Amish. Find another life.* He couldn't say that, because what would she do if she weren't Amish? He couldn't say, *Come away with me.* He was going back to a position where he'd work a hundred hours a week to prove himself; it was a job for ambitious men without families. He would make her dreadfully unhappy, just because he was who he was. And she'd said she didn't want a man to influence her choices the way Jacob once had.

Every fiber in him said to fight the battle of words, of wills. But he knew he could only push so far. It took every ounce of willpower to get into his car instead. He rolled down the window. "I'll watch until you're back in the house."

She turned and went down the path. The last thing he saw was her white prayer cap as she shut the screen door.

SARAH WAS DRAWING. She was done thinking, and she'd made her decision. It was going to be very hard, but she would go along with Daniel. All she had to do was think of Levi's rebellion and her father's words—that he couldn't bear it if she was shunned—to know where her duty lay. If she lacked the commitment to be truly Amish, if in her heart she was angry, well, she would just have to get over it.

She was doodling, her drawing seeming to have no

sense or purpose. The outline of a barn, then a buggy. Something kept niggling at her; some detail she wanted to draw. It just touched her consciousness, skittered away before the image took form.

She dipped her pen in ink again. First she drew Levi, in some enthusiastic pose, probably inspecting Brent's red car. Now she'd draw Rebecca. It was a shame the pen and ink couldn't pick up those blushes of Rebecca's, and Sarah smiled for the first time since Sunday night.

Rebecca. For some reason...

Her heart thumped suddenly. She pictured Rebecca as she'd looked at the sing, both desperate and happy over the attentions of Amos Troyer. Her pen didn't move. The image was somehow wrong.

She let instinct take over and drew her friend from the back. She frowned. She'd thought long and hard about this drawing of faces, and she knew now that of the many things in her heart the Amish would consider sinful, her drawing was the least of them. She'd changed. She didn't try as hard to hide her drawings as she'd once done. So why didn't she want to draw Rebecca's face?

Because Rebecca was on the path ahead of her. Sarah could see the white of her prayer cap from the back. She closed her eyes. She didn't want to remember. But for some reason, she had to remember.

Have courage, Sarah Yoder. The courage to remember what you want so hard to forget.

Then she saw him. Randy West, dressed as one of her own people. She shuddered, sick to her stomach as she remembered that precise moment.

Then the part she'd forgotten or hadn't seen consciously in the fear of the moment... *He'd raised his hand, reached out to grab...*

Rebecca.

Not herself, Sarah thought, jumping up from her chair and spilling a few drops of ink on the desk. Rebecca had been his target. Her artist eye for detail had recorded the scene in her mind: the reach of his hand, the intentness of his expression...

She cursed the lack of a phone, because she felt a powerful urge to warn her friend.

She made herself realize that Rebecca was safe at home, with her family all around. She sat down again but the shaking didn't stop for a long time.

Rebecca could not deal with Randy West, could not endure the violation of her body, the utter violence and savageness of this crime. Sarah knew it as clearly as she knew the Sunday hymns. Rebecca was so innocent. Randy West would break her body and break her spirit, too.

If Sarah Yoder let him.

She knew what Daniel would say if she told him Rebecca was the one at risk. He'd repeat what he'd told Sarah. Her community clung to the old ways even when it was most hard, and that stubborn clinging took its own kind of courage. But Sarah knew what she had to do. Maybe God had given her this terrible thing to bear so that she could protect her friend. Maybe God had given her the hot temperament, the need for some independence so that she could do this very hard thing.

God had also given her something else, something precious. He had given her Brent, to take her case to the English court.

CHAPTER THIRTEEN

"BRENT." Kelly stood in the open doorway, her voice uncharacteristically hushed. "There's an Amish woman here to see you. Sarah Yoder."

Brent, in the act of punching buttons on the telephone, stopped abruptly. "Send her in."

He met Sarah at the doorway as Kelly ushered her in. He shut the door as his secretary looked in curiously from the hallway.

Sarah stood still, looking around. She was dressed in a blue dress with her apron, but a broad-brimmed black bonnet covered her hair and prayer cap. "You didn't have to come here," he said. "I was planning to come to the farm this afternoon."

"I drove the buggy in. I didn't want to wait."

"You've decided then?" Excitement gripped him.

"I'm going to do it," she said a little breathlessly.

He wanted to pick her up and twirl her around. He settled for, "I'll make sure you won't regret it."

Her eyes turned luminous. "I'm afraid, but not sorry. Oh, Brent, it wasn't me Randy West was after! It was Rebecca!"

Rebecca? "But—"

"I remembered some things about that night." She went on to explain about what she'd seen and the conclusions she'd drawn. "So now I have no choice, don't you see? No matter what my people do, I have no choice any longer."

"You're very brave," he said, and his throat got thick on the words. "I swear, I'll get this guy to pay."

"I know that. If I didn't know that...what I have to do would be so much harder." She paused. "I'm not brave at all. I'm afraid of the judge and the jury and the crowds and I'm afraid of what Daniel will think he has to do..."

He didn't know what to say. She was right to fear all those things.

"The thing is..." Her voice went lower. "I've been thinking about telling my story, and thinking about it brings it all back, even the parts I made myself forget, and now I have to make myself remember... So I'm afraid..." She looked up into his eyes and for a heartbeat neither of them moved. Then she whispered, "Will you hold me?"

His gut tightened. "You're my chief witness now that we're going to court."

"I don't care. You're my friend. Hold me like a friend."

He gathered her in his arms. Comfort, he vowed. Just comfort, although it was hard not to respond to her on a much more visceral level. He kept his lower body from hers. He gathered her to his chest instead, and felt her begin to cry.

"It's all right to cry, Sarah. You're not alone. Lots of women have gone before you, and though it's hard, things are easier in the courts than they once were."

"Then thank God for those women," Sarah whispered fiercely.

He rocked her a little and held her tight, and gradually the quivering in her shoulders eased. "Are you ready to talk about this?" he asked finally.

She nodded and raised her head. "You'll have to tell me where to sit. All this space—these big windows and those velvet drapes. I knew you were an important man, but this office is so fancy."

"Don't think about that. I'm your friend, remember?"

She smiled, her upper lip a little swollen. Brent longed to soothe her in earnest. Instead, he took her over to a table and pulled out a chair. She needed him to be a lawyer. He sat down across from her and pulled out a pad. "What I'd like is for you to tell me everything that happened that night, from the time you left your house until you came home from the police station. Can you do it, Sarah?"

She took off her bonnet and straightened her shoulders. "Yes," she said simply, "I can."

"THAT'S RIDICULOUS, Your Honor. The defendant's dangerous, not just to Mrs. Yoder, but to another Amish woman, as well." Randy West's bail hearing was not going well. For the sake of his promise to Sarah, Brent kept his temper in check.

Judge Jonathan Jones scowled down from the bench at him. "So the prosecution says. That bit about the defendant going after some other Amish woman—that's something Mrs. Yoder recalled later, because she's an artist of sorts, right?"

"Right." Brent ignored the sarcasm in the judge's voice. "In the heat of the moment, I think she can be forgiven for forgetting a bit. After all, the defendant had raped her. Naturally, seeing him again would cause panic."

"She remembers a lot of things later, it seems." The judge pushed the glasses higher up on his nose. "It's taken her, what? Over five months to come forward on her own case?"

So what? Brent thought. "Yes, it's taken her quite a bit of time because as a modest Amish woman, it's been a hard decision to come forward."

The judge shook his head and made a caustic comment about the evidence being stale, then something else about the Amish "moving to their own clocks." Brent counted to ten under his breath.

Unlike this hearing, the one before the grand jury had gone well. Sarah had performed like a seasoned witness. She'd faced the grand jury and told her story in a clear, firm voice. One of the jurors had winced at one point, and Brent knew then that they were going to get their indictment.

Randy West had been indicted on one count of rape. Of course, the grand jury was the easiest part. No spectators, no reporters, and most important, no defendant. But it was good practice for Sarah.

Now they were here to set the defendant's bail. In view of the violent nature of the crime, Brent had asked that the judge refuse bail, guaranteeing that Randy West would remain in the county jail until the trial.

He glanced over at the defense table. Randy West sat in a cheap gray suit, his hair cut, his cheeks freshly shaved. He looked innocent—the picture of a humble man who couldn't possibly do something violent. His attorney, a public defender, looked young and a little scared.

Judge Jones finally put his head up. "Mr. Hancock."

The public defender shot to his feet. "Your Honor."

"You say your client is still needed at work."

"Right, Your Honor. They're in full canning season at the vegetable factory. Tomatoes, you know. And the defendant has never missed a day of work in almost two years there. He has a few juvenile offenses for theft. But he's never been accused of a violent crime, and he's lived in this community all his life."

Brent got to his feet. "He's accused of a violent crime now."

The judge shot him a quelling look. Brent knew he was taking a risk, speaking out of turn, but he was starting to get a very bad feeling.

The judge scowled again. "Our Constitution says a person is innocent until proven guilty. Therefore, in most instances, a defendant should be free before his trial, as long as he posts sufficient bail to insure his presence at trial."

Hancock spoke up. "The state of Ohio hasn't asked for a high bail, they've asked for *no* bail. In view of the defendant's record, that's a crock."

The judge nodded.

Damn. Brent quickly changed tactics. "We'll ask for two hundred and fifty thousand dollars."

"That's ridiculous given the defendant's job and record," Hancock said.

"It's more than fair considering the seriousness of the crime," Brent said doggedly.

"That's high bail for a little town like Wheatland," the judge said. "The alleged victim waited five months before bringing charges, left this defendant free all that time…"

"With all respect, if Your Honor lets this man out

until the trial, and another woman is raped in Wheatland—Amish or non-Amish—I'd rather have it be on Your Honor's conscience than mine.''

The judge turned a dull red. He was known for his hot temper, and now Brent waited for him to blow. Jones wasn't the worst judge Brent had practiced in front of, but he tended to seize on an idea and not let it go.

The judge looked at Brent. Brent looked back at the judge. There was a long trial ahead, and Brent wanted the man to know that he wouldn't be intimidated. Abruptly, Jones banged his gavel on the bench. "Bail is set at fifty thousand dollars."

Brent leaned forward. "At least no ten percent, Your Honor." Usually, a defendant could make bail by giving a bondsman ten percent of the bail amount. If he had five thousand dollars, West would be out of jail pending his trial.

"Fifty thousand," the judge repeated. "The hearing is concluded." He stood and left the bench.

Over at the defendant's table, Hancock looked stunned, amazed at what he'd accomplished.

Randy West worked for near-minimum wage, Brent thought, willing down a flash of unease. He had no family, no friends to stake him.

He looked over at West, who was getting to his feet.

There was something about the set of the guy's shoulders that seemed fake. His humility was fake. West looked at Brent and smirked.

And suddenly Brent knew the bastard had the money.

Brent had promised Sarah he'd protect her, and he'd failed.

BRENT GAVE UP trying to sleep and got out of bed at one o'clock in the morning. He got dressed again, but instead of his suit he put on a T-shirt and jeans.

He'd made things worse for Sarah today. West was undoubtedly very angry that an indictment had been filed. He might well decide the elimination of a witness—through intimidation or worse—was the best way to guarantee that no trial ever took place. In trying to put together this case, Brent had never envisioned a scenario where Randy West would be free.

The trial had been set for two weeks from today. Sick at heart, Brent had gone out to the Stolzfus farm yesterday after the hearing to tell Sarah and Adam the result. Sarah had said, "I know you did your best," with a sincerity that made him feel worse. His best hadn't been good enough.

It was his own arrogance that had put Sarah in danger. He'd been so hell-bent on getting no bail that he'd misread the judge until it was too late.

Brent stuffed his wallet into the back pocket of his jeans and found his keys on the dresser. He'd asked his cop friends to keep an eye on Sarah's place, but he couldn't sleep until he made sure West was at home. The Roadhouse closed at midnight, and West never seemed to go anywhere else.

Brent got into his car and drove toward West's neighborhood, all the while chewing over the events of the rest of the day.

When he'd got back to the office from the bail hearing, there had been a phone call waiting. Teddy Forman had said that he'd contacted one of the reporters he was acquainted with at the regional paper. "The guy wants to do a story on you and the Amish case. You're stuck down there, so you might as well get some favorable publicity out of this case,'' Teddy had said.

The reporter called, of course. Brent had shielded Sarah as best he could, but the indictment was public. All the guy had to do was check the courthouse records, and he'd know all about Sarah. Might even turn up at the Stolzfus farm, wanting an interview.

Brent had West's address in his legal file, and now he looked for the house numbers. There. West lived in the top floor of a duplex, the bottom half of which was vacant. There was no garage. The driveway was empty. Quickly, he scanned the street. There was no sign of Randy West's truck.

The guy never went anywhere.

Brent shoved his gas pedal down hard. He went through a stop sign at a deserted intersection and pushed the speed limit all the way out of town.

When he got near Sarah's, he scanned the roadside, the ditches and the areas where trees came closest to the edge of the road. No truck.

He zoomed into the gravel driveway and had barely parked before he was out of the car, and knocking on the kitchen door. Adam came to the door and Brent could see the outline of Sarah and Levi behind him. It was too dark to see more.

''What's happened?'' Adam asked.

Brent explained.

There was a pause. ''Well, he isn't around here. The house is quiet.''

Brent said, ''I'll stay for the night.''

''There's no need,'' Adam replied. ''Even though the night is warm, we've been locking the windows.''

''I'll stay,'' Brent insisted.

''Let him stay.'' Levi said.

"It wouldn't be seemly," Adam replied.

Seemly, hell. Brent opened his mouth to speak.

"Let me handle this, *Vater,*" Sarah said quietly.

After a moment's hesitation, her father agreed. "Levi, you've argued and argued that this is all about what Sarah wants. Now we'll let her decide what she wants to do about this West man apparently running around the countryside. Go on up to bed."

"Wait for me on the porch," Sarah told Brent. "I need to get dressed."

He circled the house and barn and found nothing. So he returned to the porch, feeling foolish. The house had been so quiet, and the barnyard so peaceful.

Sarah came out, shutting the wooden door behind her. She was wearing a dark dress, blue maybe, but she didn't have on her apron. In the dark, he could see the gold of her hair, hanging around her shoulders.

No prayer cap. The knowledge, after all those fantasies of his, sent his already keyed-up system into overdrive. He willed down his reaction.

"I thought—" He interrupted himself. "I'm sorry I disturbed your sleep."

"It doesn't matter. I don't sleep so well nowadays." She paused, then said, "Let's sit down."

They sat in the big old porch swing. In the slight moonlight, her hair shone faintly, and it was so long it touched the seat of the swing. She spoke. "I didn't want to be alone tonight anyway."

He pressed himself to the arm of the swing, trying to stay as far away as possible. Even a few inches in the right direction was something.

"Are you okay with everything?" he asked.

In the dark, he thought he saw her almost smile. "Sometimes," she said, "I think I should be the one asking you that. You're taking too much of this on yourself."

"I promised to handle this case, to keep you safe. I screwed up."

"You're not responsible for what the judge did."

"I am. I misread him today."

She was very still. He could hear the sound of the katydids, and a cricket started a loud song from underneath the porch floor; it was nearly autumn. Finally, she said, "Nobody expects you to be perfect."

She was too generous—this soft-spoken Amish woman. Brent knew himself better. Although he'd faced hard truths about himself, there in Toledo, he hadn't changed much. The truth was, when his idealism worked against his ambition, his ambition came first. What he'd done to Sarah was proof.

He cleared his throat. "I want to say..." He paused. What *did* he want to say? He took a breath. "I wanted you to prosecute Randy West. I kept saying it was the right thing for *you*. But I was really thinking about the right thing for *me*."

"Were you?"

He couldn't tell by her quiet words what she was thinking.

He continued. "All my life, it's always been about me. Selfish."

"I don't believe that." Her voice rang with conviction.

"After I'd decided I was leaving, I wanted to win your case so I could go back as a big shot. Even today, I wanted to get no bail because that would make me look good."

She reached across the space between them to take his hand. It was perhaps a measure of how far they'd come that she made the gesture. His own hand tightened in hers.

"Sarah, I always just wanted to be somebody, to belong to something, to fit in. Those lawyers—" He cut himself off with a quick shake of his head.

"I understand," she said. "The thing is, I understand because I've tried to belong, too. But in so many ways, I don't fit in." She paused, obviously trying to find the right words. "In some ways, you don't really fit in as a lawyer. I mean, as the lawyer you think you want to be, so important and powerful. You care about your cases, Brent. You care about the people, the women. This isn't just a job for you."

He gave a harsh chuckle. "Because that's what makes my career, prosecuting and winning these sex-crime cases."

"Would a lawyer who was only interested in winning his cases have gone out in the middle of the night to see if Randy West's truck was in his driveway and then come flying over here?"

"I wanted to be sure you were safe, that was all."

She smiled. "You could have called the police."

"It didn't occur to me."

"Because you care so much. Even in the beginning, I knew. When my own people thought I should put this whole thing behind me, you alone knew I couldn't. You alone knew how I had to finish it, and you didn't give up. Everyone else might think you're just ambitious, but I know better. If you're ambitious, it's mostly because you care." She paused. "We've both wanted to belong, and neither of us really does.

We're not so different, after all. Who would have ever thought it?''

He released her hand to cup her chin. "How did you get to be so wise, Sarah Yoder?" he asked softly.

She touched his hand with her fingertips. "It's not so hard to understand. I think you're lonely, Brent.''

He took his hand away. "When I was in Toledo, I was around people all the time.''

"People who abandoned you when you needed them.''

He was silent. Then he said, "I never thought about being lonely. I just worked, and socialized, did whatever it took for my career. Only, since coming here, I've thought…'' He trailed off.

"What?'' she prompted him. "What have you thought?''

"Never mind.''

"That you want something more? That there has to be more in life?''

He could barely hear his own answer. "Yes.''

He turned toward her. "How do you know these things? When I was in Toledo, I thought I was perfectly happy. Everyone else thought I was perfectly happy.''

"The world thinks I'm happy as an Amish woman, but—'' She cut herself off.

"Sarah, I want you to be happy.''

She hesitated. "Were you really *happy* in Toledo? I think you were playing it safe there. You found a place that was comfortable enough, so you thought that was where you belonged.'' She paused, then added, "I've been playing it safe, too.''

He turned toward her, a movement so swift it rocked the swing. "You don't want to be Amish?''

She put her foot down on the porch floor to stop the swing. "Wanting doesn't have anything to do with it. I *am* Amish."

"Yes. But you don't really play it safe. You're drawing. You're testifying."

"Yes, I am." Sarah took a deep breath. She'd crossed a line the day she'd decided to let Brent take her case to court, and she was terribly afraid, but she felt an energy she hadn't felt in years. It flowed through her fingertips when she reached for her pen. It kept her awake, staring at the patterns moonlight and leaves made on her bedroom ceiling. Energy as much as fear kept her awake. Now she wanted to take other chances.

No wonder the bishops feared change. Change was heady and belly-pinching and it made her feel…*alive*.

Alive and in love. So she said a small measure of what was in her heart. "You're a good man."

"I'd like to believe that." His voice had gone thick. "I…want you to think that."

"Then believe it, because I do think you're good."

There was a pause. "But I'm not good. If you knew what I was thinking now…"

Don't ask, the Amish part of her, the cautious part of her urged. "What are you thinking?"

"I'm thinking that you haven't been just a case for me for a long time. That you mean a lot to me."

Her heart started a peculiar thumping. "You mean a lot to me, too." On the surface, those words—the way he'd phrased it, the way she'd agreed—sounded so cautious. But she knew the words were not cautious at all. "I'm glad I'm not just a case."

He said, "You're wearing your hair down tonight."

She was surprised at the change of subject, and at the change in his voice, which had gone rough. Then she knew what he meant. She didn't look Amish to him. He saw her as a woman. *Only* a woman. It was suddenly hard to breathe.

He said, "I've dreamed about your hair that way."

Desire rushed over her, pure and honest. "What…what are your dreams like?"

"If I told you, I'd scare you."

She whispered, "No, you wouldn't."

There was a long pause. Then, "For one thing, I dream about kissing you again."

"Do it."

He was facing her, and his whole body went taut. "You're a witness in my case. I can't…"

"I don't care." Oh, this freedom! It was like the English electricity, humming through her body.

"*I* care." He paused. "I don't have anything to offer you but my services as a lawyer."

"What if *I* kissed *you?*"

He let out a sharp breath.

Only in the dark could she do this. She leaned over toward his face.

He didn't move.

The cricket that had been calling to a mate suddenly went silent. The night was warm and hushed.

She put her mouth on his, pressed it, coaxed it to open. Against her lips, he said, "Ah, Sarah, we shouldn't…"

She used the opportunity to deepen the kiss. She took his cheeks in the palms of her hands and kissed him. He hadn't moved, and she sensed rather than felt his arousal.

She reveled in it all. His stillness, contrasted with his rasping breath.

Abruptly, he thrust his fingers into her hair. He groaned. He tipped her head back, pressed her against the arm of the swing.

The door opened. "Sarah? Are you all right?"

Levi's voice. Brent released his hold on her so abruptly her head bumped the arm of the porch swing.

Levi came out onto the porch. "When you didn't come back up, I got worried—"

She jumped off the swing. "Levi—" She stopped, because what could she say? He'd seen. She knew it.

Shame washed over her. She'd been thinking of herself and Brent, not her family. A lifetime of duty and example had been thrown away in one grand moment of freedom.

Brent came over to her side. He said, "Levi, this is my fault."

"You were kissing." Levi sounded stunned.

"Your sister didn't do anything—"

"I'll handle this," Sarah interrupted.

"Let me try to explain."

"Brent, you're making it worse," Sarah said. She hated how her voice quivered.

Levi said, "Sarah, I can't believe it."

"Please," Sarah said, low and fierce, "Brent, let me handle this."

"All right. What do you want me to do?"

"I think you ought to go."

He nodded. "Yes, all right." He strode across the porch floor, down the steps and into the driveway. Before he shut his car door, he said, "Sarah, lock your door."

Tears pricked her eyes at the concern she heard in

his voice. She straightened her shoulders and went into the kitchen.

Levi followed. Once there, she lit a lamp and waited for his questions. When he didn't ask any, she said, "It was only a kiss. There's never been…anything else."

Levi sat down slowly. Sarah lit the camp stove to reheat the coffee. Then she sat down too. "So," she said, taking a deep breath, "when will you be doing your duty, and telling *Vater?*"

Levi's hand, which had been resting on the table, fisted. "Did Brent…take advantage of you? Like— like—"

"No!" Sarah rose from the chair. "Never think that. Never! I started it. I kissed him."

"But why?" Levi sounded confused, little-boy lost.

Sarah took a deep breath. "Because I'm Amish, but I'm a woman, too. I love him, Levi. I tried not to, but I love him."

The lamp flickered. "I didn't intend it to happen. I didn't want you to know." She lifted her chin. "I'm ashamed of my foolishness for letting you see us kissing, but not of my love. He's a good man, and worthy of it." Brave words, but her lower lip felt wobbly.

"They'll shun you. Father will feel he has to tell Daniel, get advice." Levi's voice cracked, the way it had a few years before when he was coming into adolescence.

Sarah's heart lurched. "They may shun me anyway, over the testimony."

Levi shook his head. "I don't think so. Daniel tried to scare you, but he thinks too much of you to shun you. Not for that."

Sarah went to the counter and started to pour the coffee into mugs. Her hand shook and she slopped coffee over the rim. She gave up and turned off the stove.

Levi said, "Are you going to run away with him?"

"No!" She mustn't let Levi romanticize this, look upon it as an adventure. "I know he's going away. He has his own world, and I have mine. I've never told him how I feel. When the trial is over, he'll go. He has a job waiting for him."

"Good."

Good? Her heart would break the day he went.

From behind her, she heard Levi get up. He came up beside her, awkwardly put his arm around her. "I'm not going to tell them."

"It's your duty," she reminded him, but relief weakened her knees. If Daniel knew, he'd ask her to repent, to deny her love, and she wouldn't be able to do it. They would be at an impasse that would change her life.

Levi said, "You talk about duty. But I'm learning things about the world. I'll make my own decisions about how I want to live."

"I'm not going to bargain with you. I'm not going to tolerate things like your driving just so you'll keep my secret." What an example she'd set for her brother!

Levi dropped his hand and averted his eyes. "No bargaining. The thing is, I love you, Sarah. No matter what, I won't tell anybody."

Sarah pulled him to her and hugged him fiercely, the first time she'd done so in years. All her life, she'd tried to do what was expected. Perhaps Levi couldn't do that. Perhaps he shouldn't. For the first time, she faced the fact that he might not be Amish in a few years. That would leave a void in her life, in her father's. But, as unprepared as an Amish child was for the English world, maybe that would be best for Levi.

She fervently thanked God that Levi would make his choices before he joined the church. Before he'd made a decision that— like hers years before—would last forever.

CHAPTER FOURTEEN

SARAH SAT in what they called the witness-box and looked at Brent. Not at the jury, as she'd done when she'd told her story. Not at the judge, though she'd looked at him when he'd asked her a question about her testimony. Not at the oak tables or the fancy fence that separated the courtroom proper from the visitors' gallery. Certainly not at the spectators, which Brent had told her consisted mostly of newspaper reporters. She looked at Brent standing in front of her.

He gave her a small, tight smile, then went back to checking his legal pad. But it gave her courage, to know he was there for her, both as an attorney and as the man she loved.

As an attorney, he was awesome. She'd known only by instinct and her observations of his personality that Brent was good. Now she knew it for a fact. He was the first on his feet for what they called objections. When he talked, everyone got quiet and listened, and when he lowered his voice persuasively at just the right time, the jurors leaned forward.

He'd prepared her well, sitting in his office every afternoon these last two weeks, going over her story and telling her about how the courts worked.

He'd had to explain so many things. He'd been like a man driven, going through page after page of notes, reading to her out of law books.

For the first time, she'd really understood how much Brent loved the law, that he reveled in the intellectual challenge. In understanding him better, her admiration—and her love—for him grew. But Brent had put up walls. Since the night Levi had caught them kissing, Brent had made clear that he intended to keep a distance between them. That first morning, he'd only asked, "Everything okay?" She'd said yes, and that had been the end of it. They were lawyer and witness and that was all.

He took her out for casual dinners at the end of the day, where he told her light stories of the law and lawyers, all to relax her for the next day, when the grueling preparation would begin again. But he never said anything personal.

She was grateful for his concentration and expertise. She treasured every moment with him. But it had still been a difficult two weeks.

Despite the preparation, testifying in front of the jury had been the hardest thing she'd ever done. Her knuckles ached from clenching her hands in her lap. She couldn't have told it at all—not here, not when there were so many strangers and not with *him* at the defense table—if Brent hadn't been asking the questions.

Now she waited for him to ask the next question. He looked up. "Do you see the man who raped you here in this courtroom?"

She had to look at Randy. She had dreaded this part most, because Brent had said that to help persuade the jury, she had to look Randy West in the eye.

She took a breath. "Yes." The word hadn't come out as loud as she intended. And, oh heaven above, she didn't want Randy to see her cry. She blinked away threatening tears. She'd cried plenty in private, but she wouldn't let Randy or these strangers see her cry. Brent didn't taken his eyes off her. Without changing his expression, his steady gaze gave her the impression that there were two of them involved, that they were sharing this moment. He took one step back, giving the jury a clear view of the tables. "Would you point out, please, the man who raped you."

Sarah turned her head and looked at Randy West. She tried to look him in the eye, but he kept his head down. She focused on the top of his head instead. She pointed. "There," she said.

And, oh, suddenly it felt good to say the words. *"He did it."*

Brent turned to the judge. "Let the record reflect the witness has indicated the defendant, Randall West." There was a pause, then he said, "No more questions."

Sarah thought, *I looked at him. It can't get worse than that.* But it could, because the defense lawyer was getting to his feet.

"Miss Yoder."

"It's Mrs.," she corrected. Brent had emphasized her marital status.

Hancock looked down at his notes.

Brent had said, in dealing with Hancock, "to take no prisoners." He'd had to explain what the expression meant.

Now she had to endure questions from Randy West's lawyer. Brent had said the Amish reputation for modesty would work in her favor. Sarah hoped so, because Hancock forced her to go back over her story in detail. Sarah knew that her cheeks were red.

The questions were endless. Yes, it had been dark. Perhaps fear and the foreignness of her attacker's English clothing had confused her? Just what time had it happened, anyway? She wasn't sure, hadn't been wearing a watch. When Hancock finally said, "No further questions," Sarah sagged with relief and fatigue. She'd been on the stand for more than four hours.   Numb with exhaustion, she hardly heard the judge say they'd be breaking until tomorrow. The jury filed out, and finally most of the spectators left.

She looked up to find Brent standing in front of her. He said very softly, "You did fine, Sarah. You're the best witness I ever had."

She managed a shaky smile. "That's because I got to coast on the Amish reputation for honesty."

"Yes. But you were calm and you told your story well."

"My voice quavered."

"The jury understood. They know you were frightened. They're ordinary people. They may not get a complete picture, sitting in this room, but you'd be surprised at how well they can tell if a person's sincere. We're going to win." He picked up his briefcase. "Now let's go get something to eat."

Sarah doubted she could eat, but she'd come to treasure Brent's casual offer of a meal. She rose and he held the inner door for her as she passed through. Suddenly, she couldn't wait to get out of the courthouse. Without waiting for Brent to help her, she pulled hard on the heavy glass and oak outer door.

The sun was bright; she blinked. She started down the steps.

Straight ahead, a foot away, was a man with a television camera.

Sarah stopped dead. A woman with red hair and a purple suit stepped up next to her. Sarah saw that the woman held a small microphone.

"Mrs. Yoder, how are you feeling after your testimony today?" The camera moved closer.

All her life, she had been trained to shield her face. She'd been taught that if tourists asked to photograph her, she should refuse. Some didn't ask, they just did it, but she'd gotten adept at turning away quickly enough to spoil the picture. She turned now, and the man with the camera pivoted so that she was facing it again. She took a step back, and her heels hit the back of the step.

"What the hell..." Brent had come up behind her. He gripped her elbow.

"Mr. McCade!" It was the woman in purple again. "How did your witness do today? Did the jury believe her story?"

Brent reached out and covered the camera lens. "Hey!" said the person behind the camera, a skinny man with a lot of hair who didn't look much older than Levi. "You can't do that!"

Brent said, "The Amish don't like to be photographed."

The man wrenched the camera out of Brent's hand and took a step back, still filming. Brent said tightly, "What's your choice, Sarah? Want to let the guy keep the camera? Or should I make it go away?" This last comment was leveled at the man, who took an extra step back.

The woman with the microphone got so close to Sarah that she was only a few inches from her face.

"What do you say about reports that you might have compromised your case by taking so long to file charges?"

Brent, still holding Sarah's arm, took a step forward, literally forcing the reporter to take a step back. He kept on coming, Sarah in tow, down the steps. The camera was still filming her, and she'd never felt so exposed.

"Let's get out of here," she whispered urgently to Brent.

"That's what I'm trying to do."

It wasn't easy. The print reporters who'd got their quotes earlier from Brent now started milling around, trying to see what all the fuss was about. Suddenly, Sarah found herself in the midst of a crowd. Everyone was talking, and still the camera rolled.

Brent just kept walking. Amazingly, the reporters gave way. Sarah kept her eyes straight ahead, though she could feel the fire in her cheeks. They were almost at the street.

From behind her, the woman with the microphone was still trying. "Are you going to win, Mr. McCade? I hear you're going back to Toledo. How will it feel to take a big win back with you?"

They crossed the street, reporters following. Brent put the key in the lock of the car door, got the door open, and Sarah scrambled in. Brent went around to his side of the car. The reporters were crowding around on the curb. Brent threw the car in gear and it jerked out of its parking place. Sarah's head snapped back.

"Sorry," Brent said between clenched teeth.

"That's okay." She was so relieved to be away from the reporters that she almost missed the sight of an Amish man seated on a park bench across from the courthouse. He sat alone amidst the tumult of the reporters.

Daniel Yoder.

SARAH PRAYED as Brent drove her home after dinner that her father and Levi would be working late in the fields or in the barn. She needed some time alone, time to take a cool bath, time to make sure she could get any quaver in her voice under control. Brent could help her with the court, but dealing with her family was up to her.

He let her off in the driveway. There was no sign of Levi or her father. She went up the steps and into the kitchen and locked the door behind her.

She started when she saw her father standing in the doorway that separated the kitchen from the living room. "I thought you were out in the fields or the barn." She peered at his face. It was peculiarly gray. Her own fatigue forgotten, she took a quick step toward him. "*Vater,* are you ill?"

She saw then that he was holding a small roll of paper. Knowing what it was, she couldn't move, and for a second, father and daughter stood there, looking at each other.

Adam came into the kitchen, walking with the gait of an old man. He said, "I needed a pen. I knew you kept some in your desk drawer, and I went to borrow one. I found these." He laid out her drawings, one by one. A pen-and-ink drawing of Amish women at a quilting bee. Then portrait after portrait of Brent.

He said, "There are so many of them."

There were almost a dozen in all. Brent, with a tiny

smile around his mouth. Brent, with those honest gray eyes.

Sarah felt a trickle of perspiration on the back of her neck. She said, "I love him, *Vater.*"

The silence was longer after that. Her father took the drawings, one by one, and turned them over until all of them were facedown. Hurriedly, Sarah stacked them up, then held them against her chest. "Let me explain to you how I feel—"

"No. We will never speak of this again." Her father's voice had gone utterly cold. "You will not see him again. You will not return to the trial."

Sarah reached out with one hand and gripped the back of a kitchen chair. "If you love me, you won't ask that. I have to go back. Until Brent goes away, I have to see him."

Her father slammed a fist down on the table. "I'm not asking you! I'm telling you! Last week I went to see Daniel, and I persuaded him not to shun you for testifying. But this! To love a man not of our faith!"

"I have to finish this," she said desperately, willing him to understand. "I'm going to be there to hear what the jury says."

"Look at these drawings—Amish faces. Thinking you're in love with an English man." He spread his hands in a sweeping motion. "I'm trying to have a care for your soul!"

She gripped the chair so hard her knuckles showed white. "I'm an adult, and responsible for my own soul." The oddest sort of thrill rose in her, but she also knew how dangerous this was. Everything she held most dear was threatened. "I'm sorry, *Vater,*" she whispered. "But I love a good man and I can't be ashamed of that." Holding her drawings, she crossed the room and went up the wooden stairs to her room.

She sat down hard on her bed, shaking from all the events of the day. Now she had drawn a line, taken a stand, and God alone knew what would happen.

RANDY WEST FINISHED his testimony, and Brent could only imagine what Sarah had gone through, listening to him. Randy West had claimed to be at the Roadhouse until eleven o'clock on the night Sarah was raped. Since police records showed she'd come in at eleven, if West could prove he was at the Roadhouse, the case against him would collapse.

The defense called Sam Wingham to the stand. Hancock asked the questions. "What is your occupation?"

"I'm the bartender at the Roadhouse."

"Are you acquainted with Randy West?"

"Well, sure. He's in my bar every night. Always has two beers and leaves exactly at eleven."

Brent made a couple of notes as he listened. Finally, Hancock finished and sat down. "Your witness," the judge said to Brent.

He left his legal pad on the table and approached the stand. "Isn't it rather odd that someone sits in a bar every night—"

"Not in my line of work."

A juror tittered.

"...sits in a bar every night," Brent continued, ignoring the interruption, "until precisely eleven o'clock?"

"Sure, it's a little strange."

"But if, say, he left an hour early one night, you would notice?"

"Well, like I said, I probably would because he's there every night until eleven."

"You *probably* would?"

"No, I would for sure."

"Now, I suppose you're pretty busy."

"People think that all bartenders have to do is pour drinks and listen to drunks. But I'm busier than you'd ever guess." Wingham puffed his chest up a little.

"I'm sure you are. Like answering the phone, making sure you don't run out of glasses, going to the storeroom for more liquor." The witness nodded. "And then there are nights when some of the guys get drunk and you have to spend time settling things down, right?"

"Right." Wingham looked pleased. "Sometimes, when they've had too much and you have to cut them off, you have to talk to them for a long time, you know? It gets pretty intense."

"Requires a lot of concentration?" Brent asked.

"Yeah. "

"So it's possible that someone who you're used to seeing for a few hours every night could come in, stay a while, and then leave maybe an hour early, a half hour early, and you wouldn't notice, say, if you were talking to a guy you had to cut off, or you were answering the telephone, or you had to make a few trips to the storeroom?"

The witness shifted. "Yeah, I guess."

Brent didn't push further. He didn't want to get Wingham's back up and have him insist that he hadn't made a mistake. His testimony was enough to get the jury thinking. What Brent planned to ask next was far more important.

"Would you describe Randy West as friendly? After all, he sits in your bar every night."

"He keeps to himself, mostly."

"Mostly? Is there anyone he does talk to?"

"He used to talk to somebody. Tried to, anyway."

Brent paused. He'd been waiting for this moment. "Was the person he was trying to talk to a woman by the name of Julie Ann O'Neal?"

The witness said, "Yeah. Like I told you that night you came into the bar, looking to know about Randy, he liked Julie Ann."

"Did she like him?"

"God, no. He would look at her every night, like all the time. Once he tried to talk to her, and she said she'd seen him watching her and that he was scaring her."

Hancock sat up a little straighter.

Brent asked, "He scared another woman just by watching her?"

"That's what Julie Ann said."

Hancock was on his feet. "Objection. Hearsay."

"Sustained," the judge said.

Brent was unperturbed. He'd deliberately chosen not to use Julie Ann as a prosecution witness. He believed her story would be more effective in cross-examination. "How did you know that Julie Ann was scared, other than by anything she said?" he asked.

"Well, I knew she was scared because she held her hands over her ears when he was talking to her, and she kind of screamed."

"Screamed?"

"Screamed."

There was silence in the courtroom now. In West's

defense, Hancock had relied heavily on how normal West's life was, that he was a little rigid but essentially a harmless man of routine. That he was quiet and unassuming. Hancock got to his feet again. "Your Honor, I don't see the relevancy of this. How is another woman's reaction—a non-Amish woman's reaction—relevant to Sarah Yoder's case?"

Brent said, "How he makes another woman feel is highly relevant, Your Honor, especially if he manages to scare her in a public place."

The judge rubbed his temples. "I see the relevance. Continue."

Brent breathed a sigh of relief. Jones might not be the world's most sympathetic judge, but his rulings in this trial had been fair and accurate.

"Did Randy West realize he'd scared Julie Ann O'Neal?"

"Couldn't hardly miss it. I mean, the chick screamed."

"Did he do anything after that?"

"Yeah. Got mad as hell. Sorry," he added quickly.

"Out-of-control angry?"

"Definitely. The guy sits there, so quiet every night, you know. Then Julie Ann blows him off. Julie Ann is kinda like that sometimes, and besides, no guy expects to score every time he meets a chick— woman. But this guy got so mad he broke a mirror throwing a glass at it."

"Thank you," Brent said. He felt it now, the anticipation of a win. He'd given the jury a far different picture of Randy West from the pleasant—if peculiar—loner. Now all they had to do was believe the eyewitness testimony of a soft-spoken, gutsy-as-hell Amish woman.

A FEW VISITORS remained in the gallery, but most were milling around in the halls of the courthouse. Brent sat at the counsel table, Norm beside him. His friend had come to wait for the verdict. On Brent's other side sat Sarah. Her face was pale, and she'd been quiet and strained.

It had been an intense day, the judge taking few breaks because he was trying to wrap up the trial. The jury had been out for three hours, and Brent was starting to get edgy. That was a long time for a jury to be deliberating over a simple case like this one should be. The dinner hour had long since passed, and his stomach growled.

Norm produced a crinkled bag of peanuts from his pocket. "Heard that," he said with a smile. "Why don't you have some peanuts."

"No thanks," Brent said.

"Sarah?" Norm held out the bag.

"No thank you," she said softly.

Norm opened the bag with his teeth. "People got to eat. Now listen, you two. This is going to work out. Juries in Wheatland are sensible."

"And some of them don't like the Amish," Brent reminded him. He'd tried, in jury selection, to weed out anybody who had a prejudice against the Amish, but people weren't always candid about things like that. "Anyway, Norm, what the hell is taking so long?"

"Don't know," Norm said placidly, chewing a couple of peanuts.

Brent's gut was raw from stress, and he could only imagine what Sarah was going through. He appreciated Norm sitting by him. But right now, Norm's being here meant Brent couldn't really have the kind of conversation he wanted to have with Sarah.

The bailiff stuck his head into the courtroom. "Judge just got a message, guys. The jury has a verdict."

Impulsively, not caring who was watching, Brent reached over and squeezed Sarah's hand. Her hand was cold, and he kept his own there a second to warm it. As the jury filed in, he took his hand back. Behind him, he could hear the buzz of conversation as the print reporters took their seats. But he ignored the sound, instead concentrating on the faces of the jurors. Randy West came in with his attorney and sat at his own table. Some of the jurors wouldn't look at West.

Good sign, Brent thought. It was harder to look a guy in the eye if you'd just pronounced him guilty. But Brent couldn't relax. In spite of his encouraging words to Sarah, in spite of knowing he'd covered all the bases, he was worried.

It seemed like an eternity until the judge entered the room, and the ritual of rising then sitting was finished. Finally, the judge asked the jury if they'd reached a verdict. "We have, Your Honor," said the foreperson. She held a slip of paper out to the bailiff, who took it to the judge.

The judge directed Randy West to rise. Hancock stood with him. The judge said, "Ladies and gentlemen of the jury, how do you find the defendant, guilty or not guilty on the charge of rape?"

"Guilty."

Yes! *Yesss.* Brent leaped from his chair, caught Sarah by the wrists and pulled her into his arms. He gave her a great big hug. It was hard to release her;

she felt warm and vibrant against him. Norm clapped him on the shoulder, offered congratulations.

Sarah whispered, "Oh, Brent, thank you," and he felt on top of the world.

Slowly, he released her, then pumped Norm's hand. The reporters were on their feet, an excited buzz came from the visitors' gallery. At the defense table the sheriff's deputy approached with the cuffs. Randy West put out his hands and the cuffs were snapped on. Brent felt a surge of relief so powerful it was hard to draw his next breath.

Sarah was safe at last.

"Let's celebrate!" Norm said. "A huge pizza with extra cheese and every topping they've got. I'm buying."

Brent felt a quick stab of disappointment. He'd wanted to be alone with Sarah... But better this way. With the exultation he was feeling, God knew if he could keep his hands off her. Her smile was radiant, her cheeks flushed and pink, her eyes the clearest blue he'd ever seen. "Pizza okay?" he asked Sarah.

She nodded, still smiling. "Pizza it is."

"We'll have to face the television cameras again on the way out," Brent warned her.

"I don't care. I don't care! It'll be over after that, won't it?"

"Yes, they'll go away for good." His mood changed abruptly. The reporters wouldn't be the only ones going away. After today, he had no excuse to see Sarah. A powerful sense of loss washed over him. He shook his head. That was ridiculous. For so long, he'd wanted only one thing—a second chance to prove he could be the best in his field. And now he was getting that chance.

Randy West was being led away. But seconds before he turned to follow the sheriff for the ride to the jail, he looked at Sarah. It was a look of pure hate.

Not sparing West another glance, Brent took Sarah's arm. "Ready for the celebration?" He had this evening with her, he reminded himself. Then he'd have to steel himself for the moment when he and Norm would drop her off at her home for the last time.

"Ready," she said with a smile that seemed just for him. He couldn't help looking into her eyes a moment too long. Her lips parted. He made himself look away.

Brent opened the gate and allowed her to pass, then he went through, followed by Norm. The reporters clamored for a quote, and Brent gave them a generic one about justice being served. They asked Sarah a question or two, but she only smiled and looked away. Norm pushed open the heavy glass door. On the steps were the television crews. Brent turned to gesture for Sarah to go out ahead of him. As he turned, someone caught his eye. Dark colors, a broad-brimmed black hat.

Daniel Yoder stood in the foyer of the courthouse, staring at him. Funny, Brent thought. The Amish said they wanted nothing to do with the English system of justice. Yet Daniel had apparently come to hear the verdict.

Well, good. Because now Daniel knew Sarah had done the right thing. With no help from her own people, she'd taken the steps to put this behind her.

TEN DAYS LATER, Brent had made his final preparations to leave Wheatland. Teddy had been calling regularly, urging Brent to come as soon as possible; the associate Brent was replacing had found another position and left the firm. Brent put him off because of Sarah's case.

Randy West's sentencing had been canceled and rescheduled. Brent didn't want Timothy Smith, the new assistant prosecutor, to handle the hearing. Tim, as Norm put it, "wasn't getting the hang of things real fast" and Brent had decided to stay another week. Brent's house had been rented to someone else, but Norm had offered the use of his guest room.

"You don't have to go, you know," Norm had said. "I could find the money in the budget to keep both you and Tim on."

Which, Brent thought grimly now, ignored the fact that it was Brent's going that had prompted Norm to hire Tim in the first place. He would have grinned at the irony of it if his stomach wasn't bothering him so much right now.

His gut was burning, and he stood in Wheatland's little pharmacy reading backs of boxes of antacids.

Soon the sentencing would take place, and Sarah's case would be truly over. The newspapers and even one of the Toledo television stations had picked up the story. Brent had been portrayed as a crusading prosecutor, a genuine hero. Teddy had been ecstatic at the good press—far more ecstatic than Brent. What the hell was wrong with him these days?

He missed Sarah. He was glad the trial was over for her, glad she could put the rape behind her. It was just that he was...lonely.

He debated between two boxes of antacids, and in the end decided to buy both. He rounded the display of paperback books and there they were.

Three Amish women. His heart gave a lurch. One of them was tall and blond, and he thought, *Sarah.* Then she turned, and he could see it wasn't Sarah, after all.

They spoke Pennsylvania Dutch, and one of them laughed. Then they paid and went toward the exit. There they stopped to look at the racks of candy.

Brent took his place at the counter. He could go out to see Sarah. Surely he could come up with some excuse about needing to talk over the sentencing.

No. It was better if he didn't. He had nothing to offer her.

"Brent. Hey, I read about you in the paper." Frank Operheimer, the pharmacist, was a big man who wore ridiculously small glasses. "How does it feel to be a hero?"

"Lousy." Brent indicated the antacids he'd plunked down on the counter.

"Life in the fast lane'll get you every time." Frank laughed, a snorting, oddly infectious sound.

Brent gave him a smile because the guy expected it. He pulled out his wallet.

The Amish women left. Brent realized he'd been watching them out of the corner of his eye, as if they were some kind of link to Sarah.

Frank noticed the direction of his gaze. "Odd bunch, huh? Nice folks, but..." He shook his head. "I've gotten friendly with a couple of the young ones. They come in here for a soda pop or a candy bar, like to use their English. But they do have strange practices."

"Not so strange," Brent said.

"Oh, no, Brent, I mean st...range." Frank pulled

out the last word and nodded to himself as he put the antacids in a bag. "They shun people. That means—"

"I know what it means, Frank. But nobody's been shunned around here for over twenty years. They don't do it very often."

"Oh, but they're doing it now. Some woman over on County Road 7."

"Sarah?" Brent asked in stunned disbelief.

"Sarah, Sadie, I couldn't quite catch it. The kids were talking among themselves. They don't let the rest of us in on what goes on with them. I did overhear the kid say the woman was a widow. But you wouldn't be shunned for being a widow, I mean there's got to be more than— Hey, you forgot your bag! What the—Brent, come back, you forgot your bag!"

CHAPTER FIFTEEN

SARAH'S QUILT SHOP was closed; it was lunchtime. Brent leaped out of the car and headed for the kitchen. The wooden door stood open; the Stolzfuses apparently weren't locking their doors since Randy West had been convicted. Brent banged on the screen door.

Adam opened it. He didn't seem particularly surprised to see Brent. He didn't seem particularly welcoming, either, because he didn't greet Brent or stand aside so he could enter.

"Adam, is Sarah being shunned?" Brent asked without preamble.

Adam closed his eyes for a second. "Yes."

"Where is she? I want to talk to her."

"I'm not sure where she is. Upstairs, probably, drawing. We're at dinner, Levi and I, and she can't—" He cut himself off.

Brent knew what he'd been about to say. Sarah had probably cooked the dinner, but she couldn't sit at the table and eat it with her family.

Anger boiled over. "Damn it, Adam, this is not right!" He almost shouted the words. "Blame me. I'm the one who pushed her into testifying. For God's sake, don't blame a woman who was only trying to keep herself safe and follow her conscience."

Levi came to the door. "That's not why she's being shunned."

Adam made a quelling gesture. But Levi added, "They decided not to shun her over her testimony. But Daniel was worried about her and came to the trial twice. He says he saw an unseemly interest in her, for you." The teenager gave him a direct, challenging stare.

"But...that's ridiculous. Sarah is the most modest woman I've ever known. If the bishop thought he saw anything 'unseemly,' the responsibility is mine." He looked Levi in the eye, remembering the night Levi had seen him kissing Sarah. "The responsibility has always been mine." He turned to Adam. "Talk to Sarah. Have her tell Daniel she feels nothing for me."

Adam sighed heavily. "I found her drawings. She's been drawing your likeness."

Brent almost took a step back. She'd been drawing *him?* He knew the significance of that. Sarah's drawing meant everything to her. Could she actually think she loved him, be confusing passion and deep friendship with something more?

He had done this to her. He had kissed her knowing full well that she was bonded to her own people, knowing full well that he'd be leaving. Knowing that with her lack of artifice and sophistication she could very well make assumptions about their relationship.

Adam stroked his beard, looking troubled. "I recognized her independence a long time ago. I should have gone to Daniel then, when there was still a chance we could talk some sense into her. But even now...I should have shown Daniel the drawings, but I just...couldn't, because I feared what he'd do. But even so, he's said she must be shunned..." His voice thickened. "My daughter lives in my house, but I can't speak to her. And once Levi joins the Church, he won't be able to speak to her, either.''

By his sides, Brent's hands fisted. ''It'll be a few years before Levi joins the church. Surely they won't shun her for years.''

''Sarah will be shunned until she freely and sincerely repents. Then it's over.''

Brent felt profound relief. So there was a simple remedy. He took a step past Adam into the kitchen. ''Okay,'' he said. ''The bishop doesn't know about her drawings. So all she has to do is say she's sorry for some 'unseemly' looks.''

Adam and Levi exchanged somber glances. Adam said, ''The problem is, Sarah told Daniel she's in love with you.''

Adam's quiet words hit Brent like a punch in the gut. Why had she made things hard for herself?

''Let me talk to her.'' He knew in that moment what had to be done.

Adam said to Levi, ''Go get Sarah.'' Brent realized with a start that Adam wasn't even permitted to go to the bottom of the stairs and call for his daughter.

''There's no need.'' Sarah stood in the doorway. ''I heard Brent drive in and also heard every word you said.'' She was attired the same as always, crisp dress and apron, her golden hair contained. Her eyes were sadder than he'd ever seen them. Her skin was way too pale. Still, she was the most beautiful woman in the world, and he couldn't look away.

But he had to remember what he'd come for. He had to fix what he'd done to her. ''Adam says you're being shunned,'' he began.

''I know. I heard every word just now,'' she reminded him. Her gaze was steady and direct, but now her white cheekbones had taken on a tinge of pink.

"So then you heard Adam say you think you have…feelings for me." God, he hated to be having this conversation in front of Adam and Levi. "Could you leave us alone, please?" he asked.

Adam said, "Under the circumstances, I don't think that's a good idea."

Sarah leveled a long look at her father. "Come outside," she said to Brent, and she pushed ahead of him out the screen door. Brent went after her, willing Adam not to follow them. He didn't.

Sarah said, "Shut the big door." Brent reached behind him and shut the inner door. They were alone on the porch where they had spent so much time together. The trees were in the full color of autumn, but it was a warm Indian Summer day. The windows to the kitchen were open; for all Brent knew, Adam could hear every word. But there was at least the illusion of privacy, one that would give Sarah some dignity.

Sarah didn't sit. "This has nothing to do with you," she said.

"It has everything to do with me. It's because of me that you're being shunned."

"I'm being shunned because I've broken the church law and I won't repent," she corrected him in a low voice.

"You can repent," he said, leaning forward a little. "You can fix this. Just say you were mistaken, that you don't have feelings for me, after all."

"I love you," she said, looking straight at him. A deep flush spread upward from her neck to her face.

His heart lurched, and for a moment he wanted

to— No. He had to persuade her to change her mind. "You don't love me. You just think you do because—"

"Don't tell me how I feel! Allow me at least to say what I feel, to speak freely." Her voice had gone low and fierce. Her hand gripped a fold of apron, and he saw that her knuckles were white. "Don't worry, I'm not asking you for any declarations. You've made it clear that this is just an…interlude for you."

He felt sick. She was speaking the truth. From the day he'd come to Wheatland, he'd been planning to leave. What he'd done in between was unforgivable. "The newspapers call me a hero, and you think so, too, because I won your case. Your case wasn't that complicated. Any good lawyer could have won it for you."

She shook her head. "No, because I couldn't have made myself testify unless *you* were the lawyer."

"Sarah, I'm no hero." He winced inwardly at the need to hurt her, perhaps even humiliate her. But it had to be done. She had everything: the love of a family, stability, security, work she enjoyed. She was throwing it all away. "I don't love you."

She was very still for a moment, then she nodded. "I admit, I had hoped—"

"Don't. Don't hope," he said harshly. "You're pretty and you're brave, but we don't belong together."

She didn't cry. She was so much more than pretty and brave. He'd never met anyone like Sarah. But he didn't deserve her, and he'd make her unhappy. She was better off here, as long as she wasn't shunned.

He swallowed hard. "I kissed you because I was

lonely and I hadn't met any women here. I thought it would be...intriguing to kiss an Amish woman.''

"I see," she said faintly.

"So you're throwing everything away for nothing. For a man who used you."

She looked away, across the barnyard toward the barn, her chin held way too high.

"Talk to Daniel," he urged. "Tell him you were wrong, that you were mistaken, that you don't care about me. Soon I'll be gone, anyway."

For a moment, neither of them spoke. Then she said, "If I talk to Daniel, I'll say what I please. You think you know what's best for me. Once Jacob thought so, too. And *Vater,* and Daniel, all my friends. It's so hard to tell those you love that you'll make your own decisions." She took a visible breath. "But I'm not the same woman I was before Randy West pulled me into the brush. I'm not the same woman I was when you first came to my shop. Now I make my own decisions."

"Don't throw away who you are," he said. "Independence isn't everything it's cracked up to be. You told me once that independence was lonely. And you were right."

She laughed a little, but it was a strained sound. "Imagine. You lecturing me about how lonely independence is. But this isn't about independence, not really. It's about self-respect. It's about honesty." Her voice picked up speed. "I won't beg you to love me, and I won't beg them not to shun me." She turned from him. "Now you'll have to excuse me. I do the washing on Mondays, and I'm very busy." She picked up the empty laundry basket and walked down the porch steps, heading toward a clothesline where

dark dresses and black trousers waved in the breeze.
Her back was very straight.

IN THE GLOW of a lamp, Sarah picked up her pen
again. The pen wasn't the kind she used with India
ink for drawing. Instead, it was a ballpoint pen, her
paper a lined yellow tablet. She had the classified ad-
vertisements from the newspaper on her desk. On the
yellow paper were two columns of figures.

It just wouldn't work. She wasn't even sure she
wanted it to work. She rubbed the bridge of her nose.

There was no way she could rent a store in town
for her quilt shop and make ends meet, even if she
rented the shop with an apartment over it that was
advertised in the *Post*. Wheatland wasn't that large,
and there was a competing fabric shop and a big dis-
count store just out of town. Since her shunning,
Amish women no longer came to her shop, and her
friends weren't allowed to help make the quilts for
her. And by moving, she'd even lose the tourist business.

It didn't matter anyway. She couldn't leave. If she
left, who would listen to Levi when he needed to talk?
Who would make her family's meals, can their vegetables, clean their house, strain their milk? Those
tasks were valuable, even necessary, to the survival
of the family.

More to the point, how would she stand the loneliness of it? These ten days of shunning had nearly
killed her. Her father never sang as he went about his
work anymore. Even Levi was sulking and angry with
her for not doing as Brent said, for not going to Daniel and saying she'd made a mistake. But she could
not lie and say that loving Brent was wrong. Even

after he'd wounded her so deeply four days ago. Until then, she'd thought maybe he'd changed. She'd seen him with Norman during the trial, and with others, too. He had friends here, a life.

The problem was, he didn't know how to value those things. Friends. Home.

It didn't matter. He was going. He hadn't asked her to go with him, and she wouldn't anyway, because whatever decision she made, she had to make on her own. The step would be irrevocable, and she had to be the one to take it.

Randy West's sentencing was in three days. Until then, he was being held in the county jail; after that, he'd go to the penitentiary. At least, when Brent left, he'd leave her with the precious gift of safety.

Maybe after he left she would gradually stop loving him. His face would fade in her memory, so she'd no longer have sharp images to draw. Her case would fade in the memories of others. Someday she would forget it, too, in the endless round of days, of cleaning house and measuring fabric and making dolls. Then one day she could go to Daniel and say, *I'm over him, and I'm sorry I caused dissension in the community*. Daniel wouldn't ask for more. He would be relieved she'd come to her senses. Yes, she'd pray to forget Brent, but it would be a bleak prayer.

Out on the gravel road, she heard a car. It slowed. Sarah glanced at the clock, its face illuminated in the glow of her lamp—1:00 a.m. Now, who... Jumping up, she went to the window. Even in the dark she could see that the car was sleek and red.

Quickly, she pulled her big pinafore over her nightgown. Her hair streaming behind her, she flew down the steps. She dashed across the kitchen in bare feet.

She unlocked the door. Brent pulled on the door and she pushed. "Thank God you're all right," Brent whispered fiercely, and he pulled her to him and held her tight.

"What's happened?" she asked quickly.

"Randy West escaped from jail tonight. The sheriff's deputies are coming, right behind me."

No. *Noooo...* She squeezed her eyes shut as she willed down her fear. "Will this ever be over?"

"Yes," he said. "I'll put this guy in the penitentiary if it's the last thing I do."

"But you're going away."

"Not now," he said firmly. "Not until he's put away."

In that moment, through the shock of Randy West's escape, she thought, *Everything he said that day on this porch was a lie. He might not know he loves me, but he cares. And he's a better man than he thinks he is.*

A squad car pulled up with the light on top flashing, and two deputies leaped out. The commotion woke her father and Levi. They all ended up sitting around the kitchen table. Sarah locked the heavy kitchen door and then took her place at the table. "How did it happen?" she asked.

The younger of the two deputies said, "Food poisoning at the jail. Not a stunt, the real thing, and everybody got sick, even some of the guards. They sent for doctors, but in the commotion, nobody was where they were supposed to be. We don't know how he escaped, exactly, but he might have walked right out of there behind one of the docs, or ended up in the ambulance with the prisoners who were sick enough to go to the hospital.'' The deputy swore in disgust, then made a quick apology.

Her father waved it off. In the light, his face looked grim, almost biblical.

Brent leaned forward. "Now we have to discuss your options, Sarah.''

As usual, Sarah thought bitterly, there weren't any. Any that her family would accept. She listened as, a few minutes later, her father firmly rejected the idea of a cellular phone in the house. "I won't make it harder for Sarah with the bishop and our people," he said.

Brent said, "If he hurts her, none of that will matter.''

Her father got up and paced the kitchen.

In the end, he agreed to allow a deputy to spend the night. Sarah was grateful for the protection, but she knew she'd go back to enduring sleepless nights and having to have Levi with her all the time. She clenched her hands and wondered if she could bear it, thought of the stories in the Bible of suffering and wondered what was in store for her.

NOTHING HAPPENED. Randy West had not been caught, but he hadn't been seen anywhere around town or in the vicinity of the farm. After three days, the sheriff took the deputy off night duty. As the sheriff explained, Randy would only be intent on escape and was probably far away by now. The State Highway Patrol had been given his description and was looking for him farther afield.

Sarah wanted to be reassured. But the sheriff hadn't been raped. The sheriff hadn't looked into Randy's

eyes and seen the wildness there. West had been a far
different man in court—not the true man at all.

She shivered, afraid. All the logic in the world
didn't help. Even drawing didn't help, because she'd
find herself putting down her pen and listening every
time a board in the house creaked or one of the animals pushed against a gate or knocked something
over in the barnyard.

Everything was hard. Waiting. Most of all, the silence. Sarah had shut the quilt shop for a few days
on the advice of the sheriff; she agreed that letting
strangers onto the farm was probably not the wisest
course.

She missed her customers. The Amish women had
stayed away because of the shunning, but the English
women had come. They had talked about their babies
and their grandchildren and their problems with their
jobs. It had been a balm to Sarah just to hear their
voices, to know that the world out there was big and
filled with noise and laughter.

In the house it was different. Levi was still sulking
and angry, and he went out at night after the chores
were done, driving the buggy to town. In court, he'd
paid a fine and listened to a stern warning, and as far
as Sarah knew, he wasn't driving a car. But she really
had no idea how he was spending his time. The shunning was upsetting to everyone; no wonder he escaped from the tenseness of the household whenever
he could.

Sarah worked in silence; she served supper in silence. The men ate in silence. Then Levi would leave
and her father would find chores to do in the barn
until bedtime.

So they had a routine of sorts, a silent routine. It

was quiet at the morning milking, it was quiet at dinner, it was quiet at supper and it was quiet during the long, long evenings. At night she'd check the locks three times. Then she'd lie on her back and try to sleep in the quiet, quiet, *quiet* night...

And try not to go stark, raving mad.

The day the sheriff took the deputy away was the quietest of all. Levi had gone to spend the night at the home of a cousin, to be there early in the morning to help load some cows for auction. Her father had had some task to do in the house. He was both underfoot and pointedly silent, and Sarah had gritted her teeth until she had a splitting headache.

Then Rebecca and her mother had driven into the barnyard, presumably on their way to town, and Adam had gone to meet them. Looking out the window, Sarah watched the conversation. She didn't go out. What was the point? Her friends couldn't speak to her. Rebecca looked up once and saw Sarah standing in the window. Rebecca started to wave, then caught herself, and the little, fluttery gesture looked forlorn.

She would not cry, Sarah told herself, and really, she didn't feel like crying. Instead, her eyes felt dry, burning, her throat thick. She turned from the window. Well, there was always work.

She threw herself into activity. She turned mattresses and aired blankets out on the clothesline. In the shop, she sorted fabric and restocked shelves and took inventory of the sewing notions. Back in the house, she washed the lanterns and meticulously trimmed lamp wicks. She scrubbed and blackened the woodstove.

She ate a silent supper—alone, of course—and did

the dishes and then, exhausted and grimy, started to pump water for a bath.

Someone rapped on the wooden door. Sarah jumped.

But when she looked out the window next to the door, she saw Brent. Brent. Not Randy, not Daniel, but the only person in the world she really wanted to see. After days of silence, she could have wept with relief. Then she thought, Could he have brought good news? Had Randy been caught? She knew that Brent would come to tell her immediately.

She stepped out onto the porch, her heart thumping. Adam came to the barn doorway, then slowly across the gravel barnyard.

"Is it good news?" Sarah asked immediately, before he could even greet her.

Brent shook his head. "Nothing new."

"I'm glad you're here," she said, her voice low but vehement. "I need someone to talk to me."

"The shunning's still going on then," Brent said, but it wasn't really a question. "I had hoped maybe you'd persuaded them by now—" He cut himself off, his mouth going into a grim line. "Damn it! How can those bastards do this to you?"

Brent's words were fighting words, and she needed to hear them. A powerful anger surged through her. Daniel was doing what he thought was right. But how could it be wrong to love this man? The fact that it pained Daniel to shun her might make his actions more understandable, but not right.

"Thank you," she said.

He gave her a look of pure surprise. "For what? And how come no chastisement for swearing?"

"I'm thanking you for taking my side. And I'm not chastising you tonight. Oh, especially not tonight."

By now her father had reached them, so she fell silent. "I hope," Adam said, "you've come to tell me this criminal is back in an English jail."

Brent said, "Nobody's heard a thing. The conventional wisdom is that Randy West is far away. I've never been one to bet everything on conventional wisdom." He glanced at Sarah. "I don't want to scare you unnecessarily, but I talked with the Wheatland police chief today. He's been in contact with the sheriff. He didn't agree with the sheriff's decision to pull the deputy and neither do I."

"You aren't scaring me any more than I've been scaring myself." She tried to keep her voice calm, but having Brent confirm her worst fears sent an icy shiver up her spine. "I've been locking my doors."

He nodded. "I've come to take the deputy's place."

Shock replaced the shiver. "You?"

"I've got my cell phone with me. Where has the deputy been sleeping?"

On a cot in the living room," she said in a kind of daze. "We have beds upstairs, but *Vater* thought it would be unseemly for the deputy to be upstairs."

Brent nodded. "Can you make up the cot for me?"

"No," her father said.

Brent made an impatient gesture. "Adam— "

"No. Everybody but you and one policeman thinks Randy West is gone. If you stay in this house, you'll confirm Daniel's worst suspicions."

"I don't care what Daniel says," Sarah said recklessly.

Her father addressed Brent. "I can't let you do

something that could mean Sarah might never be able to take her place in the community."

Brent nodded. "I thought you might feel that way, so I'll sleep in the barn."

The barn? "But you have to go to work in the morning."

"I'll get up at dawn. After all, you do it. Then I'll shower and change at Norm's and go to the office."

Her heart felt full. "Thank you. I'll feel better knowing someone who doesn't have to be passive is around. But you have to be careful."

Brent nodded. "I will." She looked deeply into his eyes. They were clear and glowed with sincerity.

Brent might not want to acknowledge his feelings for her in words, but she could read them in his eyes. For a moment, she simply looked back, communicating everything she'd vowed not to say in words. She wouldn't try to hold him; she wanted the best for him, and if he thought he knew what he wanted... But surely she could look and show her feelings this way.

Her father cleared his throat.

Brent broke eye contact. "I brought blankets, everything I'll need tonight. They're in my car."

Belatedly it dawned on Sarah that his car wasn't in the gravel driveway.

"I left my car down the road," he explained. "Despite what Adam thinks, I am concerned about your reputation." He turned to her father. "So, are you going to throw me out of your barn?"

There were a few seconds of silence as her father stroked his beard and thought. "I couldn't throw you out of the barn if I wished it. We Amish are too peace-loving." A hint of a smile started to turn the corners of his mouth. "Also, sometimes to get along in the modern world, we have to fudge things a little. If, for example, an English man were to seek shelter in my barn, and I didn't see his car, I might not even know he was there. And if I did know he was there, I couldn't deny my fellow man a night's shelter.''

So it was decided. That night, Sarah checked the locks three times and thought of Brent in the barn and felt safe for the first time since Randy West had escaped from jail. Safe.

But she was restless too, because Brent was only a hundred feet away—almost a part of her world.

CHAPTER SIXTEEN

BRENT TENSED, awakened by the sound of footsteps crossing the gravel driveway. It was so dark on the farm, but he wouldn't light the lamp. Surprise was to his advantage. He reached for the piece of wood from Sarah's woodpile that he'd placed beside his pallet earlier.

The footsteps were closer now, hesitating, then starting up again. Brent rose from his makeshift bed and crouched behind one of the big timbers that held up the loft floor. He raised the piece of wood to waist height.

The big barn door slid open. The night sky outside was marginally lighter than inside the barn, and Brent could see a figure silhouetted in the doorway. Too small for West. What the...

"Brent?"

Sarah. The breath whooshed out of him. "What are you doing here?" he asked, his voice harsher than he intended.

"Where are you?"

"Over here." Brent stepped out from behind the timber, now feeling a little foolish for the adrenaline that pumped through his veins. He dropped the piece of wood and went toward her. "Is anything wrong?"

She stepped into the barn. "No. Not really." She

laughed a little, a high, nervous sound. "I just...
needed someone to talk to."

Of course she did. For days she'd endured silence.
"I'll talk to you," he said. He went back to his makeshift bed in the tack area of the barn and lit the lantern. He hung it from a peg on a beam, then turned
to look at her. She wore a dress, but her hair was
loose, hanging about her shoulders.

Quickly, she shut the barn door. "I can't let anyone
see me here."

"Is this wise, your coming here?"

"No," she said softly. "It isn't wise. But I had to
come. I had to know." She took a hesitant step toward him.

"Had to know what?"

She took a couple more steps. "I said I wanted you
to talk to me, and I do. But I really came out here to
find out..." She stopped. In the yellow light, he saw
her put up her chin in a gesture that was familiar and
gutsy and endearing all at once. "I came out here to
make love with a man I love."

Shock took his voice away. Shock dried his throat.
He raised a hand to her, whether in protest or invitation he wasn't exactly sure. He'd dreamed of making love with her, but those dreams had always involved starched white sheets, lovemaking in his bed.
His world. And never in his fantasies had he imagined
this kind of boldness from her.

She took another step. "Say something," she said,
her voice sounding soft and strained. "I think I can
stand anything but silence."

He swallowed. "We can't do this. You don't deserve to make love on a pallet in a barn. You deserve

a man of your own kind, one who can promise you—''

"I'm not asking for promises." Another step, and she was very close now. "Don't you…" She was trying to hold his gaze, he knew, but she couldn't quite manage it. "Don't you want to?"

He gave a harsh chuckle. "Yes. And every time I think about it, it starts with your hair. Down just for me." He could barely restrain himself from touching it. She was so near he could see where her hair was parted, the delicate curve of her eyebrows, the anxiety and anticipation in her eyes.

Under his gaze, she lifted her chin a fraction. "I'm Amish, but I'm a woman too." Then she put a light palm on his chest, and through his T-shirt his skin burned. High above him towered the ceiling of the barn, but here in the circle of light the world was very small.

He was alone with the woman he'd wanted more than any in the world, and she wanted to make love and they stood over a bed and argued about it. He would have laughed if it was at all funny. If it was anything other than excruciating. If the tension wasn't like a live thing between them.

Her hand moved higher, along the column of his neck to his cheek. "It's been a long time since you shaved."

He had to clear his throat to speak. "Since this morning before I went to work."

She said in a quick and shy voice, "I like that. Just a bit of whiskers."

He felt a lurch in his groin. He couldn't believe she was saying something like this. He'd guessed at the passion so carefully hidden, had a hint of it in their kisses, but now... She traced his lips with a finger. She leaned in to kiss him. He held himself stiff, willing himself not to respond, bracing himself for the moment when.... Her lips touched his with promise.

Promises were exactly what he couldn't give her.

"Aren't I doing it right?" she whispered, her mouth against his. "That was the only thing I was afraid of. I know I'm not good at this, but I thought..."

Ah, hell. His arms went around her. "Sweetheart, you are the best at this." Despite his best intentions, his hands went to her hips, and he pressed her against his hard shaft. It was exquisite and wrong and as inevitable as summer's turn to fall. Her breathing quickened and she rubbed against him until he thought he'd die.

"I don't want to frighten you," he whispered.

"You're not frightening me," she said. "I know what happened to me has nothing to do with making love. So now I want...I want new memories...with you."

He held her tightly. "I'll never hurt you, I swear."

He felt her swallow. "I know that."

"I want to make love to you," he said, urgency stripping him of everything but fundamental honesty. "But what about tomorrow, Sarah? If they ever find out—"

"What could be worse than what they're already doing?"

He had to know what she expected. He needed to know what she wanted, because suddenly it occurred to him that people seldom asked her. Although he was afraid of her answer, he took a breath and asked, "Do you want to leave them?"

She was still pressed against him. "I don't know," she said softly.

The oddest sense of disappointment gripped him, even though he knew she'd be better off with her own. "Then we can't do this." He wondered if a man could die from wanting something so much and letting it go.

She leaned backward and looked up into his eyes. "Making love has nothing to do with tomorrow. I don't want anything from you except tonight. I don't know how to say it any clearer than that."

A better man would have put her aside and told her to go back to the house. Brent knew in that moment that he wasn't as good a man as he should be, as he wanted to be. She moved again, and he groaned. She gave a little whispery moan in response.

He lost it then, lost it utterly. His hands fisted in her hair, then flexed, drawing silk through his fingers. His mouth found hers, and he kissed her hard, trying to taste all of her in one instant.

They fell together onto the pallet. They rolled, her hair in the way, tumbling around them, strands getting caught between their bodies, being impatiently pushed aside, sometimes by his hand, sometimes hers. He fumbled with cotton, got her skirt up, felt bare thighs.

He groaned again, groped for the fastenings that held her dress. *Straight pins,* he thought, pricking his thumb in his haste.

She was pulling at his shirt. He helped her, yanking the thin cloth of the T-shirt over his head. He wore only a pair of cutoff jeans, no belt. She reached for the snap.

He pushed her hand away. Sarah deserved more

than a quick lay, the deed done before his conscience could override his groin. "Slow," he said, looking down into her eyes. "We'll go slow."

"You...you won't change your mind?" she asked breathlessly, but he caught a hint of relief in her eyes.

"Nothing will change my mind." He kissed her and undressed her slowly, carefully. When he got to her plain cotton bra, she turned her head, embarrassed. He reached out and tipped her chin toward him. "If we only have one night, we don't have time for embarrassment." He unhooked her bra with far more deftness than he'd managed with her straight pins.

When she was bare, she was everything he'd ever imagined. His blood flowed so thick and hot at the sight of her that he could feel even his ears start to burn. He bent his head, brushed aside another errant lock of her hair with his nose and took her nipple in his mouth. Her soft cry made his groin throb. The way her nipple stiffened against his tongue made him want to abandon slowness and make her his now. Instead, he flicked his tongue over her nipple and felt sheer joy when she wriggled and sighed. Suddenly, he was more complete, more alive than he'd felt in years.

But when her hands went again to the waistband of his jeans, he pushed them gently away. He had to keep his sanity, and the only way to do that was to keep his pants on. "Let's wait," he said, but he touched her between her legs. She moaned and parted her legs slightly. He put his palms on her thighs and urged her to part them farther. When she did, he stroked her.

Her head turned restlessly. "Talk to me," she whispered. "Please. No silence."

So he talked in the quiet barn, whispered words. Nonsense, praise for her, anything that occurred to him. He knew his voice was raspy. Then he stopped as he bent his head. He trailed his tongue down her belly, into the crevice between her thighs. When he stroked her there with his tongue, she started and grabbed his head and tried to sit up.

"Shh," he said, pushing her gently back.

"I don't...I never...we didn't..." Helplessly she let her head fall back, but instead of pushing him away, her fingers on his scalp tightened.

"We're making love English style, and we're going to go very slowly," he whispered, pleased by the sounds she was making and the way her fingers told him what she wanted. She was modest, but not really shy, and that pleased him too. It pleased him even more that they could—in Sarah's words—make new memories. That despite what had happened to her, she could respond so powerfully.

When she shuddered and cried out in climax, he held her thighs and pressed his face to her skin and almost shuddered himself.

When the aftershocks died, he kissed his way up her body and settled in beside her. Her eyes were closed, and strands of her hair spilled onto the rough wood of the tack-room floor. His groin still ached, but he felt better than he had in a long time.

She smiled, lifted her eyelids, touched his face. "Some things are better than talking."

"Yes."

"But I needed the talk too."

"Yes." He kissed her ear, marveling at her dishevelment, the sheer eroticism of it.

"I like the English way of making love." She put a hand over his zipper and touched him as if she were the boldest woman on earth.

He groaned and pushed himself harder into her palm. She reached for the fastening of his cutoffs again, and again he put his hands over hers. "No?" she asked, her eyes going to his in confusion.

"Sweetheart, I don't have anything with me. Any protection," he clarified. She still looked puzzled. He gave a frustrated laugh. She really was one of a kind. "A condom," he added finally.

"Oh. I understand now." She frowned, wrinkling her nose. "But for me it's not that time of the month... I mean, I really don't think I'd get pregnant."

"We can't take that chance."

She bit her lip. "But we could do it the English way."

A shaft of pure desire went through him. Did she mean what he thought she meant? It seemed she did, because she pushed him back as gently as he'd pushed her. This time, when she went for his snap, he let her. Knowing she'd never done this with a man, he held himself still, not wanting to scare her. Instead, he looked up at the cavernous blackness overhead and endured her wrestling with something so unfamiliar as a zipper. Her fingers kept straying, splaying over his shaft, her fingers pressing through worn cotton denim and his briefs.

His zipper came down. "Help me," she finally said, tugging at his cutoffs. He helped her finish undressing him. His jeans and underwear landed unceremoniously on the floor. He fell back on the pallet.

She touched him, there, curling her fingers around his bare, sensitized skin.

He almost leaped off the bed.

"Do you like this?" she asked shyly.

"Yes." He almost hissed the word. "I like it." In fact, he liked it too much. She kept on stroking, and kissed him fully on the mouth. She smelled of perspiration, a good earthy, sexy smell. He thrust his tongue inside her mouth as his desire built and built.

They'd have to save the "English way," for later, because he couldn't let her go. She was half atop him, and he welcomed her soft weight, the feel of her hair on his skin.

He groaned and she stroked a little faster. He shut his eyes on the cavernous space above and saw other images. Blue sky above the raw gold shingles of a barn roof. Pure gold hair flowing, flowing...

When his climax came, it shattered something inside him, something hard and tight. On the surge of release, he only knew one thing: he loved her.

IT WAS HOT where Brent's body was pressed to hers, but cold on her back. Yet she didn't want to move to pull the covers up farther. She didn't want to give up this extraordinary closeness. After all, she didn't have much time. Soon she'd have to return to the house, and this would be the last time she held Brent. She couldn't risk coming out here again.

Brent's nose tickled her neck. He was quiet, asleep. She welcomed this silence of completion. She'd needed to know again what it was like with a man she loved. In making love with Brent, she was whole.

She'd put away the ugly memories forever. She smiled again, her lips against the barbered edges of his hair. No matter what happened now, she could recall lovemaking as pleasurable, a gift between man and woman.

"Sarah?"

"I thought you were asleep."

"No. Just thinking about some things." He pulled slightly away from her and looked into her eyes. "You said not long ago that you weren't ready to leave the Amish. But...if you are, I'd like to marry you."

Pleasure spiked in her. She'd never expected... For a moment, an incredulous joy beckoned. But she had to remember Brent had never said he loved her. In fact, he'd denied his love on her porch not two weeks ago. "Why do you want to marry me?" She knew Brent's sense of duty. Surely he didn't think that because they'd touched each other so intimately, he had to offer to marry her.

He gave a quick laugh. "You have to ask after what we just did? How it felt?"

"That's passion," she said, feeling her cheeks heat. Now that she was not caught up in that passion, it embarrassed her a little to hear him mention it so boldly.

He was still staring at her intently. "Passion is important." He took a deep breath. "But what's also important is that I love you."

Her hand on his upper arm tightened, so that she could keep from leaping from the pallet onto the barn floor and laughing and spinning and dancing like an English woman. "You do?"

"I do, Sarah Yoder," he said with utmost solemnity. "I never would have guessed that we'd fall in love. But I love you."

"But that day you came to my house, you said you didn't care for me."

"I had to say that. I didn't want your people to shun you. I thought if you came to your senses—"

"I've never taken leave of my senses."

"No, I don't think you have. So, it's up to you." The lamplight flickered over the planes and angles of his face. "I know what I'm asking, what it would mean for you. What do you say? Will you marry me?"

She'd imagined many scenarios—of him staying in Wheatland, of seeing him sometimes, of having him for a friend. But she had never contemplated marriage with him, never dreamed that he'd ask her, never thought for a moment that this passionate, ambitious English lawyer—

"Where would we live?" she asked abruptly. Doubts were nibbling at her initial euphoria.

"Well, in Toledo, of course." He kissed her forehead. "I'm not making light of the fact that you'd have to move. But if you marry me, the shunning would last forever, wouldn't it?"

She suddenly choked up. The shunning might last forever anyway, because after their lovemaking, she doubted she could ever tell the bishop she didn't love Brent. But if she married him, she'd have to leave the community permanently. She pictured saying goodbye to her father, knowing he couldn't say goodbye back, or wish her well. She tried to breathe normally, but her breath caught; she couldn't help it.

"Oh, baby." Brent gathered her to him. "I'm sorry it has to be so hard."

She swallowed down tears. She wanted so much to marry him. But she thought hard, and knew there were some things they had to talk about. "Will you be in politics, back in Toledo?"

"No, not this time. But I'll be working a lot. You can do your drawing, whatever you want."

"That' s all that's expected of an English wife?"

"Well…" For the first time, he really hesitated. "I'm going into a private firm. There, we do a lot of socializing because we do business when we get together socially. I'd like you to come along to those events. It's expected. And we'll do a little entertaining of our own."

She tried to picture herself in his world and failed. She simply didn't know enough about it, and the thought of trying to say the right things at a party was frightening.

"You don't have to worry about a thing. I'll take you to the symphony, the opera, theater openings. We'll travel."

A part of her yearned to do these things. A part of her longed to dress up in those beautiful English clothes, to let the world see her hair down. She squeezed her eyes shut and tried again to see herself in that world. Those places he talked about. But all that came to mind was her and Brent, walking on a beach by a lake as big as an ocean. Maybe making a meal together. She knew that some men cooked, helped their wives with dinner. Would Brent do that, or would he be too busy? She pictured herself with Brent's baby…

"Do you want children?" she asked.

He hesitated again, and she felt a lurch in her heart. If he didn't want children…

"Sure," he said finally. "Someday. I was ready back in Toledo. But after the scandal, I'll have my reputation to work on. I'll have to work extra hard. It wouldn't be fair to have a child with that hanging over me."

"Not everything can be planned, Brent." She thought, *If you stayed here, you'd have a good job, and you'd have time for children too.* But she understood that Brent envisioned one future. He was inviting her to share it, but there was only one future being offered.

The knowledge sobered her, took away, finally and completely, the giddiness that had swept her when he'd proposed. "No," she said. "I can't marry you." Her voice cracked on the words because it was so, so tempting to say yes. "Brent, I do love you. But you have only one vision of your life, and I fear I can't share it. If you could stay here—"

"You want to stay in Wheatland?" His head whipped around. "With them shunning you for the rest of your life, for the terrible sin of marrying a man you love? Knowing you're only a few miles away but not able to share anything with them?"

"Yes," she said simply. She wouldn't lose all contact that way. She'd still be able to watch over them, albeit from a distance, and make sure her family and Rebecca were all right. If Levi decided not to join the church, she could still have a relationship with him. Most of all, she understood that she and Brent could be happy here. He could keep his job, do good work. Wheatland was a halfway point between her life and his. They could live quietly, have a family.

"You don't expect me to give up everything I've worked for, do you?" he asked incredulously.

"You're asking me to give up everything."

He swore. She had to bite her tongue not to correct him. He said, "Don't you understand? If I stay here, every attorney in the state will think I had to settle for being a small-town prosecutor. Every attorney in the state will realize I've lost the battle for my self-respect."

He was so wrong, because if the last six months had taught her nothing else, it was that self-respect came wholly from within. If Brent couldn't see that by now, she didn't know how to reach him. Besides, who was she to teach him how to live? Heaven above, she'd made a real mess of things herself.

He touched her lightly. "Come to Toledo. Things will work out. I can make them work out for us."

He'd make things work out. *He'd* protect her.

Her hands fisted. She'd nearly done it again. She'd nearly let a man she loved set the course of the rest of her life. The thought chilled her to the bone. This time, how she lived had to be her decision. When things got rough over the next years, when the inevitable problems of life intruded, she at least had to know one thing: that she'd chosen her own course.

"I can't," she repeated, sitting up. Quickly, she reached for her dress, pulled it over her head, worked her arms almost frantically through the sleeves. She snatched up her underwear. Unwilling to put it on while he was watching, she was forced to hold it in her hand because without her apron and its voluminous pockets, she had no place to put it.

He put a hand on her arm, preventing her from getting up. "I'm not trying to be selfish, I'm just trying to tell you who I am. How do you know you wouldn't like the city if you tried it? I'll do my best

to make you happy. I swear it.'' In the glow of the
lantern, his eyes looked dark and sincere.

"That's the problem.'' Her voice was high and
tight with her effort to control it. "*You'll* take care of
me, *you'll* try to make me happy. In Toledo, *you'd*
have to tell me every day what to say to your attorney
colleagues, how to dress. I can't do that anymore. I
can't let a man tell me those things.''

"The bishop tells you what to do.'' She could see
from the tight set of his mouth that he was angry.

She wavered a little, because in part he spoke the
truth. "But I decide if I'll follow the bishop. I decide
if the consequences are worth it.'' She stood. Looking
down at him, she said, "We're too far apart. We've
always been too far apart.''

She turned to go. She would not cry, and she
clutched her underwear so tightly her knuckles ached.
"We're worlds apart, you and I.''

CHAPTER SEVENTEEN

ALL OF THEM—Sarah, her father and Levi—pretended Brent wasn't sleeping in the barn. During the day, he packed up and went to work. Every time he left, she wondered if he was coming back. But every night he *was* back. Apparently, he was still parking his car down the road. Some time every evening, from the garden or the porch or the window of her house, she'd see him coming down the driveway or across the fields, his duffel bag in his hand.

She wondered why he still came. Surely two weeks was plenty of time for Randy West to be far away.

But every night he'd go in the barn and shut the big door behind him. She'd imagine him making up the pallet, lighting the lamp, maybe reading before he went to sleep. When it was her own bedtime, she'd check the locks three times and tell herself that tomorrow he'd surely go back to Toledo.

This evening, she'd been busy. After supper, Levi had driven her into town to do the grocery shopping. The store had been crowded, and it had taken far longer than usual to have her purchases rung at the checkout. At home, Levi had helped her carry the groceries into the kitchen and then had taken the frozen food to one of the English farmers a few roads over, one who rented freezers to the Amish.

When he left, he'd grinned and told her not to expect him back too soon. Sarah had understood. Katie Hershburger had been standing on her front lawn when they'd passed her farm.

Now she stood in front of the pantry shelf stacking staples. Then she got out the big canister and poured flour into it from the bag she'd just bought.

Her mind kept conjuring Brent. She hadn't seen him go by, but if he did come in the next few minutes, she knew she'd fly out there and ask inane questions, just to see him and hear his voice. Loneliness swept her, more powerful than ever, because she knew all she had to do was say, *I've changed my mind.*

She heard her father come across the porch floor and into the kitchen. He stopped at the sink, a pail of milk in his hand.

Suddenly, Sarah couldn't stand the silence. "Hello, *Vater.* How did the milking go?"

He stared at her, startled. She waited, her heart in her throat. She didn't really expect him to defy the ban, but she longed for one word from him. A smile, a quickly grunted "good" and she would be all right.

He didn't smile. Instead, his mouth hardened, and he plunked the milk pail on the counter and left the kitchen. A moment later, she heard his slow tread on the stairs.

Tears pricked the backs of her eyelids. She blinked them away and picked up the milk strainer. Suddenly, she flung it down on the counter and began to pace. She looked out the kitchen window as she passed it. A small movement caught her eye. There was a lean-to shed attached to the barn, and the press of other work on the farm meant that the building was in some disrepair. A gray cat slithered out from between the cracks in the shed walls.

Sarah smiled. Woodsmoke was her favorite barn cat, a sweet little thing that had disappeared a few weeks ago. Now following her out the crack in the shed wall were three tiny kittens, two gray like their mother, one coal-black.

Quickly, Sarah grabbed the pail of milk. There were a few dented pans hanging on nails on the porch wall. She opened the door and went out to the porch. Grabbing a pan, she called to the cat.

Woodsmoke's ears pricked, and she made a dash toward Sarah, the kittens scrambling to keep up.

"Woodsmoke, here you are, already teaching your babies that Sarah Yoder is the soft touch around here." She stepped off the porch, and passed the corner of the shop.

From behind, an arm wrapped around her throat, choking her. Milk sloshed her feet as the bucket fell and rolled.

Dear God in heaven. She struggled, trying to breathe.

"Don't move, Amish girl," Randy West hissed. "I have a gun."

Sick, hot fear shot through her limbs and weakened her knees. She could feel what must be the end of a gun poked in her side.

"Now," he whispered, "I know your father's in the house. I can use this gun on him, or you can help me. What's your choice?"

Her father would go passively to his death if confronted by Randy. "Help you," she mouthed, unable to speak.

He must have understood because he slackened his hold.

She took in a great, gasping breath, her lungs on

fire. She braced her legs so they wouldn't crumple. He stank, and her stomach turned as she sucked in air.

Randy gave her a shove. "Get moving. We're going to the barn. Now, don't do something stupid, or you'll regret it."

Somehow, she made her legs move. Fear made her mind numb, and she fought to clear it.

Brent. He'd been right all along. But he hadn't come to the farm yet. Maybe he'd decided not to come tonight.

She started walking slowly to the barn, her eyes scanning her surroundings, looking for anything she could use as a weapon to save herself. A lifetime of passivity flashed before her eyes, and she knew she'd do whatever she had to do to survive. To help her father survive.

The Stolzfuses were neat, she thought inanely, fear making her feel dumb and slow. There was nothing, no sticks of wood, no metal machinery to pick up and use.

Randy shoved her again. "Hurry up!"

She picked up her pace fractionally, trying to put off the moment when he got her alone in the barn. She prayed, a short frantic prayer. *Dear God, help me!*

She got to the barn door. "What do you want?" she asked in as calm a voice as she could, loud enough so that he wouldn't know how scared she was. "You could have escaped. Why didn't you run far away?"

He spat, and pushed the gun harder into her side, a jab that caused her to gasp. "I couldn't. The flamin' highway patrol was everywhere. I couldn't go home, either. I'm smart, and I knew they'd look for me there. So I stole food and water. I stole this gun the very first night. I've been sleeping in the barns and sheds. Waiting. Now you're going to help me escape. After all, it's thanks to you, bitch, that I have to run at all."

Maybe Brent would come, she thought. Maybe even now he had hidden his car and was walking down the road. Maybe if she stalled here in the barn doorway, he'd see them.

Or maybe Randy would see Brent first. What kind of chance would even Brent have against a man with a gun? He could die.

Yes, it was better to do what Randy wanted as quickly as possible.

Her stomach turned. She didn't want to go into that barn with Randy West. Her whole being rebelled against it. "Let's go inside," she forced herself to say.

"Eager, aren't you? Not like that night. Come to think of it, I owe you for a couple of black eyes." He planted a sloppy kiss on her neck and laughed when she shuddered.

He reached around her and pulled open the barn door.

If she could help him escape, get him away from the farm and her father, she would. But if he tried to rape her again... She shut her eyes on the thought. She'd fight him all the way.

He pushed her hard, and she stumbled but caught her balance. She turned in the barn doorway and looked at him for the first time.

Shock went through her. Randy West looked so much like an Amish man that for a second she thought someone was playing a cruel joke. "Your...clothes."

"Yeah." Randy aimed the gun straight for her chest. She focused on that gun. Was it her imagination, or was the hand that held it quivering?

Was he scared or just excited?

Could she use his fear or excitement to help herself?

Her heart pounded. She barely heard him say, "Mondays are wash days for you people. I know that, see. So I took a shirt from one place, pants from another, you know, so that nobody would see that something was missing and put two and two together. And I stole a razor from the place I took the gun. How do you like the beard?"

She raised her eyes. Like married Amish men, Randy West had shaved his mustache area, so that his beard was a half moon on his chin.

"I asked, Amish bitch, how you liked the beard." He gestured with the gun.

"Fine," she managed to say.

"Authentic. Like everything else about my disguise. Now." He gestured again with the gun. "You're going to hitch up that buggy, then you and me are going for a little ride in the country. No cops going to stop a flamin' Amish couple just going for a ride." He used his free hand to tap his forehead. "When I escape, everyone'll know how smart I am. McCade, the damn judge, and you most of all, Sarah. Because you'll have the chance to be...close to me." His eyes were hot. "This time you'd better not give me any black eyes, you hear?"

She didn't answer. Her palms had gone so damp that she wasn't sure she could hitch up the buggy.

"Get a move on. It's getting dark."

She went to the stall for the horse. Perspiration soaked her clothes. It was hard not to scream and run. The thing to do was to get Randy away from the farm, away from those she loved. Once on the road, there were sure to be people. If she could just hold herself together...

She caught a movement out of the corner of her eye. *Brent.* Relief and terror became one emotion in the instant she saw him. He crouched behind a stack of straw bales, a hunk of wood in his hand. He motioned her to go ahead to the stall.

She forced herself to turn away from him. *Think. Think!* Randy was still standing by the barn door, too far away for Brent to have the advantage of surprise.

Her hands were damp and clumsy as she struggled with the latch on the stall door. The horse inside got excited, stomped a little.

"What's the matter with you? Hurry up," Randy directed from the doorway.

Sarah had an idea. "I can't open the latch. I need somebody stronger."

He swore, then she heard him approach. The horse, smelling a stranger, became even more restless. She turned. Randy was almost upon her, but he'd let the hand that held the gun drop to his side...

Yes. She dived for his knees at the same time Brent tackled him.

"What the..." Randy fell back, his gun hand coming up. A shot went off toward the rafters. Then the gun flew in a high arc, toward one of the dark, cluttered corners of the barn. One of Randy's fists landed on Sarah's cheek, knocking her aside.

Brent and Randy rolled on the dusty barn floor. The

wood in Brent's hand skittered away. Sarah scrambled to her feet, ran to get it.

Brent's head thwacked on the barn floor. When he rolled with West again, drops of blood flew. Sarah, wood in hand, ran back to the struggling pair.

Brent was on top now, Randy underneath him. Brent held him by the shoulders, but Randy was struggling hard. Randy turned his head from side to side, his jaws snapping like a wild animal's as he tried to bite. Sarah held the piece of wood high, ready to bring it down on Randy's skull.

"What on earth... Sarah!" It was her father's voice, coming from the doorway. He rushed over. Grabbing Randy by the hair, he pinned his head to the floor. Randy lay there, gasping.

"I'll kill you," her father said fiercely. "I swear to God I'll kill you."

"No need," Brent said, his voice a harsh pant. He was kneeling, his knees planted in Randy West's stomach. "Not now. Though it's tempting as hell." He spit some blood onto the floor. "You sick, sorry bastard," he said to West. "The only things keeping you alive are the vows of some good Amish people and my belief in the law. A belief I'd suggest you don't test." He turned to Sarah. "Are you all right?"

"Yes." She was dizzy, but exhilaration flowed through her at the sight of Randy West pinned to the floor, his Amish clothes dusty and torn. "You're bleeding. Are you okay?"

"Think I lost a tooth," he said. "If you're all right, can you use my cell phone to call the sheriff?"

"You'll have to tell me how."

"No problem. You, Sarah Yoder, can do anything."

When the sheriff came in response to her call, Sarah and her father let Brent tell the story. He'd come to the farm extra early, and had been setting up for the night when he'd heard Sarah at the barn door. He hadn't had time to get to the doorway, but he did manage to conceal himself before she and Randy came in. Then he could only hope that Randy would get close enough for him to help Sarah. He held a bloodstained handkerchief against a fattening lip, but he told his story with a coolness that Sarah admired. Her own legs felt like jelly. But she was happy. Randy West had been taken away in a squad car, and she was free of him at last.

Sarah stood in the crook of her father's arm while Brent filled out forms. Her father said, "Even now, I'm praying. I'm giving thanks you're safe."

"You'll have to pray for forgiveness instead," she said, so giddy now that she could tease. "I heard you threaten to kill a man, don't forget."

"I would have done it too, to protect you."

She was astonished, sure her father would recant his fighting words. "You would have been shunned."

There was a pause, then her father said, "Some things are worth being shunned for."

Warmth and love washed over Sarah because she knew he wasn't just talking about himself. "Thanks for understanding."

Her father nodded. "I've been thinking. A lifetime of service to the group is worth something. Worth another talk with Daniel, I think. Surely, after this night, after what you've gone through, he'll relent on the shunning."

"It's worth a try," she said softly.

Brent pretended to fill out forms as he watched

father and daughter. Sarah would have her family
back, he was certain. He had faith in Adam's powers
of persuasion, his love for his daughter. Daniel Yoder,
for all his sternness, loved Sarah too.

And Brent loved her more than he'd ever thought
possible. She was brave and strong, with a strength
of character that was beyond anything he'd ever ex-
perienced. She was a quiet Amish woman who had
stood over Randy West and wielded a piece of wood.
She'd kept her cool as she'd faced down the man
who'd violated her body but not broken her spirit.

"Brent?" The sheriff spoke. "Can you finish those
forms? I'll have a ton of paperwork to do at the office."

"Sure." Brent printed his name and address on the
form. "I'll give you my address in Toledo, too.
You'll need me back to testify at West's trial for at-
tempted kidnapping."

"Okay. Hey, too bad you're going. It was great to
bring a case down to the courthouse and know it was
in good hands, you know."

"Thanks." Brent finished the form and handed the
clipboard to the sheriff. Levi had just come home, and
there was a little commotion as Adam and Sarah explained what had happened. Levi exclaimed something at one point, in excited Pennsylvania Dutch. After all his months in Wheatland, Brent scarcely knew
a word of Sarah's native language.

Profound sadness swept him. He told himself it was
just the letdown, the aftermath of the fight. But he
knew better. He knew it was because he wouldn't ask
Sarah again to come away with him.

She'd been right to turn him down. The little family
stood in a circle of lantern light. His chest squeezed

painfully at the sight of Sarah, her cheeks red, her eyes sparkling, her white prayer cap askew as strands of golden hair curled all around her face. They were a family. She was part of a community that had loved her and nurtured her. She was where she belonged.

He'd go to where he belonged. And as usual, he'd go alone.

PEOPLE STARED. Sarah looked straight ahead and held tightly to the reins, pretending, as she'd done for years, that she didn't notice the stares. Of course, those stares were to be expected today. Even a few gasps were not out of order, she thought with grim humor. After all, how many times did the tourists see an English woman driving a buggy?

She stopped the horse and tried to get out of the buggy. Her skirt, though modest, was still tighter than anything she'd ever owned. She had to hike it up to climb down. The buttons of her blouse felt so unfamiliar, she was conscious of the weight of each one. As she turned to tie the horse to the hitching post, her hair fell in her eyes. Cut a few inches below her shoulders, it swung free, and thick bangs tickled her forehead. That was the oddest sensation of all, to feel her hair free and blowing in the breeze.

"Please don't cut too much off," she'd said to the stylist as the beauty parlor, a woman so initially stunned to see her there that Sara had had to repeat her request for a haircut three times.

"Not too big a change at once," the stylist had said in a falsely bright voice. The other patrons had stared openly.

Brent liked her hair long. The memories of their lovemaking were still with her, even though a month

had passed. And though she knew he'd never see her
in her new haircut and clothes, it made her feel closer
to him somehow to have this tangible reminder of
their night together.

Her stomach hurt. Her palms were damp as she
reached into the buggy for a cardboard portfolio. The
rest of her life depended on the next few minutes.

She went into the gallery and nervously asked to
see the owner. The owner came out from the back
room and introduced herself as Sylvia Manning. Sylvia had on some flowing thing that reminded Sarah
of a nightgown. Her black-and-gray hair was frizzed.
She wore huge silver jewelry, and her eyes were hard
and knowing.

Sarah handed over the portfolio and asked with a
timidity that shamed her a little whether Sylvia would
like to buy a drawing or two. She'd brought only her
traditional scenes, the ones that shielded the Amish
faces. She didn't want to exploit her friends.

But most of all, she needed the drawings of the
Amish faces for herself. If all went well, she'd need
those drawings for the memories they captured. No
wonder she'd been in a hurry to draw them. Soon,
memories of her people would be all she had.

"I'll take a look," the woman said, taking the portfolio and already sounding bored. "Pen-and-ink, you
say? I don't know. Maybe too highbrow for the tourist
trade. The tourists like a lot of color—" She cut herself off and frowned as she picked up the top drawing.

It's no good, Sarah thought with a sinking heart.
Now what? Would she have to go home with her hair
cut off and say she'd decided to change her life but
she'd failed because she couldn't support herself?

Sylvia paged through the seven drawings. Finally,

she said, "I'll give you two hundred dollars for this one with the children, and three hundred for the one of the barn raising. I'll pay a hundred and fifty each for these three little scenes. The tourists don't always want to cough up for the bigger stuff, so I sell a lot of the smaller pieces. In fact, if you could do a few more simpler, smaller scenes, I could buy all of them, no problem."

"Nine hundred and fifty dollars?" Sarah swallowed hard. That was so much more money than she'd ever dreamed she could earn with her drawings. With sales of her drawings to supplement the earnings from a fabric and quilt shop in town—

"Not a penny more. I've got to make money too, you know."

"Oh. Of course. I mean, I accept." Belatedly, Sarah put her hand across the counter and, as Sylvia Manning said, "shook hands on the deal."

"I'll buy two or three drawings a month if you promise to bring them only to me. Will you take commissions?"

"Sure," Sarah said recklessly, not having the faintest idea what a commission was.

As she was going out the door, Sylvia called her back. "You know this drawing of the barn raising? The one with the American guy on the roof, with a hammer in his hand? Could you do a few drawings of him, but make him an Amish man? Wow, is he a hunk. The tourists will go nuts for him."

So this would be her life now, thought Sarah. Sitting at her desk in her English clothes and drawing Brent as an Amish man. Sadness touched her heart. Brent McCade would never see her with her hair worn down.

CHAPTER EIGHTEEN

AT HOME an hour later, her father took one look at her and sat down hard on the kitchen chair. "No," he whispered.

"I have to, *Vater*." She put her chin up because it helped her find courage. "This is who I am now."

"I thought when Brent left—"

"This has nothing to do with Brent." Although it did, she knew. In loving Brent, she'd found the courage to be herself. That was the power of love, the good side of love, the freeing side of it. And though he'd never know what she was doing today, she thanked him silently in her heart.

"Brent has only been gone a month," her father said desperately. "That's not long enough to be over him, to get any perspective on all that's happened to you."

"*Vater*, I—" She broke off. How could she make her father understand that it had been long enough for her? And long enough for Brent, too, to have figured out what he wanted. If she'd entertained any hope that he'd changed after that moment when they'd worked together to subdue Randy West, that he wanted something different out of life, she'd had it firmly dashed. He'd gone and he'd not looked back. She hoped he was happy. Surely one day she'd see his picture in the newspaper and know that he was back to prosecuting big cases, that he was important in his world.

"I won't support you in this," her father warned. "There won't be any dispute about your shunning now. If you walk out of this house, you won't be coming back."

She shut her eyes for a second. "I love you. I love my family and my friends. That's why it's taken me five years to leave." Tears formed in the corners of her eyes, her voice thickened. "I never wanted to hurt anyone."

Her father leaned forward. "Levi might follow you into the outside world. Have you thought of that? If you do this, you might be responsible for turning him from the faith."

She took a deep breath. "I don't think that's fair. Levi needs to make his own decisions. Trust him. Let him do what he thinks is right. You've been a good father—you tried to teach us both, but living our faith—it's extremely difficult. If a person isn't sure that's what they want..." Her voice dropped. "It can tear a person apart."

"But all your friends...Rebecca is being courted by Amos. Her father told me he's going to plant celery next spring. Don't you want to come to Rebecca's wedding?"

She'd vowed to herself she wouldn't cry. She'd vowed to explain her decision and to keep her courage up. But her father was right. She was losing everything. "I have to go," she whispered. "I have no choice."

Her father folded his hands and bowed his head.

Her eyes full of tears, Sarah went upstairs and packed. In a few minutes, she came back down to the kitchen. Her father hadn't moved. She placed her hand on his shoulder, but when he made no response, she moved to the window where she stayed until she saw the blue van driven by one of her customers come up the driveway. She and Colleen Simmons had become friends. Though the friendship didn't begin to compare to the depth of friendship she'd had with Rebecca, Sarah had hope. Real friendship, real connections, took time. Soon, she hoped, the constant ache of loneliness in her heart would begin to lessen as she embraced this new world.

She picked up her bag. "I'm going now, *Vater*. I'll be seeing Levi and I'll try to explain what I'm doing so he doesn't think my life is exciting or glamorous, or..." She was unable to go on.

Adam looked up, and his face was wet with tears. "Please," he said. "I've raised you to be a good Amish woman. I've loved you. I've been so proud of you."

She started to cry. "I...have no choice. I know I'm hurting you. If there was any other way, I'd take it. But if I stayed here, every day of my life I'd live a lie. You raised me to be truthful. Please understand. I want to be your daughter, but this is something I have to do."

Her father gave her a long look, his eyes full of pain. Then he shifted in his chair, and very deliberately turned his back on her.

Sarah said softly, "I'll always love you, *Vater*." Then she swiped at her eyes, opened the door and walked away from her home forever.

"COME FOR A BEER." Teddy raised his voice in order to be heard over the hubbub outside the Toledo courtroom.

"I've got to work," Brent said for the third time. "It's late. I've got depositions to prepare."

"Come on, how many times do you win a case as big as this?"

Not often, Brent conceded. He'd defended an insurance company in a class action suit brought by its customers. The case had been years in litigation, but Brent had recently been added to the defense team in order to do the actual trial.

He'd told his insurance clients to expect a several-million-dollar verdict against them. It was what they deserved, he thought. The company had taken millions in premiums but had a history of being very slow to pay claims. Nobody had been as surprised as Brent when the jury had delivered its verdict. His clients had gotten off without having to pay a penny.

"Man, we'll get tons of referrals off this win." Teddy kissed his fingers. "You're on the fast track to partner as of tonight. Not to mention making me look good bringing you on board. A win-win."

Brent was coming to hate that expression. "The whole defense team won. Not just me."

Teddy rolled his eyes. "What's with the modesty? Our associates just finished interviewing the jurors. Those jurors liked you, figured you'd tell them the truth. It was you who really won this thing."

Rub it in, Brent thought. It shouldn't make any difference how he felt about his clients. A good lawyer could represent anybody. In fact, it was a lawyer's responsibility to represent his client to the best of his ability, regardless of personal feelings. What he'd done in that courtroom today wasn't wrong.

So why did it feel wrong?

Teddy lifted a hand to his mouth and made gulping sounds, pretending to guzzle a beer. Brent was suddenly disgusted. After a big win, lawyers acted like college kids at a party. The pressure of a trial was intense. Whooping it up afterward was part of the drill, the code, the fraternity of law. Now it suddenly seemed stupid and pointless and childish as hell. So he refused Teddy's offer of a drink and headed home.

Driving the dark streets, he acknowledged what was really bothering him. He missed Sarah. He'd only spent one night with her, and in a barn, no less. But he missed her in his bed as if she'd always been there, as if there was an indentation in the mattress where she'd lain, a warm spot he could reach out and touch. He missed her quiet wonder when he'd tell her of the sights he'd take for granted. He missed how sensible she was, how she could put things in perspective in a way that his driven colleagues couldn't. He missed her quiet courage.

All that didn't surprise him. He'd given her his heart, and he didn't give his heart lightly.

What surprised him was that he missed other things. He missed Norm. Teddy made him grit his teeth, but Norm's manner was easy to live with. He missed his clients in Wheatland as well.

Had he made a mistake?

He hadn't. Sarah didn't want him, and life in Wheatland would be bleak without her. He wasn't going to spend the rest of his life looking into buggies as they passed, staring like some nutty tourist for a glimpse of golden hair and a white prayer cap.

When he pulled into his driveway, his headlights illuminated a figure sitting on his stoop. The figure stood. Brent stared. His fixation on Sarah had him seeing things. He swore he saw a black hat like the kind an Amish man wore.

"Brent!" Levi Stolzfus came running down the walk.

Brent pushed open his car door and sprang to his feet. "Levi! How did you get here?" A sudden fear gripped him. "Is Sarah—"

"She's all right. I took the bus. I had to see you." Levi stood under the garage lights and tipped his face earnestly toward Brent's. "Sarah's an English woman now."

Brent was stunned. "She left the Amish?"

"Yes, and she's rented a shop and she's selling drawings. But she's sad, Brent." His voice picked up speed. "I know she misses you. I thought, maybe you were missing her, too, because I remembered how you two were kissing and—" Levi turned his head in embarrassment. "She doesn't know I'm here. I just thought I should tell you that she isn't Amish anymore."

Sarah wasn't Amish, Brent repeated to himself in a kind of daze. Excitement gripped him. Sarah still loved him. Sarah had made her decision on her own, *and…Sarah…wasn't…Amish.*

SARAH WAS PUTTING bolts of fabric on the shelves when she heard the doorbell ring. Thanks to the convenient town location and the big room in the back that she used as a classroom, her shop was surprisingly popular.

None of the Amish came, but many of the townsfolk had signed up for quilting classes. In fact, one of her beginning classes had just let out, leaving a lot

of fabric to be put away. "What did you forget?" she
called without looking up.

"I'd like to buy a quilt," said a familiar voice.

Sarah gasped and turned, dropping the bolt of calico she was holding. "Brent!"

"Hello, Sarah," he said. As she watched, a smile
came and went on his face. He stared at her. "You
look...beautiful as an English woman."

She walked toward him in a trance. "What...what
are you doing here?"

"Levi came to see me. He took the bus."

"Levi came to you? All the way to Toledo?"

"Actually, it's not so far, not in miles anyway."
He paused. "I thought when I left, well, when you
were standing there in that barn with your father, I
thought you'd made your choice. That you wanted to
be Amish."

She swallowed. "It was hard to leave," she said in
a low voice. "But I had to do it. And I had to do it
on my own."

He nodded. "You're a brave woman. I've always
said so." He took a couple of steps toward her. "Are
you happy, Sarah?"

"The nights are long, and I miss *Vater* and Rebecca. But I have some friends, and I like my work
and the world seems big."

He nodded. "I'm glad."

For a moment they just stared at one another.
"How about you?" she asked finally. "Did you find
what you wanted in Toledo?"

"No."

No. No? Did that mean...? And just why was he

here, anyway? Her heart was thumping, a peculiar, heavy thump, thump, *thump*.

"There's an English saying," he said. "It goes something like, 'Be careful what you wish for, because you just might get it.' I got big cases in Toledo. I was already on the fast track for partner. And it didn't mean a thing. Not without you."

Her heart thumped even harder, so loud she was sure he must be able to hear it.

"I want to stay here. I want my old job back. Tim Smith isn't really good at trial work, and Norm is glad to have me. I found things here I didn't even know I needed. Peace. Quiet. The chance to have something more than a career. Friends and a family."

He paused. "Actually, I figured all that out about a week after I got back to Toledo. The only thing keeping me there was knowing I couldn't bear to live in Wheatland with you still Amish. I couldn't stand knowing you were only a few miles away, but that it might as well have been another world away. That's what I couldn't bear."

"Oh, Brent." She went directly, boldly, impulsively into his arms. "I've missed you so."

He crushed her to him, and he chuckled a little. "And here I was, nervous as hell, thinking maybe now that you were English, now that you had choices, you'd decide that you could live without one stubborn, driven man."

"No way," she said fiercely. "That stubborn, driven man is the man I love."

"Will you marry me?" he asked solemnly, his mouth against her hair.

"Yes. Oh, yes."

"Soon?"

She leaned back in his arms. "I never finished that quilt you ordered. If we put off the wedding for a little while, I could make it for our bed. I'd like a wedding quilt."

The disappointment on his face would have been comical if she hadn't been so full of love, if she didn't know as well as he that waiting would be too hard.

"Do you have to have a quilt?" he asked, sounding endearingly desperate. "You do beautiful work, but... Couldn't it be a first-anniversary quilt instead?"

An Amish woman wouldn't think of going to her marriage without a wedding quilt. So it was a measure, perhaps, of her newfound freedom that Sarah said, "A first-anniversary quilt it is."

He kissed her and kissed her. "Did I tell you I like your hair?"

"Not exactly."

"I like your hair," he said, running strands of it through his fingers. "If we danced, it would swirl around your shoulders. I know you want to do things on your own. But could your husband teach you to dance?"

"Oh, yes." She imagined herself dancing with Brent. Dancing, of all things. Dancing at her wedding.

EPILOGUE

Dear Daughter,

I need to write in Pennsylvania Dutch because I don't trust my English for what I'm about to say. But you may read this letter to Brent if you wish.

All my life, I've tried to follow the faith, and though I haven't been tested as you have, I too have had my troubles to bear. So I hope you can forgive me for turning my back on you the day you left. I was doing what I thought was right then.

I'm doing what I think is right now. This once, on your wedding day, I'll defy the ban to write you this letter.

You may not be part of my life now, but you'll always be part of my heart. I've been thinking about you all day. Levi said you were pretty in your white dress. He said you and Brent looked happy, and Norman and some of your new English friends came. I thank the Lord that this day was a happy one for you. I'm also grateful that Levi was there, that you could have one of your family at your wedding.

I've been thinking about Levi, too, praying he'll do what's right when the time comes. But

I will respect his decision. Levi must follow his own conscience. As every Amish must. As you did.

I could not see you married, but you have my blessing, daughter, and my love. I will never speak to you, but I hope to catch a glimpse of you when I come to town, I hope to see my grandchildren playing in the yard of your home. More I cannot offer.

Except one thing. In this package is your mother's quilt. It's the one she brought to her own marriage, the one I've had on my bed for over thirty years. I hope you'll put it on your own bed and have as much happiness as your mother and I had.

Also know this: if you ever need me, I will come, ban or no ban. Because never doubt for a moment that I love you.

Sarah finished translating the letter for Brent. He hugged her. "Are you okay?"

"Yes." She blinked back a few tears. "*Vater* has gone far beyond what he ought to do, to write to me. But I'm so glad he did. It makes my day so much happier to know I have his love."

Brent nodded, his eyes full of concern.

"I'm fine, Brent. Just a little emotional." She smiled. That smile was a tad shaky, but it was real. Now that she knew she could stand on her own feet, Brent's concern felt good. "Come on now," she said. "Help me put this quilt on our bed."

Sarah unfolded the quilt and laid it on the bed. With her on one side and Brent on the other, they worked to straighten it.

She smiled more broadly as he pulled a little too hard from his side, getting the diamond pattern off center. "Gently, remember? Not everything has to be done at breakneck speed." Sarah tugged, bringing the center medallion back into place.

She ran her finger down a row of tiny hand stitches and thought about her mother's patient work. She thought about her father and Levi and her friends. She thought about good people, Amish and English. Most of all she thought about Brent, and how much she loved him.

She knew somehow that this quilt brought everything together.

Welcome to *Love Inspired*™

A brand-new series of contemporary inspirational love stories.

Join men and women as they learn valuable lessons about facing the challenges of today's world and about life, love and faith.

Look for the following April 1998 Love Inspired™ titles:

DECIDEDLY MARRIED
by Carole Gift Page

A HOPEFUL HEART
by Lois Richer

HOMECOMING
by Carolyne Aarsen

Available in retail outlets in March 1998.

LIFT YOUR SPIRITS AND GLADDEN YOUR HEART
with *Love Inspired!*™

Steeple Hill™

LI498

DEBBIE MACOMBER

invites you to the

★ ★ ★ HEART OF TEXAS ★ ★ ★

Join Debbie Macomber as she brings you the lives
and loves of the folks in the ranching community
of Promise, Texas.

If you loved Midnight Sons—don't miss
Heart of Texas! A brand-new six-book series
from Debbie Macomber.

Available in February 1998
at your favorite retail store.

Heart of Texas by Debbie Macomber

Lonesome Cowboy	February '98
Texas Two-Step	March '98
Caroline's Child	April '98
Dr. Texas	May '98
Nell's Cowboy	June '98
Lone Star Baby	July '98

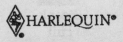

HARLEQUIN®

HPHRT1

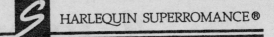

COMING NEXT MONTH

#786 A FATHER'S HEART • Karen Young
Family Man

Daniel Kendrick wants the one thing he can never have: his children. Thanks to the testimony of Tessa Hamilton at his custody hearing, he's a marked man. Now his daughter has run away to the uneasy streets of the Big Easy. The only person who can help him find her is...Tessa Hamilton, and Tessa has begun to have second thoughts about Daniel. Could she have been wrong all those years ago?

#787 SHE'S THE SHERIFF • Anne Marie Duquette
Home on the Ranch

Virgil Bodine is the onetime sheriff of Tombstone, Arizona, and a former bodyguard to the stars. Sick of Hollywood life, he's come home, his reluctant ten-year-old son in tow. Desiree Harlan is a former Phoenix D.A.—she talked herself out of one job and is looking for another. Tombstone needs a new sheriff, and Desiree decides to run. So does Virgil. Next thing he knows, he's calling her sheriff. And boss. And... wife?

#788 CUPID'S REVENGE • Ruth Jean Dale
The Camerons of Colorado

Jason Cameron, ex-rodeo champion and all-around ladies' man, is back in Cupid, Colorado. Jason's friends and fellow ranchers consider him too much competition on the romance front; they want him to fall for *one* woman and leave the rest for them. He does. He falls for newcomer Diana Kennedy and he falls hard. There are plenty of sparks flying between them, but Diana's not sure she wants any of them to catch!

#789 THE FAMILY NEXT DOOR • Janice Kay Johnson
Count on a Cop

Judith Kane moves to a small obscure town for one reason—safety. She's afraid of her ex-husband, afraid for her children. So she moves to Mud River, Washington—right next door to a cop. But Chief Ben McKinsey doesn't *want* a family next door. He doesn't want to get involved with an attractive woman like Judith—or her kids. But they seem to need help, and who can you count on if you can't count on a cop?